PRAISE FOR *PSYCHOPATHS ANONYMOUS*

'Another wild ride from Will Carver, this is a darkly delicious page-turner' S J Watson

'I read this in one sitting. Dark, gripping and yet surprisingly warm, I fell in love with Carver's murderous Maeve. This is an *Eleanor Oliphant* for crime fans. Carver truly at his best' Sarah Pinborough

'I LOVED IT. The voice is laugh-out-loud funny one moment and brutally dark the next. The story is vivid and engaging and completely unexpected. Will Carver is one of a kind: a true original. Bravo' Lia Middleton

'Wow! It's totally insane and I mean that in the best of ways. Maeve is a brilliant character – you shouldn't root for her but you really do. There's an amazing twisted logic to all of her actions. Incredibly dark and very funny' Harriet Tyce

'Will Carver's most exciting, original, hilarious and freaky outing yet … I loved it' Helen FitzGerald

'Dark in the way only Will Carver can be … oozes malevolence from every page' Victoria Selman

'Gripping, addictive, and leaving you with the faint, uneasy feeling that you probably shouldn't have enjoyed it as much as you have, *Psychopaths Anonymous* is a wickedly dark and funny novel, with a protagonist you can't help but root for. I've recommended it to everyone' Lisa Hall

'Maeve is the best female fictional character since Marla Singer' Christopher Hooley

'Move the hell over Bret Easton Ellis and Chuck Palahniuk, Will Carver's newest transgressive crime novel cements him as the new lit prince of twenty-first-century disenfranchised, pop darkness!' Stephen J Golds

'As inventive and messed up as ever. Will Carver is an incredible writer. It's funny, dark, bloody and absolutely perfect' Chris McDonald

'Utter lunacy. Utter madness. Utter brilliance ... There is a level of truth and honesty running through his narratives that is as hard to look at as it is to look away from. Addictive, much. Highly Recommended' Liz Loves Books

'A dark and disturbing masterpiece ... A fantastic book, totally original and unusual' K A Briggs

'Another stunning, brilliantly crafted novel ... If you're looking for a wild, entertaining, very dark read, then I highly recommend' Hooked from Page One

'My obsession with Will Carver and his utterly amazing, spine-chilling, sphincter-clenching and totally, totally brilliant books just grows and grows. What a book' Buzz for Books Blog

'Stunned and speechless after reading this wild ride book. Maeve is the best psychopath I've had the pleasure to meet' Mrs Loves To Read

'A must for all crime lovers. It's addictive ... and unlike anything you will ever have read' Sally Boocock

PRAISE FOR WILL CARVER

Longlisted for Goldsboro Books Glass Bell Award
Longlisted for Theakston's Old Peculier Crime Novel of the Year Award 2020
Shortlisted for Best Independent Voice at the Amazon Publishing Readers' Awards
Longlisted for the Guardian*'s Not the Booker Prize*

'Cements Carver as one of the most exciting authors in Britain. After this, he'll have his own cult following' *Daily Express*

'Weirdly page-turning' *Sunday Times*

'Laying bare our twenty-first-century weaknesses and dilemmas, Carver has created a highly original state-of-the-nation novel' *Literary Review*

'Arguably the most original crime novel published this year' *Independent*

'At once fantastical and appallingly plausible ... this mesmeric novel paints a thought-provoking if depressing picture of modern life' *Guardian*

'This book is most memorable for its unrepentant darkness' *Telegraph*

'Unlike anything else you'll read this year' *Heat*

'Utterly mesmerising' *Crime Monthly*

'A novel so dark and creepy Stephen King will be jealous he didn't think of it first' Michael Wood

'One of the most compelling and original voices in crime fiction … The whole thing feels like a shot of adrenaline' Alex North

'Twisty-turny and oh-so provocative' LoveReading

'Deliciously fresh and malevolent story-telling' Craig Sisterson

'Original, thought provoking and highly recommended' Mark Tilbury

'A masterfully macabre tale … a whole new level of creepy magnificence' Louise Mumford

'Magnificently, compulsively chilling' Margaret Kirk

'Fans of Chuck Palahniuk in his prime will adore Carver' Christopher Hooley

'Another great novel written in true, unconventional, Will Carver style' Catherine McCarthy

'A taut, highly original novel from one of the most underrated crime writers out there' Simon Kernick

'Beautifully written, smart, dark and disturbing – and so original' Steve Mosby

'Possibly the most interesting and original writer in the crime-fiction genre' Luca Veste

'A genuinely creepy thriller … completely enthralled' Margaret B Madden

'A twisted, devious thriller' Nick Quantrill

ABOUT THE AUTHOR

Will Carver is the international bestselling author of the January David series. He spent his early years in Germany, but returned to the UK at age eleven, when his sporting career took off. He turned down a professional rugby contract to study theatre and television at King Alfred's, Winchester, where he set up a successful theatre company. He currently runs his own fitness and nutrition company, and lives in Reading with his two children.

Will's latest title, *The Beresford*, was published by Orenda Books in July 2021. His previous title *Hinton Hollow Death Trip* was longlisted for the Not the Booker Prize, while *Nothing Important Happened Today* was longlisted for the Theakston's Old Peculier Crime Novel of the Year. *Good Samaritans* was book of the year in *Guardian*, *Telegraph* and *Daily Express*, and hit number one on the ebook charts. Follow Will on Twitter @will_carver.

Also by Will Carver and available from Orenda Books:

The Detective Sergeant Pace Series:
Good Samaritans
Nothing Important Happened Today
Hinton Hollow Death Trip

The Beresford

PSYCHOPATHS ANONYMOUS

WILL CARVER

Orenda Books
16 Carson Road
West Dulwich
London SE21 8HU
www.orendabooks.co.uk

First published by Orenda Books, 2021

A catalogue record for this book is available from the British Library.

ISBN 978-1-913193-75-1
eISBN 978-1-913193-76-8

Typeset in Garamond by typesetter.org.uk

Printed and bound by CPI Group (UK) Ltd, Croydon CR0 4YY

For sales and distribution, please contact info@orendabooks.co.uk

'Send the poison rain down the drain
to put bad thoughts in my head.'

Elliot Smith – *Miss Misery*

PROLOGUE

Jill is the fucking worst.

She thinks she's so open and poetic, and she's sooooo sixth step, all ready to let God remove these defects from her character.

I mean, there's obviously no God, and if there was, He's not sitting around thinking, 'I need to make Jill quit the booze because the red wine turns her into such a cunt.' That can't be right. Even if you are everywhere and see everyone and know everything, you don't give a fuck about Jill, she's so annoying.

Next, Jill is telling us how she doesn't remember her daughter before she was six years old, and we're supposed to care. How she would drive her to the pub, leave her outside in the car, get pissed and then drive the little fucker home like she was the biggest inconvenience to her life.

And the thing I'm most annoyed about is that I got here while Jill hit step three. I want to see this witch at step one. I want to know what her rock bottom is. I want to know that she's on her knees in a supermarket car park, taking shots to the back of the throat so that she can afford another spritzer to numb some maternity out of her.

If I can hear how low Jill was, and what made her want to take that first step, then maybe I can find some sympathy. Because, right now, I want to drink.

I want to drink.

And I kind of want to kill Jill.

But then she's holding up some chip that says she's been sober for one hundred days, and everyone claps her strength and determination.

Everyone but me.

I want to take Jill out and get her wasted. I want to drop her back five steps. I want to hear her curse about the child she never wanted and let her tell me that the only thing she's ever really loved is the house red.

Hell, I'll knock back a bottle or two of Chardonnay with her and spill my guts about things that she'll never remember.

All this talk of drinking and not drinking really builds a thirst.

But I can't today.

It's Tuesday and it's only 16:30 and this is just the Kilburn meeting. I only come here for Jill, now. There are better venues within the London North West Intergroup. I'm a big fan of Women's Reflections over in Maida Vale at 19:00; some real train wrecks there. Any time there's a New Beginnings, I'm first through the door. That's when it's most interesting, most raw. And you have to remember that people are at their most fragile when they take the leap – that's where I go when I need to get laid.

I'll avoid anything too churchy. Big Book Wednesday is not for me. And I can't stand those ones with the cutesy names either, like You'll Never Walk Alone or Sober in the Suburbs. Who comes up with this shit?

No, I can't get pissed with Jill before dinner and turn up to Camden Newcomers two hours later. It'll send out the wrong message. That I'm not really serious about this.

And I am extremely serious about drinking. I love it.

And the misery. I can't get enough of that. It's the reason I'm booked in to Simply AA Sunday and Emotional Sobriety on Monday and Midday Reflections and Hampstead Women and anything else where I can see some truth, no matter how ugly.

The only other time you see that kind of honesty is when you look into the eyes of someone who is about to die.

I walk into another cold hall where the natural light is the bluest shade of depression. This isn't one of those meetings where you sit around in a circle, you have to go up to the front and tell them how you got to this point. I have a few stories that I use. I can't even remember which ones are true any more. Tonight I'm thinking of doing the my-husband-shot-himself-in-the-face bit.

When they ask if anybody would like to speak, I raise my hand and move myself to the front.

'Hi. My name is Maeve and I'm an addict.'

PART ONE

STEP **ONE**

'Admit that you are powerless over your addiction, that your life has become unmanageable...'

You can't drink away alcoholism. And that's one of life's great shames.

You come home from work early one day to find your girlfriend is banging her personal trainer: a twenty-four pack of beer can sort that right out. Sorrow can be drowned.

The sad, the tired, the lonely can pick up a bottle of gin and something to mix it with, and get some temporary happiness or drink themselves to sleep or feel like they have a friend. The feelings they don't want to feel can be alleviated for just a moment.

Even the poor and the homeless can give it a go. Sure, Johnnie Walker Red isn't as smooth as the Blue, but you can afford a bottle even if you can't afford your rent or a place to live. And who needs that much food, anyway?

I'm one of those I-can-stop-anytime-I-want-to (I-just-don't-want-to) drinkers. I'm fucked if I know when or where or why it started. There was no seismic event. Uncle Lenny didn't like to bounce me on his knee until I turned sixteen, and mum and dad hardly drank at all, so it's not some genetic thing. They didn't really talk at all, either, but that's no excuse.

I think that drinking on a Saturday night out turned into Friday and Saturday, which morphed into Friday and Saturday out, then Sunday night in with a bottle of wine. That evolves into a Wednesday night tipple, to get you over that midweek hump. Eventually, you're filling in the gaps.

And you tell yourself that you're not drinking too much, because it's only a couple of glasses and you're not actually getting drunk per se. But it is every day, and it's the first thing you think of when you clock off from work or walk back into the house after a long day in the office.

It's not an addiction, right? You're just taking the edge off. You don't wake up in the morning and crave vodka. No. That's what alcoholics do. They need it all the time. You're not an alcoholic, you don't even really like the taste. But it relaxes you.

You're not smashing your fist against the glass door of your local pub at 9:01 because they're opening up slightly late and you should already be at your favourite table with a pint of the cheapest bitter in the land. You're not burying four empty rosé bottles in the garden to hide the evidence of your pre-lunchtime guzzling.

You still talk in sips and swigs. There are no glugs or quaffs. You're not even a gulper. So you can't be an alcoholic.

But it's every night now. And what was once two small glasses is now half a bottle. Sometimes more.

You don't call yourself an alcoholic but you are a fucking drunk. Not a mean one, sure. Not overly promiscuous. There's no gateway to other substances. But you are a drunk.

You're a drunk.

And the only difference between a drunk and an alcoholic is that alcoholics go to meetings.

This is what I was planning to say when I walked through the door of Simply AA for the very first time. I'd looked online and found that there were two types of meetings: open and closed. Closed meetings are for your hardcore members, which I'd hoped to be one day. Those who were both committed to getting their lives back on track but were also the most committed to the booze.

The open meetings felt a bit like a gym trial, where you get free sessions for a week to work out whether you like it or not, whether you are one of those people who goes to a gym. You don't even really have to be an alcoholic. Maybe you're questioning whether you have started to drink too much or your partner has brought it up with you. Maybe you don't think you drink a lot at all and coming to a meeting will prove that. Perhaps it will give you something to aim for. A target.

That Simply AA meeting took place on a Monday afternoon at 15:00 in Edgeware. It was mostly men, because the drunken housewives were heading out for the school pick-up. I thought I'd get up and give my long speech about being a drunk, not an alcoholic, but none of it went to plan.

Because I shouldn't be here.

At best, I'm trespassing.

It was one of the circle ones. The chairs looked like they were used for school PTA meetings or church prayer groups. I arrived a little after the start time because I didn't want to be the first person there, the only person there, or get caught in some conversation with the only other person there.

Eighteen seats and twelve of them were filled. I managed to bag one so that I had at least one side that was not occupied by another person. The man to my right was probably the same age as me. He looked ruffled but deliberately so. He hadn't just rolled in off the street for the free coffee. He tilted his head up to me as I sat down as if saying, 'Hi. This is a bit awkward, right?' And I appreciated that.

The first guy to tell his story was in the wrong place. Some ex-military type, said his name was Castle. He looked like shit and he smelled like Christmas pudding. But not in the festive, brings-a-smile-to-your-face way. Without a doubt, he had been drinking all day.

He couldn't look up from the floor. The entire time he spoke, his eyes were down and his head was shaking a little. It made him no less captivating, though. I searched around that circle for another person who, like me, might've been thinking, 'Now THAT'S an alcoholic, pass me a shot of sambuca.'

He'd got drunk and hit his wife. They'd been together for ten years and he'd never laid a hand on her. That's what he said. Then one night, he had come home late – they'd been out together – and she'd said something that was slightly provocative and he pushed her on the bed. Jokingly. 'Like a "don't-be-silly" or "get-the-hell-out-of-here" way.' He re-enacted the push as he said it.

His wife didn't like it. She didn't see it as a joke. So she got straight back up and started slapping him, telling him that he does not lay a finger on her. Ever. She was attacking him. So he punched her in the face.

He lost the room at that point.

He remembers the noise it made and the way her nose felt under his knuckles as he made contact. She kicked him out right then. And he left straight away. He knew he'd done wrong. He hardly ever sees his daughter now and boo fucking hoo.

Turned to the drink. Yada yada yada.

No amount of liquor can make him forget the sound of her delicate nose breaking or the feeling of it crushing beneath the weight of a strong right hook.

I glance at the man next to me, who grits his teeth to demonstrate the awkwardness in the room. I roll my eyes.

This fucking lowlife beat up a woman and became a raging dipso, and has the cheek to gatecrash an open AA meeting and bring the mood down like this.

A man on the other side, closely cropped hair and highly groomed beard, gets up and walks out. I look at his face, trying to drink in his problem with the situation. He doesn't seem disgusted or offended, or angry, even, that this gin-drenched mince pie of a man is ruining everyone's Monday with his tale of woe.

It's relief. And focus. He's experienced some kind of epiphany. Nothing puts you off dinner like somebody throwing up in front of you, maybe this guy realised that he wasn't going to end up that way; it wasn't worth it. Losing your home and your family. Not for a drink. Maybe the utter misery of this drunken bore has helped some other idiot pull their life together.

Skip straight to step twelve.

Or maybe, like me, he can't quite bring himself to care about the wretched dope, who is still whinnying about his self-inflicted mental torment. Maybe he's just escaping. Maybe this is not the club membership he was after. Maybe he knows of a decent bar nearby, or better, an awful bar nearby. I'm tempted to follow him.

But I want my turn.

Because I've got this whole witty speech planned. I know what I have to do. I know the answers. I'm woke, as they say.

That stinking yawn is still droning on, looking at the floor, he hasn't even noticed that one member of the audience has already asked for a refund. I'm hoping that the steady shaking of his body is Parkinson's Disease, that way it might rock him to sleep, but it'll be just my luck that it's withdrawal from the booze. He clearly hasn't had a drink for the three hours it seems his sad story has lasted.

It must be killing him.

He's probably better off dead, I think.

What kind of a life is this?

Then he cries. And the guy at the front who seems to be moderating proceedings utters some platitude about bravery.

'It is so difficult to admit defeat, to say out loud that alcohol has become a destructive obsession.' When he speaks, I sense a genuine compassion within him, though he must have heard every kind of story a hundred times before. This is the first time I've been to one of these and I can't force myself to feel anything but annoyance and frustration.

Then he turns a little more evangelical.

'There is no bankruptcy as potent as addiction. It is an allergy. An allergy to your body that manifests in self-destruction. You must accept it.'

As if that wife-beating pickled onion had not been humiliated enough, the sponsor was making it absolute. Though I'm not entirely sure what the whole 'allergy' thing really meant. Sounded like he'd delivered that line a thousand times before. Straight from AA scripture.

'Your admittance of defeat is a requirement for you to make that all-important first step. Your powerlessness will become the foundation for your success and eventual happiness.'

It's too preachy. I'm not here for that. I can understand why people can be put off when the guy running things is trying to proselytise the virtues of a twelve-step plan before you've even had the opportunity to express how your own mind has apparently been warped by drink or drugs or sex.

I guess he's playing the percentages. The guy in the middle, the woman-puncher who smells like ash and cloves and burnt cinnamon, looks utterly beaten down; worse than when he got here. There is nothing else that can be done but build the idiot back up again. He is at the bottom and wants to be saved. He's buying into this. That's how easy it is to recruit.

I raise my hand.

Fucking the guy next to me was inevitable. I didn't want to leave that place empty-handed.

'Yes. This is excellent. Very courageous. You cannot recover alone. We are a community. Thank you for offering to talk to us, too.'

Everyone starts clapping and I finally lower my hand, not realising that I've had it up in the air like an eager school kid the entire time the group leader has been pontificating.

'Thanks. I'm … er … I'm … Wait, I don't have to say my name, right? That's what the second A is all about.'

He shakes his head.

I take a breath and run through a few things in my mind. All that business about weekend drinking bleeding into the week, and being woke or awakened or whatever the right word is. I'm going to keep it rational and deliberate, and hopefully as captivating as the mouldy clementine who opened up before me.

But instead: 'My husband died. He was shot. Or he shot himself. The police are fucking useless and won't give me a straight answer.

You think they can tell those things from angles and tiny molecules of powder. But they won't say for sure.'

I can see that I have them. Even the port and stilton who spoke before me has stopped crying.

'We used to drink together, you know? It was our thing. It was just fun and silly and a release,' I give the guy to my right a subtle glance, 'and sexy.'

A pause for it to register.

'But then he's gone and I still have all that wine in the house and the drinking isn't fun or silly any more because life is neither of those things. It's an anaesthetic, I know that. I'm not stupid and I'm not drunk now. I'm alone, I guess. I have nobody to say these things out loud to. And that's what I'm supposed to do, right? That's what you want me to do.'

More platitudes fly my way from our inspirational mentor. He's handling me with kid gloves. Maybe because I'm a woman. Maybe because I'm not as flammable as the guy who spoke before me.

'I'm drinking for two, I guess. Trying to keep him alive or something.' Now would be a great place to cry. I'm sure I could do it but I don't want to. I don't want to be told that I'm weak, because I'm not. I don't want some guy who has known me for ten minutes to tell me that I'm not ready for the road ahead, the one that will help me lift this unrelenting obsession, because I have to admit what I am.

I don't want that.

I want to screw the other guy I've known for ten minutes, the designer stubble to my right, after sharing too many bottles of something that burns our throats, mangles our brains and loosens our underwear.

Another wino talks after me about how the men in his family all drink too much. His story is not interesting but I can't pull myself away from his melancholy. It's intoxicating to witness such vulnerability. That's more of an addiction than the Sauvignon Blanc, for me.

Show me your misery.

Afterwards, it remains relaxed and we can all wander freely around the room and grab ourselves a tea or coffee and talk to one another. I avoid eye contact with everyone but my target.

'Didn't want to speak tonight?' I ask him. It's obviously playful.

'I prefer the anonymity part over the alcohol part.' He smiles and drinks some tea. He's a swigger, I can tell. A beer guy. His elbow stays at his side. Whisky drinkers lift their elbow. Spirits drinkers hold the hand higher against their bodies.

I sidle in closer to him.

'Well, we don't have to talk about the alcohol if you don't want to but we can certainly drink it if you know somewhere nearby.'

Last week was so amazing that I almost didn't come to the meeting tonight.

Lisa and Kim went at it. Gloves off. Nails sharpened.

It was some swanky restaurant in Amsterdam and Kim was giving a heart-wrenching account of how she lost her sister to an overdose when she, herself, was still a kid. The other ladies around the table are empathetic and nodding their heads in solidarity. I can't help but smile because I can see that Lisa is seething about something and she is waiting for her moment to blow.

This is a normal night for me. I had a bottle of wine to myself and a comfortable sofa. I was still in my work outfit but I'd loosened some buttons and kicked off my shoes and taken off my tights. Those Real Housewives of Beverley Hills were enjoying their fine dining while I had heated up a chicken supreme meal in the microwave. It was disgusting.

Lisa couldn't let it lie. She'd been sober for three years and felt aggrieved that Kim had got on her back about drinking. Sure, she's got some issues when it comes to drugs and alcohol because of her sister's overdose but what right does that give her to lecture somebody else?

'Shut your fucking mouth, I've had enough of you, you beast.'

I had to live pause because I was laughing so hard when Lisa said that to another 'friend' at the table.

Then she called out her sister for not being supportive.

Then she attacked Kim, saying she knew a truth about her husband and Kim didn't want her to say what it was.

I did.

Then Kim threw a wine glass at Lisa.

It was gold. Televisual perfection.

Lisa behaved horrifically in the eyes of everyone but I could understand where she was coming from. My issue was that she let it fester for too long. She should have had it out with them individually long before that meal, got rid of a few of them.

And tonight is the follow-up from that carnage. I have wine in the fridge and three meals to choose from, though I was thinking of heating up the prawn linguine, which will now leave me at a calorie deficit.

I need my shows, my doses of reality that are anything but real. And I know I need my wine or gin or whisky. There's more to me than that, though. My father always used to say, 'It's important to have a hobby'. So I've recorded the show and I opted to attend the meeting. The one where I know I can usually pick somebody up.

I have other needs.

And it's important to make time for all of them because if that balance is thrown off, if I don't get a little of all the things I need, if I don't make time for the hobby, things go wrong.

He still doesn't tell me his name. Even after pulling out and hosing me down. You'd think the guy would tell me his name. Or *a* name. Any name. It was fun and flirty in the beginning and I like that he was riffing on the whole AA thing, but enough is enough.

I reach across to the bedside table and pick up the bottle of

Johnnie Walker Red. He has his own on his cheap pine bedstand. I take it straight from the bottle. He's doing his best to keep up. He has been all night.

There's no way this nameless guy should have been at Alcoholics Anonymous, my dead grandmother could outdrink him. She'd probably outfuck him, too. I wonder whether he goes there to pick up needy women. He could be married. His wife has called him a needle dick or she no longer puts out and he has found that drunk women give him a more favourable critique.

I'm not sure.

But I know he doesn't belong at AA with that fake thirst, and he's never going to cut it as a sex addict.

'My name is Audrey, by the way.' I figure this might get him to open up.

'I'm Jack.' He stares at me and I can see he is trying to hold back a grin.

'You are full of shit. You are not cool enough for Jack.'

'And there's no way you're an Audrey, so let's leave it at that.'

I sit up, the covers are sticking to my stomach where he left his mark. I take down more of the cheap whisky. This guy is a piece of shit.

'You're married, right?'

Drink. I see how much he has left in his bottle. What a wimp.

'What do you want me to say? Look, it doesn't matter. You don't know her. You don't know what it's like. I know what I'm doing. It's not your fault. Don't feel bad. She cheated first.' He sits up now, to add some kind of gravity to his sentiment.

'I don't feel bad. I can't. It doesn't bother me if you're a philanderer. I guess I'm just ... disappointed that you're not an alcoholic.' I'm guessing that he's too stupid to understand the word 'philanderer', so definitely won't get how I undercut him with the rest of the comment.

I want to tell him that he actually doesn't know what he's doing. That the clitoris is about another inch higher up the boat than he thinks.

There's always more damage through suggestion.

'Like you, you fucking drunk bitch.' Obviously he lashes out. Instant aggression.

Men throw punches while women throw nuance.

I get out of the bed, bottle still in my hand, and move towards the bathroom door.

'I may be drunk but I'm not a fucking fraud. So please leave your bottle on the side. I'm taking mine in here to shower the poison off my body and finish myself off.' I turn my back on him, but it's only for a moment before I'm in the bathroom and have locked the door. It's flimsy but I feel safe.

I think about smashing the bottle over his head and throwing a match at him. The fucker probably wouldn't burn, there's so little flammable liquid in him.

I do exactly what I told him I would do and, when I emerge from the steam-filled bathroom – wrapped in a towel, the cheap whisky is half an inch lower in the bottle – and the dick with no name has gone.

He left his drink on the side table, of course, and opened the curtains. Weirdly, he also made the bed. With military precision, Not Jack made the bed we fucked in and he came over.

Clearly the behaviour of a psychopath.

The hotel isn't one of those charge-by-the-hour places but it's cheap enough that I don't feel the need to stay there overnight. I put my clothes back on – I'm surprised No Name didn't fold them into a neat pile and place them delicately at the bottom of the bed for me. I'd have been less shocked if he'd cut them up or stolen them. Or I'd come back into the room and he'd been wearing my underwear.

I take his bottle and put it into my bag, keeping my own in my hand to swig as I make my way home in the cold dark of the London streets. It's past the time when pubs and clubs kick out but there are still signs of life. Others, like me, taking that early walk of shame home after some one-night stand. The lucky ones, who don't fall asleep afterwards and have to wake up to that early-morning awkwardness the next day.

I see a couple who haven't even made it to a bedroom yet. He pushes her against some railings by the side of the road and reaches a cold hand down the front of her skirt. Anyone can see. But it's mostly homeless people hunkering down in shop doorways, cardboard boxes for mattresses, swathed in filthy, bare quilts to protect them from the cold and their limited possessions from being seen or stolen.

It's too late in the day to be asking for money, they're just hoping to make it to the morning.

But there's always one that doesn't adhere to these unwritten rules.

I take a right between two buildings. On one side is a shop that sells camping equipment and the other side used to be a cinema but is empty now. There's a guy sitting on the floor next to some rubbish left outside the shop. He mumbles something at me and I hesitate because I want to make out what he just said.

As I pause for that moment, I take him in. He's drunk and filthy and it looks as though he's pissed himself. I can smell it. Urine and booze and the cinnamon aroma I always associate with Christmastime.

It's not. Surely. The man opened up and stated in front of a bunch of strangers that he was at his lowest point. He was going to get help.

This point seems lower than earlier.

He murmurs another sentence, which I work out is a question that contains the word 'drink'. I lean down to look closer at him. I didn't really see his face properly at the meeting because he would not take his eyes off the floor.

He takes a swipe at my bottle but it's laboured and I manage to move it out the way.

Then he's pawing at one of my legs with his gnarled fingers and taking a second shot at the bottle. I pull it away again and feel that both his hands are high up my thigh. I know this isn't a sexual attack, he just wants the whisky.

But so do I.

And I don't want his fucking hands on me.

So I grip the top of the bottle and hammer it down into his forehead. It's not a swing, I'm not trying to break it over his face or anything, I want to preserve it. I chop into his right eye with the thick base of the bottle and he lets go.

He's defeated.

But I'm not done.

~~You piece of shit.~~

I hit him with it again and again, cracking into the front of his skull. He drops to the floor and I kick him. And I hit him twice more in the face, crunching down on his nose, the same way he did just that once-was-enough time on his wife.

If it is him.

I don't know.

I don't care.

Does it even matter?

He stops moving and I can't tell if he's unconscious or dead but I know it makes no difference to the world either way. It certainly doesn't make a difference to me. Another homeless scrounger left in the shadow of a building they darkened, first, with their presence.

It's not that I spit on them as I walk past or that I wouldn't drop a couple of pounds in their cup to put towards their next fix, it's not that I spend time thinking about how disgusting I find them. I don't care enough. But nobody has the right to touch me.

That's the mistake he made.

And the ones before him.

I shouldn't need to explain. ~~And I'll never apologise~~.

There's blood on the bottom of my whisky bottle. Red on red. I unscrew the cap, knock back a mouthful, screw it back on and get walking.

I am not powerless over alcohol. Nor am I powerless over men.

I'm managing. I'm in control.

Still, I think I'd like to go to another meeting.

STEP **TWO**

'Come to believe that a power greater than yourself could restore you to sanity.'

Where the mind is rational and intelligent, there is no place for God. We don't even have to hit double figures before we start questioning how one man gets around every child's house to deliver a present on Christmas Eve. We know early on that the Tooth Fairy isn't real, we just keep our mouths shut for the money. And the whole Easter Bunny idea is absurd. As absurd as a man dying and coming back to life two days later.

Yet people still talk about God as though the concept is any different to these fantastical fables.

Successful writers, singers, actors, sportspersons, will receive an award and the first thing they do is thank God.

They thank God.

There is a belief that whatever talent they have been gifted is from Him. They may not even have a talent but have worked hard to get into the fortunate position in which they find themselves. Instead of taking the moment to reflect on their own worth and determination, they attribute it to God, which, to a sane person is the same as thanking Jack Frost for the snow.

Perhaps the marketing department in Heaven is a little avant-garde, they're thinking outside the box. They've realised that God isn't cool any more. That society is becoming increasingly secular. And the best way to get His message out would be through a song called 'Bootylicious'. Or a last-minute goal against Barcelona.

The Lord may work in mysterious ways, but none are as batshit crazy as His PR team.

God is for the desperate. The people who have nothing, who have lost everything, including who they are. God is not for the rich and successful, they just say that they have Him because they want everything.

Father Christmas is for the innocent, the ones still with hope. But God, He is reserved for the hope*less*. The miserable. The suicidal. He feeds on despair and anguish and is undoubtedly the reason that He finds Himself to be so prevalent with those who struggle with addiction.

God doesn't see everything. He is not everywhere.

He's at an AA meeting.

Hell, He's at all of them.

And I'm at one. It's in Highgate. I said that I'd never attend this type of thing but intrigue got the better of me and I'm paying for that now. It's called Footprints In The Sand. Or FITS, if you work in the events team at Heaven HQ. They are going to make sure that we all get through this tough time in our lives. They want us clean and sober, and when that happens, they want us to stand up in front of everyone and thank God.

Christina Rossetti is buried in the cemetery nearby and I'm thinking about visiting her grave afterwards to explain to her what a truly bleak midwinter looks like.

There are three types of addict:

The ones who won't believe in God.

The ones who can't believe in God.

And the ones who do believe but have lost any faith that God will help them.

It does not matter which one you are, by the time you start this twelve-step journey, your thoughts will be turned around.

You will believe.

You can believe.

And you will regain your faith.

It works. It absolutely works. And the perfectly constructed get-out is that if it doesn't work and you go back to the booze or stuff your face with six glazed donuts or suck a few cocks for rocks, it's not God's fault. It's yours.

Here's how they get you:

If you're one of the first two types of addict, the *won't believes* and the *can't believes*, you are not made to feel lesser than the person who embraces the idea of a higher power. Far from it. You are already at your lowest. You have made an admission and there is no need to try to knock you down further.

It's all cotton wool and kid gloves and empathy. You do not have to jump through hoops to get to a better place of sobriety and control; there is but one hoop and it is wide. The sponsors can help you through the experience.

They tell you that the steps are suggestions rather than commands, and step two does not have to be swallowed immediately. It's a wide hoop, so just keep an open mind. That's all they're asking. If you can stop debating God then it opens up the opportunity for you to feel. In fact, forget about all the God chat, AA itself can be your higher power.

It's manipulative and it works. Because once you believe that there is a higher power at work – whether that is fate or community – you can put your faith in something you cannot see, that isn't there. And you will be more open to believing that the higher power is God.

You'll come around eventually.

But what if you are that other kind of addict? You believed. You got to that point of desperation where you asked your God to help and He did nothing. He failed to come to your aid and fulfil your demands. You've tried faith and you've tried no faith and found both to be deficient.

This third type of addict is not treated to the delicacy of the kid gloves. They are told that defiance is the stance of many alcoholics.

'Belief means reliance, not defiance.' That's what the sponsor keeps saying. Quoting the plan like he's regurgitating scripture.

You are told that you asked God for help, to fix you, maybe, but at what time did you ask what His will is? Your faith was superficial. You were not serious about God.

That's on you.

Not on him.

Get yourself back to step one and take stock of yourselves.

He is not a genie, ready to grant your wishes, but He can restore your lost sanity if only you can relate yourself fully to Him.

They're rallying. You've been hooked and now you are being slowly reeled in.

And, if you are sound of mind and still have the ability to reason, you are probably pissed off with how easy it is for the big man in the sky to get away with everything. Still drinking? Not His fault, you should have believed better. He didn't help you in your time of need? Your fault, pal, you were too busy asking Him to solve your problems rather than checking that it wasn't His will for you to have these problems in the first place, so that you could then fix them and become stronger in your conviction and devout belief.

Nobody is questioning this great plan of His, which seems to involve war and pestilence and famine and suffering everywhere you look. If this is God's will, God is a dick.

Of course, nobody at Footprints In The Sand is sound of mind and nobody is really questioning the holy algorithm. They're a bunch of drunks and they're going along with it all.

'...grant me my wishes rather than thy will be done...'

A shake of the head or slap on the wrist. And, for the non-believers, a hug and a smile and a little more encouragement.

I haven't realised but I'm staring at the sponsor. He might think that I'm listening to his drivel intently or that I am attracted to him but the truth is that I'm gazing through him, into the future. A future where I take him back to mine or to a hotel room and tie him to a bed. Where I take his dick in my mouth and bite down hard before asking him how that is part of the great plan. Where I drink wine in front of him before smashing the top off the glass and using the jagged end to cut bloody shapes in his torso while saying, 'It's God's will, motherfucker.'

~~I'm going to enjoy killing you.~~

I smile at the thought and it catches his eye.

He smiles back.

And to think I was never going to come to another FITS session again. Now I have a job to do.

A normal evening for me looks like this: I pull into my drive and the sound of the gravel beneath the tyres is like a bell ringing in the ear of Pavlov's dog. I want to get inside and not think about how to market a soft drink or sports shoe or debut novel. I want to kick my shoes off across the floor of the entrance and feel the cold tiles of the kitchen on the soles of my feet as I saunter towards the fridge. I want to yank that door open and pull out the remains of some white wine bottle, pour it into a glass and take an emphatic gulp.

But it never quite goes that way because I always finish every bottle that I open.

Still, there's something about the ceremony of popping a cork for the first time or hearing that click as you unscrew the lid of an untouched bottle.

That's how it goes.

I have developed a wonderfully fluid technique where I can kill the ignition, pull out the key, unhook my seatbelt, grab my bag from the passenger seat, open the driver's door and get out all at the same time. One swift motion.

I lock the car with the fob as I'm switching to the house key. I let myself in and have already kicked off one shoe before I've pulled the key out of the open door. The other shoe is liberated, the bag is dropped on the floor and the door is shut behind me.

Within a minute, I am poking holes into the plastic film that covers whatever microwaveable meal I'm having that night and I'm walking into the lounge with an oversized wine glass filled with something cold that was once a bunch of grapes.

I go straight to the news. I love it. Most of my working day is spent making stuff up. I'm good at it, too. But nothing is as exciting as real life. Nothing is more interesting than the truth.

It's not about the events or the glory projects, it's the mundanities. It's the everyday things that people can relate to. If you're going to make a reality television show, you need to film real people. You need to put twelve accountants in a house with cameras on them twenty-four hours a day. Putting a feminist with a male chauvinist, a sex worker, a gay person, a wannabe socialite, a black rapper and a Conservative politician is entertaining but it is forced. And it is not reality, despite the cultural hotpot that is our all-embracing country.

There is so much reality, so much truth, in misery. That is why I love the news.

It's devastating.

More so than soap operas, which people only watch because it makes them feel better about their own shitty lives for half an hour each day. If you really want to feel good then you need to know that some innocent women and children were bombed in a village you've never even heard of as a result of a skirmish you think is too far away to ever affect you.

If you want a pick-me-up of some kind then you don't want to catch the end of the programme. You don't want to hear about a dog calling the police and saving its elderly owner. You don't want to know who won a race chasing a round of cheese down a Gloucestershire hill in the rain. The warmth you get from a fluff piece like this is fleeting.

Good news does not make you feel good.

It doesn't work.

Throw out a global epidemic. Every day, the news is reporting death tolls and lockdowns and parliamentary incompetence. If there's a report about some food innovator who has found a way of feeding the hungriest people of the world, it does not scratch your itch. Who cares if some volunteers have been helping refugees. What do you really get from clapping the National Health Service once a week?

It's patronising, not unifying.

You need some people in Syria blowing each other up or slaves being beaten on ships near China or another school shooting in the

United States. Because you don't really care about the ones on the front line trying to save lives or protect the elderly until it affects you.

The good news is too far away to make you feel good and the bad news is too far to make you feel bad. You're connected to everything now, but the distance from reality is growing.

You want to lose weight, looking at some size-zero model on a catwalk is not inspiring, you need to witness cases of morbid obesity. You want to get fit, seeing a six-pack on anybody is supposed to be good news, that what you seek is possible.

It doesn't work.

Neither do those motivational posters dotted around the office.

And those quotes that get thrown around social media, something that has been said in history by a person who has achieved something and thought hard about what message they were putting out into the world, one of those pithy sentences that is regurgitated by some nobody who takes pictures of their dinner every day, it doesn't help anybody.

It doesn't make a reader change their outlook and it certainly does not help the person who posted that drivel.

I watch the news because I need reality. And I'm not stupid enough to believe that these different news organisations do not have their own agendas. I know that sometimes we are shown a story to detract the national interest away from something else that is happening. The reality I crave is that the world is fucking awful.

You will hear those who bitch and moan about it but don't really do anything to change it. And there are those who think that half-baked, insincerity or positive thinking will have an effect. The real power comes from acceptance. Knowing that most of us won't make a difference to our immediate environment, let alone on a national scale.

It's apathy through lack of empathy.

I love the news.

I get home, kick off my shoes, pour a drink, start the microwave dinner, switch on the television, eat the microwave dinner, pour another drink, then another and another.

And I say to the group, 'I don't really know how society got to this place but, to be honest, I'm not sure that I really care.' I often lie at these things but figured, if I'm going to waffle on about truth and mundanity, I may as well do something mundane myself, like tell the truth.

And that fucker leading the session behaves like some exploited Indian call-centre employee and reverts straight to the script.

Do I believe a power greater than myself could restore me to sanity?

Do I fuck.

I don't even believe I'm an alcoholic.

Outside the room, there's a huge pinboard. Janet teaches Zumba on a Wednesday evening at 19:30 but, from the looks of the picture, which I assume is Janet twisting her hips in front of twenty other women, Janet needs to think about her nutrition because the Zumba isn't working.

Yoga with Debbie twice a week doesn't seem like a good option, either. Nobody wants to see a fitness instructor who is all legs, six-pack and perfectly pert tits but you want to know that they are at least fitter and healthier than the people they are teaching. I'm sure Debbie and Janet are both flexible and coordinated but they're not aspirational.

The people who attend these classes are not there for fitness or to push themselves in any way, they are there to belong, to be a member of something, to be able to say that they did yoga last night when they get into that first morning chat in the office.

There's a metal-detector club that meets every other week and the local weavers bring their spinning wheels and boxes of yarn on the third Saturday of each month. If you need a babysitter, there are six or seven to choose from. Someone will even walk your dog if you can't be bothered and have more money than sense or your legs are still aching from Janet's Zumba session.

If you would prefer to socialise with other dog lovers, then there's a meeting spot at 6:30 every morning, much like the gathering I can see through the windows near the entrance where the running club are assembling in their high-visibility Lycra.

And there are choirs and tap dancing and karate clubs for all ages, and badminton or youth club or Teddy's sing-a-long for parents with new babies – though the poster only mentions the mothers. The amateur dramatic society is currently rehearsing a performance of something called *Martha, Josie and the Chinese Elvis*.

It's a veritable smorgasbord of Hampstead boredom but that is the kind of snapshot I find interesting. Yet it's the piece of paper pinned to the top-right corner of the board that excites me the most:

For information on hiring any of the rooms in the centre, please call or email Calvin...

I take a picture with my phone to make note of the contact details. Apparently, he is here on weekday mornings until lunchtime because they run a preschool in the second, smaller hall.

Directly opposite the room where I just attended Footprints In The Sand – it's Steps To Christ every other week (~~The same fucking thing)~~ – there is another space of a similar size but it's empty, the lights are off.

It would be perfect for what I have in mind.

The sponsor sees me outside, looking at the notice board. Everyone else has left and he has stayed behind to stack the chairs together and place them in the corner out of the way so Janet and friends can wobble out a slow-paced merengue later in the evening.

'Oh, hello,' he says, as though I'm a five-pound note he has found in the street.

'Hello again,' I say back.

He takes a look at the board then back at me before asking, 'This club is a bit heavy, right? If you're looking for something a little lighter, I can recommend the Classics Book Group.' He lowers his voice and leans in closer to me. 'But avoid the needlework club,' he looks around over his shoulder as if somebody might be listening, 'A real fucking bitch fest.'

And we both laugh.

'You did really well in there. I know that the second step can be tough and there's always some resistance to it in the beginning. I was exactly the same.'

'Should we really be discussing it outside of the meeting?'

'I'm not your therapist or your priest. Though I am here to listen. You're me, ten steps ago and I am you, ten steps from now. I'm not trying to push you, I'm not asking for atonement, I'm just letting you know that I understand and that I'm here.'

Kid gloves?

Is this how cults are started?

'Well, that's very kind of you but I'm not sure why I'm getting special attention, there were lots of people in there.'

It feels like he might be flirting with me but I keep my distance because it still feels like it could be a recruitment technique.

'Of course. And I can tell almost right away who is willing to put in the work and who will need more help. I also know that the ones who find a way to hang around at the end often still want to talk a little more.'

He smiles a smile of a someone who thinks they have me pegged and I go along with it, I try to look coy. But not too much.

Then he asks me if I have a sponsor yet by telling me that I don't have a sponsor yet. And he offers his services.

Before I know it, we are exchanging phone numbers so that I can contact him – anytime, apparently – if I feel that I am veering off course at any point.

He thinks he knows me, he's seen my type a million times before. That I was hanging around for him at the end of the session.

He doesn't know a thing.

He doesn't know that I am going to book that empty room opposite his and start a club for people just like me.

He doesn't know that I think Footprints In The Sand is horse shit, that I'd rather take a fist than go to FITS.

And he has no idea that I'm going to kill him at some point.

~~I'm going to fuck him. And then~~ I'm going to kill him.

STEP **THREE**

'Make the decision to turn your will and life over to the care of God as you understand Him.'

Faking the first two steps was a cinch. But they are the only two on the journey that are about acceptance. Accepting that I am powerless over my addictions and accepting that there is a higher power at work that can restore my sanity and sobriety.

My sponsor, Gary, is still pushing the whole AA-can-be-your-higher-power angle but I know he really thinks it's something to do with a God. I can't bite on that one but he's staying hugely patient with my resistance.

I've told him that I'll go along with the *community* being the higher power but it is time to get moving with step three and it's no longer about acceptance.

Now is the time for action.

It's just past midnight and I'm calling him. Partly because I want to annoy him and push his good will to breaking point, but also to learn.

I've had a bottle of Merlot. I'm not telling him that. He probably thinks he knows.

'It's great to have faith in something, Maeve, but you can't do this on faith alone. You can have faith but still keep God out of your life, which is what you are doing.'

'You said that AA can be my higher power.'

'Yes, yes. I know. And I wasn't lying about that. You have done brilliantly.'

~~Liar.~~

I take a swig and look over at the clock. I know what he wants, he wants me to attempt to let the Big Guy in. It's a baby step. But the entire programme rests on how well I can pretend to do this.

It's not his fault that I'm going to kill him. It doesn't have to always be something heinous. It doesn't have to be retribution. It doesn't require some deep motivation. Sometimes a person is just in my way. Sometimes it's for fun. Sometimes, it's just that it's been a while.

He keeps talking.

'There's a blockage, right? I sense it. I get it. I was the same. Imagine that barrier is a door. You just need the key.'

'And how do I get this key?'

'The key is willingness. If you are willing to take a step forward, the door will open itself.'

Hell, it's all so flowery and preachy it makes me want to punch him in the dick.

'This is the way towards a faith that works, Maeve.'

I don't tell him that I want to finish my wine and put my hand between my legs – I freely accept that I am powerless over the orgasm. I don't tell him that I am using him, pumping him for information. I can't say that, with every call I make, I am manipulating him. I'm fucking with him. That I am making him dependent on me to give him a sense of achievement and self-worth.

I don't tell him that I am reeling him in.

Breaking him down.

Instead, I tell him that he has helped me. 'I know what I have to do, and I know that you say it is just a small step that is needed but it feels huge. Maybe because it's late. But thank you, it gives me something to think about.'

'And you haven't been drinking?'

'I've wanted to, of course, but I haven't.' I glance toward my glass. Almost done.

'And I'll see you at FITS this week?'

'Definitely.'

I sense that he nods but he doesn't say anything. Neither of us say goodbye. It seems like the right time to put the phone down.

I finish my wine, turn off the lamp on the bedside table, push my hand under the covers and accept the climax as my higher power.

Calvin looks as though his hair has never been washed. It's mostly greasy grey with the odd streak of black. He reminds me of a badger. A badger with milk-bottle glasses and three crooked teeth. He must scare the hell out of the kids when he opens up the hall for the preschool.

'That room is twenty pounds per hour.'

I tell him that I didn't know what I was expecting but that it sounded a bit steep and that I could probably charge people a small fee to help cover that.

'Oh. I'm sorry. It's not for profit? You're not a business? I probably should have asked that first. Busy morning.' He laughs to himself.

'Oh, no. It's not Zumba or anything like that.'

'That's lucky. I tried putting in a second Zumba class and Janet had a fit.' He speaks as though we both know Janet. I've never met her but I do feel as though I've got her sussed from her advertisement on the notice board.

'No. It's a support group.' I don't want to give too much away. The idea is still formulating in my mind.

'Ah, that's great. We do already have an Alcoholics Anonymous group that meets once a week. We used to have something for sex addicts, too, but there was ... an incident.'

I'm not sure how I feel about Calvin's candour. It's obviously beneficial in getting the word out there but his indiscretion is a worry.

'No. It's not that. I wouldn't be stepping on anyone's toes.'

There's a silence.

He wants me to tell him what it is and I don't want to say. It's a difficult spin to say that I want to gather psychopaths. That I want to enrol people who display elements of psychopathy. Because most people would think that I am rounding up serial killers and that's not the case. I might as well tell this custodian that I am setting up a paedophile ring.

'It's a mental-health group.' My marketing spin. People are so scared of these buzzwords that they'll bend over backward to accommodate you. It scares people. They don't really know what it means and they know they can get sucker-punched legally if they don't pay attention.

'Oh, yes. Mental health and all that. Very important. I mean, we don't offer the rooms out for free but there is a reduced rate for charity and non-profit work. Eleven pounds.'

I'm happy to cover that. He tells me that the AA meetings are subsidised by the church and it makes me hate God a little more. I roll my eyes at the idea of the 'The Key of Willingness'.

'And it's free at the same time as the Footsteps In The Sand group?'

'It is, for now.'

'I've got your number, I'll come back to you in the next day or so.'

'Not a problem.'

I leave the hall. Mothers are arriving with their toddlers. Toddlers with their teddy bears.

I'm late for work.

†

I'm late out of work and it screws with my routine.

I'm thirsty. These shoes are pinching my feet. My bag is too heavy. Hey, Gary, can we get God to carry my laptop? If He could drive me home, too, so that I can get a drink in, I would be grateful. Truly. That would really go some way to me opening that locked door with my key of willingness.

Hell, I'll turn my will over to the bearded bastard if he has an ice-cold bottle of something open for me when I get back.

I have to work through the night. Some blue-chip client is not happy with the campaign that has been put together and now it's on me to fix it. Because I delegated. I let someone else take up the slack. I depended on them and they've screwed me. I'm going to miss Cricklewood Living Sober tonight. It's not my favourite but I'd rather be there than polishing copy about a new netbook laptop or the refresh rates on a bunch of computer monitors. Apparently the screens can't be broken. They're tough enough to withstand a kid jabbing it with a pair of compasses or tipping it over onto their mouse. (Apparently the most common way for a monitor to be broken.)

What are these kids doing at school that they need military-grade equipment that can withstand an explosion? Whatever happened to a notepad and pencil? When did that become not enough?

Kids no longer talk, they text. It's all LOL and BRB. They're abbreviating single-syllable words into acronyms. More understandable if they are writing to a friend in a hurry but less acceptable when used in actual speech.

What are they doing with all the time they are saving?

It's laziness. A pseudo-language that only helps perpetuate their four-second attention spans. They can't converse, any more. Because they are too busy having eight micro-conversations at once that are filled with pointless acronyms and smiley faces.

Apparently, if you put a full stop at the end of a text to anyone under twenty, they see it as rude. Like you're shouting at them or telling them off or calling them an ungrateful sack of shit.

So it makes sense that a school lesson that lasts for an hour would bring about such rage and confusion that their only outlet would be to stab the expensive computer screen they never deserved in the first place.

That's what I'd like to say in this advert.

In fact, I'd like to tell school purchasers to save the money and restock the stationery cupboards. These screens are the reason that kids bring guns in to school to mow down their classmates and teachers. It's only a matter of time before the monitors and laptops have to be bulletproof.

Bulletproof equipment in classrooms. That will be the solution that some inbred politician comes up with instead of taking the guns away.

Handbrake. Ignition. Seatbelt. Bag. Door. Keys. Shoes. Fridge. Screw top.

And pour.
That's better.
Stab the meal. Shove it in the microwave. News on.
Drink.
I'm not going to start the work until I've eaten and I'm at least halfway through this bottle.
I couldn't even depend on some highly trained professionals to come up with a decent tech campaign for DoTrue Computers. It's their job. Their livelihood. They screwed it up. But they exist. I can see them. I can chastise them for their incompetence and hope that the lesson sinks in and they do not make the same mistakes again.
How am I supposed to turn my will over to God? Somebody I cannot see. Someone who may not even exist. How can I depend on that when I can't even depend on my team at work? How am I supposed to surrender my will and independence to Him?
Gary says that 'dependence gains independence'.
But what happens to ME if I give myself over?
Where do I go?
I like the first two steps. I think acceptance is important. I'll definitely use that when I start my group. Step three is proving to be a difficult stumbling block. I don't want to replicate this plan. I want to improve it. Maybe I don't understand it fully.
I just need to get my head around a full-HD resolution to cope with increasingly demanding computer applications, tough acrylic screen surface that delivers a longer-life solution ideal for schools and hospitals and anti-glare technology to help reduce eye fatigue associated with continuous use. And a typical five millisecond response time. Whatever that means.
Once my mind has been numbed by jargon and Riesling, I'll give Gary another late-night call and find out how the hell I'm supposed to open this goddamned door.

The real beauty about cracking a homeless guy's skull with the heavy base of a whisky bottle is that nobody gives a shit.

I've watched the news every day since I struck that hobo. Footballers are still fucking each other's wives, politicians are saying they'll do something then legislating for the opposite. A tech mogul was charged with rape. Some millionaire killed themself, leaving a note about the futility of life and worthlessness.

I checked some of the local rags, too. Another teenage kid was stabbed. A sportsman I've never heard of cut a large ribbon outside a new building I'll never use. And the country's oldest identical twins have taken up lake swimming.

But nothing about that piss-drenched drunk who tried to grope my leg the other night.

He could have bled out on the street and died. He could have crawled his way to the road and been seen by a motorist, who, in turn, called an ambulance. They could have patched him back up. Got him washed and fed before throwing him back out on the street. He could be out there now, sitting in a wheelchair with a dent in his head.

It's not newsworthy.

That's why you read about so many serial killers cutting up prostitutes. Sure, a lot of them have issues with women because their mothers were domineering or laughed at them when they were little and tried on a skirt or high heels while playing dress-up, so they have limited social skills when it comes to the opposite sex. Often it's because their own mothers were sex workers.

But that's psychological and sociological and environmental. That's only one part of why they choose to slay ladies of the night.

It's logistical.

Nobody will miss a whore.

The police are not going to put the hours in to locate some pissed-off pimp or drugged-up john. It's another sex worker off the streets. In fact, history shows that you can get away with three or four of them before anyone really sits up and pays attention.

Even then, they'll continue to walk the streets with a prostitute-killer on the loose. They'll hedge their bets. Because they need the money.

And it's the same with the homeless.

Nobody cares.

Nobody's listening.

You can give money to charity and still hate poor people, just as you can have faith and not let in God. That's what Gary tells me.

I probably wouldn't have beaten that homeless man around the head with a bottle if he hadn't have touched my leg like that. I was walking home. I was sexually fulfilled. Not by the guy I'd fucked, but still, I'd got there in the end.

The point is that I could have killed some hobo outside a camping-equipment shop and nobody would have found me. Because nobody would have been looking. I could have killed one a week since then and I'd probably still be okay.

But I'm not going to make a habit of it.

It doesn't mean anything to me. I have nothing against them. That one guy, I did. (~~Don't touch my legs.~~) But my dad wasn't homeless. My mum didn't beat me because I liked sleeping in a box as a kid.

I don't have to kill.

I'm not powerless over the need to end someone's life.

I don't get off on it. I'm not revisiting the scene of the crime in an attempt to drink in the same high I felt as I ripped somebody's life away.

It's not a necessity.

But I do enjoy it.

Gary calls me.

It begins with me feeling angry that he wants to take away my independence and ends with me repeating a mantra line by line.

'God, grant me the serenity to accept the things I can't change, the courage to change the things I can and the wisdom to know the difference. Thy will, not mine, be done.'

It's the last part that really bites.

Thy will, not mine?

Gary tells me that I am an intelligent woman, like somehow that's a bad thing. He says that I probably believe that my intelligence and my willpower can control my inner life. I want to tell him that those are the things that control my outer self. That everything he sees and other people see is quietly regulated. It's a mask, a veil. Because the things that go on inside cannot be controlled.

Not by me. Not by him.

And not by Him.

Thy will, not mine?

'If every man or woman believes that they can defeat their addiction with their own intellect and willpower, then each of them are playing God. And how well do you think that works? Ask any alcoholic and they will tell you that it doesn't, Maeve.'

I screw up my face but say nothing.

He continues. I think he likes the sound of his own voice, now that he has discovered that he has one.

'Self-sufficiency causes ruin,' he preaches. And I think of all the times I've flicked through the television channels and accidentally hit upon some evangelical fraudster, flouncing around a stage, damning Satan, non-believers and homosexuals. 'With so many different and individual beliefs and agendas, the only result is collision. This is how wars are started.'

'And no wars have ever been fought over different ideas of God.'

I can't let it go. He sounds ridiculous.

Gary brushes past my comment with a moment of silent disdain and continues his unwanted diatribe.

I realise that step three is the great fault and brilliance of the alcoholic code.

The problem is that it is going to rub intelligent people the wrong way. The pick-up will be low. People who use their brains don't want to give that up. You will end up with some cerebral types, who will rationalise that whatever they have been doing so far has not helped them, so why not try letting God in?

Letting go. And let in God.

But those numbers will be few.

The brilliance is that those of us who refuse Allah or Shiva or Yahweh or whatever as our higher power eventually break away from AA and it is our fault that we fell off the wagon. It is not the programme's fault. Because the programme works.

You have to hit rock bottom first, that way you'll buy into anything.

What Gary is trying to explain to me is how my will, my own free will, is the thing that got me drinking in the first place. It was a misuse of willpower. Flood that with a range of everyday problems and it's a cocktail for self-ruination. Again, it is your fault because you are supposed to bring that willpower in line with God's intentions.

It is a difficult step to take. Surrendering your will to God. And a God who's own objectives are muddled. Those who have tried know that it can be done. That's how the whole sponsor thing works. They get to talk from experience.

'A small step is enough. Remember, it is your willingness to depend on a higher power that can open the door. Even if we can get it slightly ajar, it's enough. The door can always be opened more. It is only self-will that slams it shut again.'

He says that joining Alcoholics Anonymous is showing that willingness. I'm already doing what I need to do without realising. I'm in a safe harbour.

Then he suggests I get on my knees and repeat after him.

'...grant me the serenity...'

It is not God that Gary will have to answer to, but me.

God is going to get Gary killed.

I think about tying him to my bed and climbing on top of him, pouring wine into his mouth even though he doesn't want it. Then gagging him and drilling through his knees before pushing a hole through one of his temples.

God, grant me the lack of empathy to kill the ones I cannot stand, apathy for the ones I can tolerate, and detachment to know the difference. Thy kill, not mine, will be fun.

DoTrue loved the new copy I puked out of my mind. I had one of the younger, more eager designers whip up some different visuals. The kid did well. Exactly what I wanted, plus some additional ideas that were more abstract.

It's always the squares and the scientific types that have a million opinions on creative work. The more artistic clients have a greater appreciation for the process.

I hate the managing director of DoTrue. Typical small-man syndrome. Pissed off at the world, insecure and full of bravado. He used to try to belittle me, undoubtedly like he does his own staff. But now he's flirty. He has forgotten that the way he probably portrays himself to the men in his office is not the person he truly is. He doesn't get laid all the time. He doesn't fuck about on his wife. He has no swagger whatsoever. His pathetic goatee tells you that much.

'I knew that we just needed a pro like you on the job.'

He accentuates the word pro so that I know he means prostitute, not professional. And I say that, 'I'm an old hand', emphasising *hand*. 'I've got all the tools for the job.'

The idiot thinks I'm flirting back.

~~I will open you up.~~

I'm just getting this across the line. It is not a stretch for me to fake my way through one of these meetings. I know what a drain it must be on people to pretend that they like a client or throw out a laugh that they don't mean, just to make someone feel special.

It's not like that for me.

This dolt, in his expensive but ill-fitting suit, posturing in front of some account manager called Jones, thinks he is sat in front of Maeve the marketing guru. He thinks the woman opposite him can fall for what he considers charm. What this jumped-up silk tie and his sidekick don't understand is that I am physically sitting in front of them but I'm not here.

I'm just not here.

'The copy is spot-on and you've made the hardware glisten. It looks amazing.'

'We've got a new guy. I got him to change his CV this morning to say that he can polish a turd.'

'I'm sorry. What did you say?'

'He's very good at his job.' I keep talking as though he may have misheard what I said and I smile like I want him. I see as he nudges his partner in crime; it's so obvious. He'll go back to the office and talk about my legs or my tits or how he'd love my bright red lips wrapped around his tiny ginger dick and the younger sales guys will punch the air, while the women he hired for customer-service positions will all baulk.

I know that, as a woman, a strong one, independent, I should not let him get away with this behaviour. It's wrong. It goes on way too much and it's been going on for longer than it should. And we should stand together to fight this outdated chauvinistic approach. I just can't bring myself to care.

Not about the wider picture. Not about the greater good.

I care about me.

And I think it sends a stronger message for me to stab this guy repeatedly in the flesh behind his balls until he bleeds out. But not before I cut off his tiny excuse for an appendage and stuff it into his mouth.

It's great to spread the word with a social-media campaign or create a hashtag for the virtue signallers. We can use rhetoric or satire to scold these Neanderthals but I think a cricket bat to the head says everything in a more succinct way.

There's real impact when a heavy piece of willow pulps a man's brain.

'Talking of new guys...' He sits forward in his chair, leaning his elbows on his thighs, which are spread apart like he is opening up shop. He thinks it's a real power pose. 'I've got someone starting in a couple of weeks. A real whizz with the retailers and e-tailers. He's taking over a lot of the external stuff so you'll be dealing with him rather than Jonesy here, from now on.' He taps Jones on the knee, who gives me a polite shrug of the shoulders as if saying, 'It was nice while it lasted.'

'It's always good to get some fresh meat.' I give an obviously furtive look between his legs and I can see that he doesn't know what to do. He plays the big man but if I told him to whip it out now and do me on my desk, he'd probably piss his pants and cry with fear.

They talk to me about nothing important for another ten minutes and I walk them out of my office. We shake hands and, as they exit, I touch the small of his back to usher him through the door but leave him with that feeling.

I want it to stay with him. To stick in his mind for the rest of the day. He can think of that touch and my legs and my breasts and my lips while he tugs at that piece of gristle between his legs later. I want him to think that he has a chance with me. Maybe I'll get an inappropriate email at some point in the next few days that I can act on.

And I'm not talking about whistle-blowing. I don't mean forwarding the words to his superior. I don't want to call him out on his behaviour so that it gives some of his customer-service women the courage to do so, too.

I don't want to be a part of your movement.

I've got my own.

It doesn't need a hashtag or an endorsement from Oprah. Just a strong piece of willow and a knife.

I tell my assistant to take a message if anyone calls or wants to come into my office. Then I slouch into my office chair, find some classical-music playlist on my computer and I listen until I fall asleep.

And Gary asks me why I drink.

I need a pick-me-up after the day I've had at work.

Luckily, it's Tuesday and I always leave a little early so that I can get over to Kilburn for 16:30 to see Jill.

There are other people there, of course, but Jill is my favourite train wreck. And it's as though she has read my mind or stalked my day because when I get there she is utterly resplendent in all her vulnerable glory as she produces her hundred-days-of-sobriety coin and throws that fucker across the room.

Glorious.

Thirty days ago, when Jill hadn't let a drop of alcohol pass her lips for a couple of months, she announced that she had got herself back into work. I forget the details but it was the kind of low-level, menial work you give to someone who is usually too pissed to operate heavy machinery. Wherever it was, she had scored herself a position in the pending team. This is the place where purchase orders go to die.

If someone places an order online and there is a discrepancy with the information they have provided, a pender has to resolve the issue. If an overzealous account manager takes an order and places it wrongly because they are trying, desperately, to hit their monthly or quarterly target, someone in pending picks that up.

They get paid by the hour. There's no commission. They get shouted at by the customer on one side and angry salespeople on the other.

It didn't matter to Jill. She was on the path to recovery. She was taking her life back after giving her will over to God. And in His great plan, which never requires question or justification, He placed Jill in the pending team of some company whose name I have forgotten.

And it made her so happy. At one point she even mentioned her child as something more than just an inconvenience.

Jill gets up at the front of the room and flicks the coin up in the air then catches it in her hand. She repeats this a few times and the rest of us watch, completely enthralled.

This is a balance between celebration and degradation.

'I don't deserve this,' she says, quietly, almost to herself. Then throws it across the room. 'I lost my job,' she continues, pausing to breathe and take stock of her situation. 'But I sure as heck deserved that.'

Most of the room have that look of fascination you get when you pass a car accident or a station platform is cordoned off because somebody has jumped in front of an oncoming train. Traumatic captivation.

It seems that Jill thought she was strong enough to attend a work event. Dinner, drinks and dancing. She could say no to the booze. She could have her meal, socialise with her team, get to know the sales guys a little better and head home before the real partying began. This is where having a kid finally came in handy because Jill could say that she had to be home to relieve the babysitter.

It turns out that it was in God's plan for Jill to give in to some light peer pressure. Looking down on everyone in the world, God chose Jill that night. He decided that the best thing was for her to celebrate one hundred days of sobriety by getting out of her skull on rum and Coke. It's hard to understand why this was His will. And harder still to fathom why He wanted her to get to know those two sales guys in particular.

'I should have gone home to relieve the babysitter. Because I ended up outside with a couple of the sales guys. One inside me from behind and the other in my mouth.'

I can't believe how open she is. I think I almost respect her somehow.

'I was out of my head on rum.'

~~And drunk on cock.~~

Part of me wants to stand up and applaud.

I'm trying to work out whether she is drunk now. She does seem to be slurring.

Nobody wants to get up and follow that powerful performance but a couple of guys try, though there's nothing nearly as interesting. Cliché after cliché.

I hone in on Jill afterwards. She's making herself a cup of tea. White with three sugars. I take a black coffee and tell her that she's brave.

'I don't feel brave. I feel stupid and used. I'm back at step one.'

'Really? You have to go all the way back to the beginning because of one minor indiscretion?'

'Two guys at once is minor? What do you do on the weekends?'

I laugh. And it's genuine.

'Honestly? Usually I drink and, if I'm lucky, I fuck.'

Her eyes widen.

I hand her my business card and tell her to give me a call when she feels ready to work again, I may have something for her. Also, if she ever feels like a drink, she should give me a call.

It was risky, but she took the card and put it in her pocket. I could see in her eyes that she wasn't sure if I was being serious or not. Maybe she was thinking that it was God's will for us to meet like that. Perhaps she was destined to come and work for me.

Fuck God.

Fuck Gary.

And fuck step three.

I'm ready for step four.

STEP **FOUR**

'Make a searching and fearless inventory of yourself.'

After surrendering your will to a made-up man in the clouds, it's time to screw around with your instincts.

That capricious, bearded warmonger apparently gave us our instincts for a purpose. It's these instincts that make us a complete human being.

We want nutrition and shelter for survival. This is natural.

Then there's social instinct. People caring for other people.

And there's reproduction. The purpose of which is to populate our planet – the planet He created in seven days. This guy, who is watching over seven billion people at once and provides the willpower to the addicted, took an entire day to divide light and darkness. Another day to focus on fish and birds. One on water. The fourth day was allegedly the sun and moon and stars, which seems like an oversight, having spent twenty-four hours on the whole night and day thing in the beginning.

Of course, there's sex. Which is nothing to do with reproduction. It's fun. It's enjoyable. There's a different category for this. It's a desire. Like wanting emotional security or material things.

Wants rather than needs.

~~What do you want?~~

These are the things that can end up ruling our lives. That's what they say at AA. All of the wonderful things that remind us we are alive are the cause of our ruin. A real bunch of killjoys.

If these desires of ours get out of control, it causes us great trouble. These troubles manifest as serious emotional problems. And it's our fault, of course. We misdirected our instincts and turned them into liabilities.

We got drunk and fucked around and bought a widescreen television for the kitchen and smoked a little weed and had a gay experience at college and drank some more and ate takeaways for half the week. And we ended up in a community-centre back room with some other people who confused their instincts with desires as a member of a club that ends with the word 'Anonymous', where a recovered addict explains that, at step four, we must discover what our liabilities are and have been.

This is my favourite step so far.

The day after you have amazing sex with someone, it's great to talk it through with them. Reliving those moments is almost like doing it all over again. This is what I love about step four. I get to go back and look at all of these so-called liabilities.

As a kid, the idea of getting drunk filled me with dread. I'd seen drunk adults – not my parents necessarily but their friends would come over and get louder and sillier. I remember how awful my dad would feel the next day. It would wipe him out completely. The king of hangovers. He would put the entire three-seater sofa out of action. Mum would make him cups of coffee and bring him glasses of water and tease him for being a lame lightweight. But she looked after him, all the same. I think she liked feeling useful.

I had my first drink at about fourteen. It was at a wedding for a cousin of one of my parents. I can't remember who it was and I don't think I've seen them since that day. There was wine on the table and one glass of an English sparkling wine that was meant for toasting. I can't remember the names of the people who got married but I can remember my mother muttering something about only getting married once and they can't even spring for one glass of real Champagne each.

I had a sip after each of the speeches but thought it was disgusting.

I recall my mother commenting about how surprisingly good it was for 'fake bubbles'.

But not to me. It almost put me off drinking entirely. I guess that was not God's will. Because later that evening, while everyone was dancing, some guy, who claimed to be my great uncle – though his story didn't quite add up to me – appeared at my table with a Malibu and Coke.

It wasn't as harsh as the toasting swill. It didn't burn the back of my throat. It didn't screw my face up like I was chewing on lemons. It tasted like Coke with a twist. I couldn't quite tell what it was, but I knew that I liked it. I had four and remember feeling dizzy when I went to the toilet.

I liked that feeling, too. Not being out of control but not being so in control that everything is deliberate. Not being so concerned with who I was hiding inside.

I washed my hands and went back to the table but, on the way out of the door, some distant family member bumped her shoulder into mine and didn't apologise. She just carried on walking past and then disappeared behind a cubicle door.

With that sweet coconut rum coursing through my body and bringing down the barriers I keep up for everybody's safety, I found that I stopped in that doorway and waited, my gaze penetrating the closed toilet stall.

Scenarios ran through my head. One where I kicked the door down. Another where I waited patiently outside until she opened it herself and I caught her off guard, yanking at her hair and smashing her head against the porcelain of the toilet.

It was my first proper drink.

And the first time I realised that I could contemplate killing another person and not feel an ounce of guilt at the prospect.

I don't think the two are linked.

It's just who I am.

Hitler. That's an obvious one.

Air travel. Maybe a little more obscure. It encourages interest in other cultures and opens up the world. It was also responsible for the death of thousands as two of the world's tallest buildings crumbled to the ground in Manhattan on September eleventh.

And there's the internet, of course. Opening the world in a way that air travel could never achieve. We can communicate with other people from every tucked-away corner of the globe, and we can do it in microseconds. That's one of the good instincts: man caring for their fellow man.

The misuse causes more damage than it does good. It's so easy to disseminate misinformation or attack a person while remaining anonymous. Or attack a group of people. Racism. Bullying. Rigged elections.

Child molesters can congregate or fool a youngster by pretending to be somebody they are not, grooming in chatrooms.

You can airbrush an image of yourself to look better than you do. You can swipe a screen for sex. You can watch a woman get screwed by five different guys who empty their balls over her face and you don't even have to pay for it any more.

There's Donald Trump and Ryan Seacrest and Ted Bundy. Was that instinct? On that sixth day, when man was created, were these part of the plan? Is that why He had to have a rest on the seventh day? Because He knew what was coming?

These are God's liabilities. Where is He? Why is He not in a church hall somewhere looking back at His fuck-ups, making His moral inventory.

†

I don't think I'm addicted to sex as much as I'm addicted to the feeling of an orgasm. I had to do that myself until I was twenty-four. I'd had a lot of sex before then but it hadn't been working.

I felt like I had experienced a decent variety, too. Every kind of dick: short, thick, long, thin, bent, circumcised. There was one guy whose penis hooked to the left at the tip. It looked a little odd but felt amazing, for some reason.

There were men who didn't last very long and a couple who just kept going until I was bored and chaffed. Ones who liked it rough and others who were more tender. The younger sexual partners I have been with lately seem to be forgetting that they are not watching their free pornography. I'm not letting some one-night stand stick it in whichever hole he wants and finish on my face. That isn't real. I'm no prude but there's a generation of males who are so sexually depraved that they'll reach the point where they won't be able to even get it up unless they have a plastic bag tied over their face and a gerbil stuffed into their rectum.

Eventually, I met someone and had a relationship. And he made me feel comfortable. Not to the point where I could be myself around him completely, but certainly more so than anyone else I'd been with.

It wasn't that we were so close that there was some magical connection that sparked a series of mind-blowing simultaneous orgasms, but something did click. He wasn't offended when I ushered him in the right direction or manoeuvred him to get the best angle. Men are so precious about being in control, they see it as emasculating when you tell them what to do in bed.

The number of partners who felt under pressure because I've told them to 'come on, do it' or 'that's it, make me come', is ridiculous. Lost wood. One guy almost in tears. Pathetic.

Suddenly, I'm twenty-four and I'm guiding this guy to bring it home. And he fucking does it and it feels insane.

I'd always enjoyed the feeling of having sex but it felt like there was something more that I was missing. After three months with him, it opened something up in me. Something primal and carnal.

And it never went away.

If I am going to do this searching and moral inventory properly, then I guess it's fair to say that I probably equate sex with love somehow. If I'm with a man and it seems as though he has grown bored of fucking me, then we are doomed. It's probably also fair to say that I have used sex as a weapon. It's a wondrous tool for manipulation.

It's the fact that you can get lost in it. When it's done right, you can lose yourself for a moment. You don't have to think about who you are or who you are trying to be or who you are attempting to not show to others.

Maybe that's what the alcohol is, too. A way to disappear. To not think. To relax.

But perhaps it's far simpler than that.

There's no need to drill down deep and over analyse it. Can't it just be that it's nice? Thirty years ago, people 'partied too much', now, everyone's an 'addict'.

Gary tells the room that he sucked a guy's dick.

His actual words are 'I took a man in my mouth'.

The problem is that life is so hard because it needs to be about balance. As soon as those scales tip too far one way, you end up at the extremes. Half a bottle of wine on a Friday night or a cigarette on Christmas Day is balance.

'But you end up thinking that you had to drink because times were tough or times were good. You're either smothered with love or you have no love at all. It's easier to spot these defects in others but you have to apply them to yourselves. You need to make a list of these.' Gary, my sponsor, bravely offers some of his own.

He rattles off a few of the classic deadly sins. His gluttony and abuse of alcohol and other substances. His lust for anyone to connect with him. And the pride that justified the excesses.

Then the night when a mixture of drugs and booze landed him at the home of some strangers he'd met in a club. People were pairing off everywhere. Some disappeared in threes. Instead of taking off, sobering up a little with a kebab on the way home, or just going into a corner alone to masturbate and get the poison out, Gary did something he'd never done before and hooked up with another man.

'Because, when you react in fear, you will eat and drink and grab for more. For anything. And it will destroy the foundations of everything that you try to build.'

He tells us that he's not gay. That he has never been gay. But that his indiscretion was, actually, the beginning of a very loving and often passionate, five-week (secret) relationship.

~~I don't know, Gary, it sounds pretty fucking gay to me.~~

The idea is that you hear from someone who has gone through the things that you have and has emerged victorious. Gary mixed his vodka with his coke and it took him all the way to blow-job city. But he made the list he wants us to make. He searched deep within and brought out all of those weaknesses, all the things he had succumbed to, all the things that took him to the bottom. He was fearless in this pursuit and now he is clean and he is paying it forward by using his experience to help others.

Don't get me wrong, it's great to know that he is – or at least was – a human being and not some automaton, sprouting off lines of scripture from the Bible and the twelve-steps. He was a mess like everyone else in that room. He did things he's ashamed of that seemed like fun at the time. There's more to him. He's flawed.

He drained another man.

With this brand new information, I'm left wondering whether I'll get to fuck him first or just cut him up.

He leaves us with a few questions to ponder:

Q1 – How did a sexual pursuit damage others and myself?

Q2 – What people were hurt?

Q3 – How did I react at the time?

There's too many to choose from my past, so I figure I can give it a week before I answer to his face.

A1 – I got blood on my carpet and he got cut into pieces and put in the freezer.

A2 – Gary. Just Gary.

A3 – Nonchalantly.

Work is a mixed bag.

Two calls after lunch.

The first is from that idiot at DoTrue. He sounds buoyant. Apparently they just won a tender to supply thousands of monitors to schools in Manchester. I don't know whether he's telling me because he thinks I care or whether he is showing off.

The new guy, taking over from Jones, is on the call.

This is apparently our introduction but I haven't heard a word out of him apart from his initial greeting when his boss mentioned his name.

I'm completely removed.

The new account manager is clearly another timid mouse who will let his director adopt the alpha-male position because he cannot relinquish control of anything. This is common with the small-to-medium businesses. Often, it's someone who has started the business from nothing and they can't let go or delegate because they are scared of losing something that they created.

In this case, it's because the director is a balding ginger with a micro penis and limited education. He's so insecure, you can taste the desperation. Pretending he doesn't care if you like him but dying inside if he doesn't get that laugh or that slap on the back.

His voice irritates me.

I think I want to add him to my to-do list.

It would be too easy. I've been buttering him up recently, making him think that he might have a chance with me. A flirt here. An innuendo there. Holding on to a glance just a little too long. It wouldn't be a challenge to get him alone and stick an axe in the back of his head. I'm not sure it's worth even minimal effort.

I keep the idea in a glass box.

Break in case of emergency.

By the time I've hung up, I realise that we've been talking for almost fifteen minutes. I have no idea what it was about and I can't remember the name of the new account manager. But I have doodled a picture of a short man with a goatee. A knife has been thrust into the left side of his head and blood spurts from the right. The spatter has almost covered the Thursday section of my weekly planner but I had nothing written in for that day, anyway.

A knock at the door.

It's my assistant. She has brought me a coffee and my lunch.

I have the same thing every day. After all, there's nothing I love more than a habit.

It's boring as hell. A mixed-leaf salad with grated carrot and tuna, dressed with a decent slug of balsamic vinegar and a crack of black pepper.

Every day.

I tend to have coffee for breakfast, most mornings, but there is the odd slice of toast or bowl of oats. Dinner is often a ready-made meal, which I can cook in minutes and the label tells me the exact amount of calories and fat I will consume.

I need this. I need to count. I need to be aware.

If you are one of those people who has a partner that enjoys cooking and prepares you meals all the time, hurray for you, don't forget to post a picture of your food every day and declare your husband or girlfriend the greatest love of your life. Who doesn't enjoy a photo of a pasta carbonara? Or a public declaration of just how much better your relationship is than the one of whoever is reading your words?

The real problem with cooking from scratch all the time is working out the nutritional values of everything you use. You have to be careful. Because adding one glass of Sauvignon Blanc with your dinner each night is 120 calories that you have not legislated for. That's 840 calories per week, which is almost 44, 000 calories each year.

And, if you are me, it's almost quarter of a million calories per year because there are 609 in a bottle.

So, I skip breakfast a lot and I have the same lunch every day because I am that committed to the booze. Those people you see who separate all their meals for the week into little plastic containers, where they cook off chicken breasts and broccoli on a Sunday night and eat it every day after their lunchtime workout, that's the level of dedication I have to not turning into a fat drunk.

I also have a strict regimen for moisturising my face because the drink ages you. I can handle a few crows' feet and frown lines as I get older but I don't want to be fat and unfuckable. And I don't want to be one of those people who goes to Pilates, either.

My assistant knows to hold all my calls for an hour and take messages.

I eat at my desk and trawl through the internet, looking at the news. Still nothing locally about the homeless guy. It seems the country's economy is 'going to get worse before it gets better'. Bitcoin shares have plummeted. As did a plane off the coast of Indonesia. Nothing I'm particularly interested in.

~~Nothing important happened today.~~

I turn the screen off and finish my lunch while looking out the window.

When I open the door to my office, my assistant, Daisy, is outside eating a sandwich she had prepared at home and brought into work in a brown, paper bag.

I startle her.

'What are you looking at?'

'Oh, my God, Maeve. I didn't hear you there, sorry.'

'It's fine. You're entitled to a lunch break. I was just interested in your quiz.' I point at her screen.

'Really? Well, it's stupid. A joke from a friend. She sent me a link to a test to see how much of a sociopath I am. It's silly, really. I think it gives you a percentage or something.'

I ask her if there have been any calls that I missed.

'Just the one. From Jill Hydes.'

The name doesn't register.

'She didn't say where she was from. Just said that you had given her your card and she wondered whether the offer was still open.'

Shit. Jill. Worst-mum-in-the-world Jill. One-hundred-days-sober Jill. Filled-up-both-ways-at-the-office-party Jill.

I try my best not to seem excited.

'Okay. Thanks. Can you send through her details and I'll pick up when I go back in? Oh, and Daisy, send me the link to that test you're doing.'

The sociopath test isn't some stupid file that gets sent around every office in the country like that Condescending Wonka meme. It's the legitimate website of a mental-health charity. It doesn't take long, it's not hidden behind any paywalls and you get your results instantly and confidentially.

The test consists of a series of statements and the user must indicate to what degree they agree or disagree with what is being displayed.

Completely disagree.

Somewhat disagree.

Somewhat agree.

Completely agree.

Simple. Crude even. But I click the pink start button.

'It's wrong to cheat because it's unfair on other people.'

I think of cheating in terms of infidelity, in which case I strongly disagree with the statement. If I'm cheating on someone then it's over anyway. The only thing that isn't fair is that we are still together. Unless it's talking about cheating in sport or work to get something you want, in which case, I don't really care about that but there is no apathy option, so I stick with my first choice.

'It would be distressing if I succeeded because somebody else failed.'

We learn when we fail. What has another person's failure got to do with the way that I feel?

'I can justify anything as long as I don't get caught.'

Seems to make sense.

'I would not lie, even if it got me what I wanted.'

This is stupid. Why would somebody agree with that?

I click through a few more and I can see the flaw. It's totally leading. You can force the answer either way because the questions are so trite. Daisy can push the results towards her being zero percent sociopathic if she wants, or she can send it back as a joke with a hundred-percent rating and a message telling her friend to sleep with one eye open from now on.

It's a joke. It's not being taken seriously at all.

I click through the last four statements randomly, without reading. When I get to the end, it says that I likely have a high level of sociopathy and can click on the message box to speak with someone confidentially.

I shut down the page, open my emails and find Jill's number.

Damn, this woman can drink.

I abandon my calorie counting for today because Jill wants to talk about a possible job opportunity – meeting at a coffee shop – and I want to see what a real alcoholic looks like. I encourage her to meet me for dinner. I know that she's struggling for money so she could probably do with a decent meal. And she certainly has no qualms about leaving her kid at home.

I don't want coffee and I don't want a caffeinated Jill, either.

She hesitates but agrees to meet me near King's Cross at a place call The Fellow. I've been there plenty of times after work. It's trendy but not too 'North London trendy'. It feels comfortable. The food is good. The drinks are plentiful and there's a roof terrace that works brilliantly in the summer and romantically in the colder months.

I tell her that she can still have her coffee and that she is strong enough to not drink. We can eat, talk and leave.

And the reason that she says 'yes' is because she wants to drink. Her resistance is for my benefit. She doesn't want to damage my sobriety. Or she wants to put across the idea that she is trying to bounce back after her carpark double-penetration debacle.

'Here are your menus. Can I get you anything to drink in the meantime?' The waiter smiles. I can see under that white shirt that his body is tight. His face is chiselled, too. I'm guessing an out-of-work actor. Beautiful. Rugged. But lightweight.

Jill looks at me, expectantly. I know she wants it.

She has scrubbed up pretty well. Too well for a quick bite to eat with somebody you met at Alcoholics Anonymous. She looks like a woman who is out for the night.

'Jill, what do you fancy?' I pretend to look down the list.

'Oh, er, whatever you're having is fine.'

I turn back to the waiter.

'I would like the Gavi Cá di Mezzo and my friend doesn't really want what I'm having because she prefers a red, so if you could bring her the La La Land Pinot Noir, that would be great.'

Jill is completely still. I'm convinced that she wants to thank me.

'I'm sorry, it's not always clear on the menu but our wines come by the bottle, not the glass. We can do Prosecco by the glass...'

'It looks perfectly clear to me. One glass with each bottle, if you wouldn't mind. Thank you.' I stare at the Ryan Gosling wannabe and wait for him to turn and leave. Then I watch the way his body moves as he does so.

'So, we're really doing this, then?' Jill asks. She looks a little nervous, but she could be shaking because the wine has already taken over fourteen seconds to arrive.

'Look, Jill. It's one evening. You went for a hundred of these without touching the stuff. You're trying to do better. Everyone can see that. You didn't drink last night, right?'

'Er, well, no, I...'

'There you have it. You start by cutting down a few days and eventually you can handle it.'

'That's not really how the steps work...'

~~And filling yourself in each end with sales guy semen is?~~

I want to remind her that repeating the steps again is not necessarily going to have a different outcome. It didn't work last time and it probably won't work this time. You just end up stuck in a loop. Surely it's better if the loop involves some semblance of joy.

Maybe some people are supposed to be drunks. In the same way that some people are meant to become postal workers or carers or dictators or fishermen. Some are destined to work in recruitment.

It's obvious to me that Jill has found her calling.

The waiter returns with our drinks. He pours a little in the bottom of Jill's glass, first, and asks her if she would like to taste. She waves her hand and tells him to 'fill 'er up'. I like her style.

I prefer to taste mine when I am out and the bottle has cost me four times what it would from a shop. It's beautiful. Hints of almond with citrus notes. I invite him to pour mine to the top, also.

When I turn around to Jill to raise a glass with her, she is already raising an empty one towards Not Ryan Reynolds for him to refill.

I give him a look that says, 'wow'.

'I don't like falling off the wagon, Maeve. I prefer to jump off.' She clinks her glass into mine. I'm both appalled and impressed.

For the first bottle, she is a terrible bore. All those playground mums with their small talk and pretending they care about the other's home extension progress. It's that kind of surface drivel. She says that her sister is taking care of her child tonight and asks me if I ever want children. I laugh.

I opt for a bottle of Merlot next because it's £7 cheaper and I've never seen a human being put the drink away so quickly. I'm thinking she must be one of those people who get drunk early and stay that way all night. I'm more of a pacer. I won't drink three bottles in an hour but I will do more than that over the course of the evening, if the mood is right.

Over her shoulder, I see two men in suits and they keep flitting their gaze in our direction. They look decent enough but I'd rather see what Jill offers up after we move on to the gin. For £115, you get something called the Half Hitch Gin Station. It includes a bottle of gin, ten mixers and garnishes. Sounds awesome.

We eat. Jill goes dirty whereas I stick to something clean. No red meat. And she talks at me. She admires me somehow. Like I, at least, have a reason to drink so much because my husband got killed – I'm glad she reminded me of the story I use at the Kilburn meetings – and she's just pissed off because the love of her life knocked her up then fucked off and left her with a kid that she would've traded in to be back with him.

I can't think of enough ways to say that I don't care.

I can't empathise, either. And not because I can't empathise, but because I've never been in love. Not enough to want to give a child up and not enough to think about calling the next day to do something other than fuck.

She is so drunk by dessert that she just points at the menu and I read out what she wants. But, somehow, she keeps putting it away. I must show on my face because she says, 'I know, I can really suck it down for a skinny one, eh?'

Gulp. Glug. Swig.

'You have this much when you ... did what you did at the work party.' I act a little coy but I'm not.

'Look, I know what I said in the meeting but it wasn't a mistake. It was a blowout. I'd done a hundred days. More than ever. I wanted to celebrate that.'

Well, fuck me, Jill, you're a lot cooler than I gave you credit for.

She leans in. 'To be honest, I don't know what all the fucking fuss was about. I knew what I was doing. Those two guys were hot. I'm a woman. I'm allowed to want sex, too.'

Then she's telling me that she has been paid for sex and that she gave her cousin a hand job once and let him film it. 'Not my face, though.'

It's everything I wanted. I mean, some of the things she is talking to me about are rotten. She does no favours to the modern woman. Hell, she's a little wrong for even the oldest profession but it's not bluster. Jill is telling it like it is. From three-day blackouts to a simulated rape fantasy.

I like her honesty. She's real.

I thought she was miserable but she is not. She is uninhibited, and more so under the influence, but she's just rough and real. She's not even stupid. She is a human. And not even an anomaly.

But she is wasted.

I pay the bill. Over £300 but absolutely worth it.

The air hits her outside and I'm holding her up by the kerb because everything is spinning.

I hail a cab, take her licence from her purse to see where she lives and put her inside. She lies down on the back seat and I take a picture of the driver's Hackney Carriage details.

'Hey. What are you doing?' He seems perturbed.

'I'm taking down your details in case she calls me in the morning and says she's been fucking raped.'

'What are you talking about?' His voice goes high-pitched.

'Look, can you just take her here,' I hold up her licence, 'and not touch her anywhere?'

'It's forty pounds up front,' he snarls, thinking that will get rid of me. I push a couple of notes towards him and turn back to Jill. Glorious, alcoholic Jill.

'Jill, this cab is going to take you home. I've already paid for it, okay.'

She nods.

I go to close the door but she calls my name.

'Yes?'

'Did I get the job?'

I want to laugh.

'Let's talk tomorrow.' And I shut the door.

Watching them drive off, I wonder how many others in that meeting are lying, how many – like me – are playing the game.

STEP **FIVE**

'Admit to God, yourself and to another human being, the exact nature of your wrongs.'

The whole set-up of Alcoholics Anonymous seems to be that we, as human beings suffering with an addiction, should go against our natural desires.

Stop drinking.

Stop fucking.

Starting talking to the Big Man Upstairs.

The idea is to deflate our ego. That's what they say.

But think of it in these simple terms: if you are driving in your car and somebody cuts you up, you get angry. You may swear or shake your fist or hold down the horn to show your annoyance and frustration. But it is your ego that keeps you in check and stops you from getting out at the next set of lights, running to their car, opening the door, pulling them out and beating them unconscious for their behaviour.

I don't have that.

I don't have that thing which tells me to stop trailing them back to their home. I don't have a voice to inform me that it is wrong to wait outside that house every day until I see an opportunity to put things right again, make them balanced.

Nothing tells me that it's wrong to set fire to their house, because they shouldn't have cut me up in the first place.

The book says that this is the biggest but most necessary step to long-term sobriety. But they said that about step three until step four came along, so I have no doubt that step six will say the same. But I don't want to jump ahead.

I like to give everything a try.

Maybe something will stick.

Maybe I'm just addicted to AA.

A year back I looked into a psychiatrist. I don't know why. Someone to talk to, I guess. I spend most of my time alone, I like my own company, but it's probably something innate in humans to be around other humans from time to time. How else would we have sex?

I tend to hold back when I'm in conversation, I don't want to give too much away. Also, my mind wanders when others are talking to me. I speak in my head about what I'd like to do to them or how I wish they could meet their demise. I call them out on their failings and unobstructed tedium.

I could sit in the sanctity of some shrink's office and do that. It would almost be like being alone but I'd still have some release.

There was a practice I found online, sounded very official. Erickson, Rossi, Milton and Artaud. All specialising in different areas. But there were too many testimonials from ex-police and military types who had been helped with PTSD from the many atrocities they are forced to face.

It was a non-starter.

What if I'd had enough of some cardigan-wearing pencil chewer asking me, 'So how does that make you feel?' and ended up strangling the guy with his paisley-print tie? The last thing I'd want is a group that is entrenched in rehabilitating police detectives.

Today, I'm at Wood Green Step. A new group that I haven't tried yet. I tell them that I started drinking because I was dating a guy who killed himself. Jumped off a bridge.

They focus on the plan here and I really want to get to grips with it. I'm avoiding Jill for the moment in case she thinks we're friends. She hasn't called, so I assume she's either okay or was raped and killed by that taxi driver. I didn't like his face. He looked more likely to kill *then* rape.

I say that I've been working hard on the steps, that I've made my searching moral inventory and now I'm ready to step it up.

I can't believe there isn't a group in the area called Step It Up, *or*

Steppin' Out or Step by Step, or Every Little Step You Take. They come up with all these fancy, schmaltzy titles and all they could think of for this one is Step.

They're looking into steps five and eleven, I'm not sure why they go together yet, so I'll probably only stay for the first half.

Here's the rub. I can't keep my problems to myself. Worse than that is keeping all the lovely defects I've uncovered in my moral inventory locked away or written on a piece of paper. We need to talk to somebody about our ghosts. Apparently.

'It is an intense step that many try to bypass.'

I had a sneak peek ahead and step six enraged me. It looked worse. I'd rather give this shit a go.

Then the fucker at the front makes some sense. It's easy to admit bad behaviour that your friends and family already know about. That isn't the goal. The goal is to open up about the things you have never said and say them out loud to another living human being.

'We keep the worst in, hoping that it will stay with us until the grave.'

~~I just cross it out.~~

This makes me think about Jill. That woman came to a meeting and told thirteen different people, most of them men, that she got double-teamed next to the food bins at the back of a restaurant. That is what she chose to share. And if this guru is correct in his assumption that we choose the easier events to divulge to others, it goes some way to understanding the depravity that lurks within the history of the wonder that is Jill.

Damn. That woman can fucking drink.

She is a real alcoholic.

And a real lady of pleasure.

It's at that point the mentor tells us that we may divert attention by accusing others of the defects that we conceal about ourselves.

Damn this guy for making sense.

I don't think I'll come back to Wood Green, this mother fucker will end up making me believe there's a God.

'So sorry about yesterday. He likes to take control of the conversation, as I'm sure you know.'

The new account manager at DoTrue calls me to apologise for his boss being a controlling, ginger dick. He doesn't say those words but I'm reading his subtext loud and clear.

It's not a long call and I can hear that it's on his mobile and he's outside because the wind is loud and he cuts out every now and then.

I like his voice. I hope he looks the way he sounds. But anything is better than that half-bald, limp-dicked short arse who is usually here, showing off about the crap I don't want to hear about.

'Have we got a date in for you to come into the office in person?'

'No. Not yet. I have to travel to Germany this week for a product meeting,' I can almost hear the yawn in his voice, 'So, maybe next week we could hook up.'

'Sounds great. It doesn't have to be formal. And you can come by yourself.'

Please.

'Yes. That works. One second...'

I wait. He's checking the diary on his phone, I assume.

'Next Tuesday? I'm in the area. I could get to you around four. Is that okay? I know it's near the end of the day...'

Fuck. I'd have to miss or be late to the Kilburn meeting.

But I'm intrigued. He knows his boss is a dick and he's not afraid to imply that. I like it.

'Let me just check.' I wait, pretending that I am flicking through my busy schedule. There's nothing in my diary apart from a picture I doodled of a man with horns, who would tip over if his erection was that big.

'I can do 16:30,' I lie, 'but forget the office, there's a place nearby called The Fellow. I'll send you the details.'

He agrees.

We have a date.

Next Tuesday at 16:30, I am going to The Fellow to meet Seth Beauman.

†

Ignition. Handbrake. Seatbelt. Bag. Door.

Out.

Keys. Shoes. Fridge. Wine. Microwave.

In.

The news is on. Some millionaire sportsman grew a conscience overnight, it seems, and is now taking the government to task over the rights of a child on their social-media platform. There's a ton of support for him because he's a celebrity but also because people like to be outraged about anything. It makes them feel like they're part of the gang. Do they really care about child literacy or poverty or school meals? Or is it just another opportunity to call the prime minister a bastard?

Outrage swings both ways, though, so this footballer, who appears to be trying to pay it forward or do some good, for whatever reason, is receiving almost as much abuse as the politicians he is questioning.

He'll probably end up getting a knighthood.

Another kid was stabbed in London. It's almost a daily occurrence, now. He was fourteen years old. Instead of tackling the cultural and educational reasons behind these youngsters hanging out on the streets with a knife, it's, once again, video games that are coming under scrutiny. Like these adolescents can't distinguish between a two-dimensional cartoon character on a screen getting into a shootout and thrusting a sharp piece of steal through the back of some kid's neck until he is no more.

This is the reason we now need hard screen computer monitors in classrooms.

I know I should feel upset about the kids being stabbed but I'm more angry that some tech company profits from this wayward generation's stunted attention span.

There are a couple of parents out there who were so pleased that they managed to get their child away from a screen for a while, made them go outside the house and be active. Alive. And now he's fucking dead and they blame themselves even though they were doing the right thing.

Fascinating.

It's hard to come back from that.

Their feelings and hurt and blame will stay with them. And holding it in will undoubtedly cause them to be irritable and anxious and depressed. Just like all the lonely alcoholics out there, struggling with step five.

I imagine that burying your own child leaves a parent feeling like they no longer belong and, instead of leaning on each other, parents isolate themselves to grieve. AA understands this. We are the ones who are tortured by loneliness.

Drunken idiots, thinking we can conquer our demons on our own.

We drink our demons away.

I understand this idea of speaking your issues out loud to another person, the part I hate is that 'only on admission will the grace of God enter'.

Fucking God. For a guy that I don't believe is everywhere at all times, He sure does get around.

Where was He when that fourteen-year-old had a blade hanging out the back of his neck?

What was His 'plan' there?

The microwave pings and I take out my dinner. Tonight is a katsu curry but, instead of chicken, it is made using sweet potatoes. 412 calories. Perfect. And I'm pairing it with a bottle of Viognier.

Seth Beauman drops into my head and I decide to open the laptop while I fork at my rice. I can't find him anywhere on social media. I like that about him. There are Seth Beaumans on there but they're not him. Almost every account I find is open for perusal. Their pictures, their birth dates and marital status, where they work, what films and music they enjoy. Privacy is dead.

I check the DoTrue website. They have updated their staff contacts list but there is no image of their distribution and retail manager.

I shut the laptop and finish my dinner while flicking through the channels. There are reality shows on every other channel. Whether it's a chef trying to help some rednecks save their hog roast diner, four gay guys giving someone a makeover, or a couple renovating a castle or a bride allowing her friends and mother-in-law to choose her wedding dress, it doesn't matter to me. I love them all. I don't know why, but I do.

I catch the end of some show where a matchmaker is trying to find a woman who will love some obnoxious millionaire for his awful personality rather than the inheritance she will receive when the dullard finally croaks.

There's still half a bottle left of my evening. After dropping the curry packaging into the recycling and throwing the fork into the dishwasher, I put my shoes back on and head out into the garage.

There's a lot of crap in there, like any garage but it's pretty organised. I know where everything is. Next to the shelving unit, which houses tools and some camping equipment I can't remember ever using, is a roll of plastic. One side is adhesive. Decorators use it to lay over carpets to protect them from any paint spillages.

I'm using it in my bedroom so Gary's blood doesn't stain anything.

I don't have another human that I can talk to, to get these things off my chest. Apparently, even the old-timers can relapse if they haven't nailed step five down because those defects they are holding on to, that they don't think another person will understand or will judge, eat at them. Even if they haven't touched a drop of liquor for five years. It's the thing that prevents real progress.

Psychiatrists are useful to many. As are shamans and priests, I'd imagine. But it is suggested that not only do I have to tell somebody the deep secrets I hold within, I also have to listen to theirs. That rules out shrinks, vicars and doctors.

Alcoholics understand other alcoholics. I could sit down with Jill and listen to her tell me how she let men beat her up for money while drilling her from behind and tearing her up. Maybe she could delve into just how far her neglect for her only child goes. She probably used to leave her at home alone to fend for herself while she went out looking to score … anything. That's why her sister stepped in. A six-year-old should not be making their own dinner, showering, brushing their teeth, then reading themselves a bedtime story and trying to get herself to sleep with the wind howling outside and people wandering past her window.

She divulges her deep-seated shame.

Then I could tell her how many people I have killed.

I could say that I started with a hobo because I wanted to know how it felt and I knew that nobody would miss them. I could say, 'Jill, I'm addicted to watching the life drain from another human being. I can't get enough of how powerful it makes me feel to get the better of someone, usually a man. All *you* have to contend with is the drink, you lightweight.'

That would go down well, I'm sure.

'A man once paid to fuck me then come all over my feet.'

'I know exactly what you mean. I cut some dude's head off to see what his neck looked like on the inside.'

Sharing is caring.

We could recognise what we are and finally feel like we could be forgiven. And, maybe, just maybe, we could both attempt to find the people we could be.

Or Jill would think that I was lying. And she'd laugh at me. Then I'd have to kill her.

Or she'd freak out and get scared and try to run, so I'd be forced to cut out her tongue.

This doesn't end well for Jill.

I try to get out of it by talking to God. I can admit everything to Him. Hell, He might even reveal Himself unto me. He may talk back.

'Gary, you'll never guess what ... You were right. God spoke to me. He is here. He is real. His will, not mine.'

Gary says it's easy to be alone with God. It's a classic cop-out. 'Honesty with another is honesty with ourselves. And God.'

~~I am honestly going to spoon your eyes out of their sockets.~~

He suggests that I could talk to a stranger. Sometimes that can make it easier. I don't know how to go about this. Sit on a park bench next to someone and extol the virtues of bathing a dead body in bleach? Maybe I could call the Samaritans. They are not there to judge, just listen. If I did it over the phone, it wouldn't feel like a real person but it would be. Quite a nifty loophole but I'm guessing that the Samaritans would have similar rules to the clergy or a psychiatrist in that they swear to keep things confidential unless you are contemplating or admitting to a crime of some kind.

Perhaps I could just grab the phone book and dial a random number and tell them my story. I wonder how many people hang up before somebody would listen and make a connection.

'What's his story?' I ask Jill, whispering as somebody in our circle prattles on about their 'journey' and their progress. I want her to tell me which ones in the group are frauds. Frauds like us. Paying lip service to Gary then getting out of that community centre and heading straight to the pub or off-licence.

She doesn't know much about him.

'He could be legit.'

He doesn't sound it.

I make her tell me a little about everyone in the room, as quietly as she can muster. She talks in clock times to mark their position.

Four o' clock lives rough. He comes here for the warmth. Outside of this room, vodka is his blanket.

Seven o' clock is a Jesus freak. Couldn't understand why God had forsaken him so. Gary has really talked him around. He talks about being born, a lot. In fact, he loves it so much that every time he falls off the wagon, he gets to be born again.

Eleven o' clock has a scheduled bi-monthly relapse.

Twelve o' clock is Gary.

If what Jill is saying is true, over half the people in here are failing. The guidelines are there but are not being followed by all. Like the weight-loss group that has this room tomorrow night. They know that they've been scoffing hot dogs and chocolate all week but act surprised when they stand on those scales and nothing has gone down.

Then Jill is putting her hand up to speak and telling the room that she went to the pub and drank however many bottles of wine. She couldn't resist the gin station. She looks solemn but I'm not buying it. I was there. She doesn't mention me, though.

'I don't even know how I got home but my purse was empty when I woke up and I'm only seventy percent sure that I went to bed alone.'

That fucking rapist cab driver.

Afterwards, Jill tells me that she added that part to make it sound worse than it was. She remembers being dropped off and he actually seemed concerned that she would get in the door in one piece, so stayed until it was closed.

Her sister was furious when she got back and they ended up arguing again.

Gary is having a coffee and someone is speaking to him. He is warm and welcoming and his face is weathered but friendly. I wait for them to finish then swoop in.

'I've been thinking, and I read in the steps that a lot of people choose to talk to their sponsor. I don't mean just talk, I mean the step-five talk. You know?'

Gary nods. He thinks I'm nervous because I'm playing it coy.

'Well, after considering the options, I think that is the best course for me. I know you but not really that well, so I think it has all the benefits of talking with a stranger but also the plus that you've been through this yourself.'

He's so genuine. I can see that he is touched that I have chosen him.

I inflate the ego that AA destroyed.

I ask him whether he would come over to me because I think I will be more comfortable doing it in my own surroundings. And Gary agrees to die sometime on Thursday after 19:30.

You can absolutely knock someone unconscious with alcohol. I'm not talking about cracking someone over the head with a bottle of Coors Light. I mean drinking so much that everything slows down and you black out. Liquid ecstasy will also do the job. These are no good if you want to knock out somebody who has been sober for years.

You want something that will act quickly and hypnotically.

You need benzodiazepines.

If you've ever struggled with panic attacks or you're afraid of flying, your doctor may have prescribed you a couple of Xanax or Valium. These are benzodiazepines. They alter the effect of the neurones in your brain that trigger stress and anxiety.

When a person feels anxious, there is an overstimulation in the brain. Certain neurotransmitters can work against this action and provide a calming effect. Benzodiazepines will enhance the effect of a neurotransmitter that will produce this effect. Chilling you the fuck out. Or, if taken in the right quantities, knocking you the fuck out.

So, here I am, at the doctors' surgery. There's a mother with a baby, suckling contentedly at her breast while her toddler moves some beads around a wire and sticks bricks in its mouth, while they wait for some kind of postnatal check-up or the Lego-eater gets a booster shot.

An elderly woman sits with her elderly partner. She has some kind of dressing on her cheek and from the way her eyes are squinting and her lips are pursed, whatever is hidden beneath is clearly sore and causing her some distress.

I want to know what it is, so badly.

Then there's another couple. Younger. Maybe late twenties. Both morbidly obese. The more male-looking keeps coughing then sucking on an inhaler. It's easier to say that he has asthma than admit that the fat around his organs is putting pressure on his heart and lungs.

He is powerless over food.

There is a power greater than himself that could restore him to sanity.

I would suggest that he make a searching and moral inventory of himself.

A few steps in the right direction.

His name is displayed on the screen and I can't help but stare as he has to rock back and forth a couple of times in his seat to gain the momentum required to stand up.

Eventually, my number comes up. Doctor Powell will see me now.

I refuse to see Doctor Kimble. He had this annoying way of asking, 'So, what do you think is wrong with you?' To which I would reply, 'Isn't it your job to determine that, doc?' He was useless. Powell is much better. She listens. She understands. She loves writing prescriptions.

'I need something this week.'

She nods at me.

'Work has been crazy and my fitness tracker says that I didn't even have twenty hours of sleep last week. I'm going out of my mind.'

She taps into her computer and reads down my file.

'I tried some herbal stuff, lavender oil, but it did nothing but smell nice.'

Another nod.

'I can't have another week like that. I think I'm starting to see things that aren't there. I just need a night with eight hours.'

'I don't think you're right about that.' She finally speaks.

Fuck. I'm busted.

'One night isn't going to fix it. Look, I'm going to prescribe you some flurazepam. This drug is only a short-term solution. I can prescribe it for a week, two at the most, it is not something you want to become reliant upon. But you need some sleep, so I'm giving you enough for seven days.'

Relief.

The printer sounds. She pulls the slip out of the machine when it finishes and signs the front.

'Do NOT go over the stated dose. Take ONE, ten minutes before you want to go to sleep. Let it do its thing. Catch up with yourself over the next week. But if these symptoms come back, there may be something deeper rooted that we need to explore. Okay?'

This time I nod. 'Thanks, Doc. Like you say, I think I just need to catch up with myself. It's work stress, I'm sure. It just hasn't affected me this badly before.'

I take the prescription straight to the nearest pharmacy, which happens to be inside a supermarket. The assistant behind the till reads my prescription and it seems like she is judging me. She checks all the boxes are ticked and signed in the right place then hands it to the pharmacist and tells me that it will be ready in about ten minutes, if I wanted to go and do my shopping first.

'No. I'll just wait here.' I look right into her and I don't stop until she hands me a paper bag with my sleeping pills inside, even though I could have done with picking up some wine and a few tins of tuna.

That night, I don't drink, because the pills can have harmful side-effects if mixed with alcohol. At 20:50, I get into bed, swallow down a pill with a mouthful of water, set the alarm on my phone and lie down.

After six minutes, I already feel drowsy. The numbers on my phone are blurred.

It's good to know that they work.

Even though I've never had trouble sleeping in my life.

East Finchley Reflections. An open meeting. Eleven of us. In a circle. A young man, early thirties, sticks out in his thousand-pound suit.

He stands up and says that he is Oli and he is an alcoholic. It has been 1,926 days since his last drink. Over five years.

And he tells us his story.

'Playing the stock market is risky. It's exactly the same when you work in it. You assume that we know what we are doing. It's high pressure, all the time. It's stressful. People burn themselves out at a young age. One way to keep going with the mental turmoil is to abuse your body with substances.

'I took the job because I had nothing. The basic pay was awful and the commissions seemed too good to be true but every car in the carpark showed that there was money to be made.

'I didn't enjoy it at first. But then I did. And I enjoyed earning the money. Until I didn't.

'I was doing drugs all week to keep me alert and bingeing on alcohol on the weekend as a recovery because it would knock me out and I could sleep.

'The short version of the story is that my candle burned at both ends and would not last another night. I lost my job, couldn't afford the drugs but the booze was cheap. Instead of saving up for the weekend, it numbed me through the week.

'A friend would show concern and I'd stay dry for seven days. But it wouldn't last. The friends faded, the drinking didn't. Eventually, I took a punt on an AA meeting. My dry week turned into six weeks before I lapsed. I was like a sportsman training for an event. The dry period was the preparation for the main competition of hitting the bottle again.

'I persisted with the meetings. Like so many, I struggled with step three. I was an atheist. I believed in myself and that I was invincible and could control my own destiny. But working through the remaining steps helped me become conscious of God. I found myself guided towards a church where I experienced a spiritual awakening. I found myself in the process.

'I would have died before I hit thirty if I had not given myself over to AA and the grace of God, as I understand Him. I stand here as proof that the plan works. Both the twelve steps and God's own.'

This is what I'm here for. Not to get 'better'. Not to find God. I want these stories. Not the last part. Success is boring. It's the start that's most interesting. How do people get into this mess? I'm not inspired by the people who are sober now. I don't want a sponsor talking about a higher power. Show me how you fucked up your life.

Feed me with your misery.

Then we can follow up with a drink.

The doorbell rings at 19:25. Gary is early. I knew he would be. There's no way he wouldn't be on time for something so important. This is my breakthrough moment.

'Good evening, Maeve.' He smiles and hands me a bottle. Iced tea. 'I didn't want to come empty-handed.' He starts wiping his feet on the outside mat. I thank him for the drink and invite him inside.

Next, I'm ushering Gary into my lounge and asking if I can fix him a drink of some kind.

'I have coffee, water or maybe some iced tea.'

He opts for some of the bottle he brought with him.

I haven't had a drink of alcohol for almost two days.

I pour myself a coffee and dig some ice out of the freezer because Gary's drink is not cold enough. I want to know if anybody knows he is here with me, tonight.

'Thank you so much for coming over, Gary. I hope it's not too out of the way and I'm not dragging you away from anything.'

'It's absolutely fine, Maeve. Not a problem at all.'

'You haven't left a Mrs Gary at home?' I remember that he told the group how gay he wasn't, after telling us that he'd taken another man in his mouth, so I rectify, 'Or a Mr Gary.'

'There's no Mrs or Mr. I live alone.' He drinks.

He might want to tell me how there used to be a Mrs Gary until the drinking and drugs and sexual fluidity got out of control. He may even have a kid that doesn't want to see him again. These are the types of things he could share when I use him as my human sounding board. And I'll have to listen. That's part of the contract.

We exchange pleasantries for a few minutes. Gary looks uncomfortable.

He drains the dregs of his iced tea and bites through an ice cube.

'Is everything okay?' I ask. He's rubbing his head and blinking his eyes.

'It's hot. Does it feel hot to you? I feel a bit dizzy. Could I get some water, please?'

'Of course. You do look a little pale. The bathroom is up the stairs and on the right, if you wanted to maybe splash some water on your face.'

Gary gets up but looks a little unsteady on his feet. Still, he makes his way up the stairs, holding on to the bannister with all his might and I go into the kitchen to pour a glass of water. Except, I don't turn on the tap. Instead, I open the door to the refrigerator, pull a bottle of wine from the inside of the door and pour.

One minute later I hear a thud above me as Gary's body hits the floor.

I finish the glass before going up to check on him.

It's even better than I planned. I crushed two of my prescribed pills into his disgusting cold tea. I thought he would just drift off on the sofa but the side-effects got him itchy and sweating. He is not a huge man but I was still dreading having to haul him up the stairs one by one. Now I just need to drag him down the hall.

I take his clothes off in the bathroom and he doesn't even stir. There's a cut on the side of his head where he fell but only a little blood. With my hands underneath his armpits, I drag him along the hallway carpet and into my plastic-covered bedroom.

Knocked-out Gary's skin squeaks against the plastic and catches. It's harder to move him but I manage to get him leaning over the mattress so that I can lift his legs and roll him into position.

I tie his hands and feet to the legs of the bed until he is spread out like a naked starfish, his penis hanging to the left, slightly. The trick is to wind the rope around the bed knobs on top of each post but tie the knot below, on the legs. It gives the victim no chance of reaching the end part to untie themselves, but also gives you the leverage to keep the binding taut.

Once I know he's secure, I head back downstairs to pour myself another large glass of wine and sit in front of the television for a while.

When it comes to pure, belly-laughing enjoyment at other people's misery, it is difficult to beat *Don't Tell the Bride*. It makes no sense as a concept. It's utterly ridiculous. And I love it.

It's simple. A young and in-love couple want to get married. They want to show their family and friends how much they love a person that they found on this planet, that they believe was put here just for them. One day. One huge celebration.

They hope that they are only ever going to get married once, as every couple does the first time they get married. Is has to be perfect. So why not let the groom arrange the entire thing and have a camera crew film it as everything falls apart and is ruined.

This week, Maria is having a breakdown because Ryan got her a pink wedding dress that looks like a belly-dancing outfit. She weeps with displeasure as her mother gets angrier and her bridesmaids try their best not to laugh.

In the next scene, Maria's mother is bawling Ryan out on speaker phone as he calmly explains that, despite working in telesales, he spent £1,500 designing the dress himself and is hurt at her reaction. Also that 'belly dancers can look good'.

In the end, he relents a little and says that she can have £200 to make alterations. He hangs up and turns his focus back to the venue he has hired for the ceremony: his old school sports hall.

It's like watching a car crash in slow motion and knowing that you could stop it from happening but, instead, you go along for the ride.

And I laugh until it hurts my stomach and tears fall down my face.

I think Maria deserves a shit wedding, a shit dress and shitty Ryan. She wanted to be on TV for thirty minutes more than she wanted to celebrate her love for that one person, for one day.

That idea of fifteen minutes of fame is more and more prevalent now. Anyone can be an online sensation. You can have your own channel, for free. You can show people how to work out or cook or play a song on the piano. You can use your skills or talents to add something to somebody' else's life, perhaps even enhance their own skills.

Or you can film yourself eating a tablespoon of cinnamon or capture your grandmother falling over in the garden or playing a video game.

No skill.

No talent.

Just some equipment and no idea.

You don't know what you want from life, what you want to do with your one chance, you just know that you want to be famous. And you don't care what that's for.

So you get your three-year-old kid to do reviews of the toys you buy them because you thought it would be cute or funny, but now a million people have watched one of the videos, you have generated some income. Your cute kid is now put to work every day. And while you are setting up better cameras and lighting to make it look more professional, your child is being robbed of a childhood where they just want to play with the toys rather than force out a critique.

Or you feel sad about something that has happened to you

personally and it makes you cry but you pause the tears for a moment so that you can capture it all on your phone and share with strangers.

Or maybe you are at school one day, in the sports hall, and some cool guy called Ryan comes up and talks to you and you hit it off and start dating and end up fucking and eventually run out of things to talk about so decide to get married. And maybe it's all costing more than you thought because, hey, it's your wedding day and you want it to be perfect. But you see an advertisement from some TV channel where they will pay for your entire wedding, the only catch is that the groom controls the budget and all of the decisions regarding venue and food and flowers, even the dress.

Something in you thinks that he understands you and will try to make it memorable for you; there may be a few things that aren't going to be the way that you would expect but, on the whole, he's got your back. There's that other thing that worries you because he is a bit laid back and could get the entire thing wrong and ruin your one big day that is supposed to all be about you.

And then you think, fuck it, at least we'll be on TV and the money we save on the wedding fuck-up can go on a really great honeymoon where we can make up for the bridesmaids being dressed as clowns or the music being played by a school band.

It's hard to understand because it's a different generation but harder still when you are somebody that, mostly, just wants to be left alone.

I guess I should go back upstairs and drill through Gary's brain.

Gary hasn't moved an inch.

I check his breathing because there were very severe warnings on the drugs about dosage and I don't want to have killed him yet. Not like that.

It is laboured but he is breathing.

I have a bottle of wine and a drill. One glass for me and Gary to share.

He's going to drink tonight.

Next, I'm undressing. I leave my bra and vest on but take off everything else. I sip the wine and watch Gary for a few moments. So peaceful and still. No idea what has happened to him or what is coming.

When I slap him the first time, he doesn't even stir.

I straddle his chest and pour some wine on his face.

Nothing.

I hold his nose and he continues to breathe slowly through his mouth.

Slap.

Nothing.

I move myself up so that I am over his face. The end of his nose puts some pressure on my clitoris and I feel his breath underneath me. I imagine him waking up and flicking his tongue out to taste me.

But there's nothing.

Maybe two pills was too much.

I sit back on his chest. I pinch his nostrils shut and pour wine into his mouth until he chokes.

Gary manages to move his head to the side so that the liquid falls out and onto the plastic I have used to coat the mattress. His eyes open and shut, open and shut. He's not very strong. I grip his head still with my knees. He can't fight it.

'This time, I want you to swallow.'

I take his lack of response as a yes and pour a small amount into his mouth.

'Drink it,' I order.

His eyes don't open but he manages to swallow the first taste of alcohol he's had in years. I remain on his chest and take a gulp myself, while I wait for that sharp Riesling to fire up Gary's synapses.

His breathing has changed and his lips and tongue are motioning like he is trying to taste something. I pour again. He takes it down. But still doesn't wake up to see where he is or who he is. And I'm getting bored of the waiting so I brush my hand through his hair –

he clearly likes the way this feels from his expression, so I turn back to see if I am having any effect on his dick.

I lean back and take it in my hand. Nothing too vigorous, and certainly not sensual in any way. Just moving it around, seeing if I can get some blood rushing south.

Now both of my hands are in his hair and my mouth is by his ear.

'Gary. Gary. Wake up. It's me. It's God.'

I ball both hands into fists and it pulls his hair tight.

He lets out an 'ow' but his eyes won't open fully, still, and I can tell that the pain isn't enough.

'Gary.'

Slap.

'It's me.'

Slap. SLAP.

'It's God.'

SLAP. SLAP.

I pinch his nose and tip the bottle upside down so that it goes into his mouth and face.

He opens his eyes. He doesn't understand what is happening. But there is horror to be seen.

'There you go, sleepy head. That wasn't so difficult, was it?'

He wriggles, realises he is completely bound and that his penis is at half-mast. Still, he wriggles again, thinking there will be a different outcome.

And I'm the insane one.

'Now, you wait here, I need to go and grab another bottle of wine because you wasted that one, didn't you, Gary?'

There's a cold bottle of Pinot Grigio that isn't as cold as I'd like but it will do.

I realise that I've left the television on in the lounge.

It's a reunion show. One of those after-the-event episodes where they get the cast of a reality show back together to go over what happened and what has happened since. Very American and cringeworthy.

I haven't seen the show in question but I still find myself being drawn into it.

Here's the premise: two people meet from different countries – one of them is the USA and the other looks to be Mexico or the Middle East, in this instance. They apply for a ninety-day visa and have that time to decide whether or not they are going to get married. The audience is left wondering whether the love is real or whether one of them is only in it for the green card.

Ludicrous.

Brilliant.

I sit down with my drink.

Having not seen a single episode of *90-Day Fiancé* I'd guess that it is almost always not for love.

It seems that Mohammed and Danielle ended up tying the knot but he had some intimacy issues. He wouldn't even kiss her at the altar, citing religious reasons.

The interviewer is trying to tease out the reasons while the other contestants stifle their knowing snickers.

Mohammed tries to deflect. 'It's a private matter. Something that no man should accept.'

Damn. I want to know why he can't fuck his wife.

Maybe he has a baby dick. Or it looks like a cauliflower. Maybe he's a thirty-year-old virgin. Maybe he was touched by a family member or was raped by a dog.

I need to know.

Danielle pipes up to defend herself.

'He has been telling people that I smell and that I peed on him.'

I wasn't expecting that.

Mohammed responds quickly.

'You do.'

I laugh loudly but not as loudly as Gary calls for me.

'What's all the shouting about?'

He's more awake now and I watch as he takes me in, standing in the doorway, bottom half naked, my left hip slightly collapsed, my right hand holding a glass of wine, the other gripping the half-filled bottle, which I intend to swap for the drill.

'What am I shouting about? I'm fucking naked and tied to a bed, Maeve. What did you do to me?'

'What's that taste in your mouth, Gary? Huh?' I wait while it registers. 'Seems to me, somebody fell off the wagon and doesn't remember how much he drank.'

'That's not true.'

'You explain it then. You tell me why we both taste like wine, why you have your dick out and are tied to my bed, and why I can still feel you throbbing inside me.'

'You're lying.' He thinks about it. 'You are lying. I'd remember.'

I finish everything in my glass and fill it back up, placing the bottle on the plastic-covered carpet and step in towards my sponsor.

'You want some more? Might calm you down a bit.'

'Maeve, just tell me the truth.' He looks like he is going to cry. Gary struggles against the ropes but I don't make mistakes. His words are still slightly slurred but adrenaline is amazingly sobering.

I kneel down next to the bed and run my finger along his left thigh.

'Are you saying that you don't find me attractive? Did you use me, Gary?'

'No. Of course not.'

'No, you didn't use me? Or no, you don't think I'm attractive.'

'Maeve, you're twisting my words. Can you just untie me, please? We've had our fun, it seems. I just ... It's fuzzy in my brain. I can't believe I drank alcohol.'

'Well, you know, even the old-timers can relapse. It's all well and good making that inventory of your defects but if you don't take the next step and reveal them to a real person, then it will eat away at you.'

He keeps pulling the ropes. It's irritating me. If you're looking for my motivation to kill someone, it can be something as little as this.

'I know the steps. I've done the steps.'

'Then you tell me why you're here like this.' I take his dick in my hand and squeeze it, never taking my eyes off his. I start to move it back and forth. His expression changes. I can see that he likes it but also hates that he likes it.

And I love that confusion.

'What are you doing?'

'What did you hold back on, Gary? What didn't you get off your chest at step five that has caused this?'

'Maeve, I came here to talk to you.' He shuts his eyes. He's so hard in my hand. 'So let me out and we can do that.'

I let go of him and I see something in his eyes.

Hope.

Gary hasn't noticed the drill. But he's about to. I place my glass on the bedside table and pick up my power tool.

'What are you doing now? What are you doing with that? Maeve?' It all sounds like one word.

I straddle him again, this time sitting lower. I have to move his dick to sit on his pelvis. I can feel it poking at the back of me.

'I'm not sure that thing is going to go down by itself.' I laugh. He's scared and he should be. 'I'm not the confessing kind, Gary, if you want me to be honest. I'm more of a grudge-holding kind. And I don't like being told what to do. I never have.'

I press the trigger and the drill whirs for a split second. Gary tries to buck his hips and get me away from him. I stand up. One foot on the mattress and one on the floor. Too high for him to touch me.

'The last thing you want is for me to make any sudden movements with this thing in my hand. Now stop.'

He does.

'That's better, Gary.'

I sit back down and move his dick out the way again but can feel that the excitement is draining out of it.

'Well, that seemed to do the trick.'

He asks me what I want and why I am doing this to him and how he only ever tried to help me, despite my clear resistance to elements of the programme.

'The God thing, right? Maybe I just don't understand it. Maybe I can't understand how everything is part of His plan. It seems sadistic, to me. How is this a part of His plan, Gary? Why does He want you boozed up and tied to my bed, with me sitting on you, holding this drill?'

I don't let him answer because I don't care what he has to say.

This is not a dialogue.

I rest the tip of the drill bit on the left side of his chest. Where his pectorals would show, if he bothered working out his body more than his mouth.

'You see how I'm telling you stuff, Gary? You see how I am talking to an actual person about the things inside of me?'

It's slight, but he moves his head to nod at me.

'You know, many addicts first feel the presence of God in step five?'

I lift the drill just above the skin.

'Do you feel that, Gary?' I squeeze the trigger to start the head spinning and lower it down into the muscle. 'Do you feel God's plan? This is what he wants for you.'

Gary screams. I'm not trying to kill him here. Just tear him up a bit.

I stop. He's bleeding. I step off him and collect the bottle from near the door before taking my seat again. Gary manages to quieten down. I take a swig straight from the bottle and empty a splash over his wound like it's his gravestone.

'Tell me, Gary, where's God now?'

'Fuck you, you psycho.'

'Is he everywhere? Is that what you still believe?' I give the bloodied drill bit a double whir.

'Why do you want to kill me? What did I do to you?'

'I'm not some movie bad guy. I'm not going to sit and explain everything to you. But I am going to give you a chance. To tell me the truth. Did you admit the nature of your wrongs to God?'

'Of course I did.'

'So your higher power is ... Him?' I point the drill towards the ceiling.

'Yes.'

'So, what if I tell you that there is a way out of this? That you can make that choice to leave yourself or you can leave it up to God, as you have surrendered all of your will to Him?'

'What? What do you mean?'

'I mean that you can decide to get out of here safely because you believe in yourself or you can choose to continue to lie and tell me that you have given your life over to God, and He will make the decision about what happens to you, based on his great and unknowable plan.'

I hold down the trigger and the drill spins ferociously. There is blood over both of us and blood on the bed. I'm glad I wrapped it up.

I appreciate that Gary doesn't answer me straight away. The adrenaline flowing through him has cancelled out the effects of the benzodiazepines and he is seeing everything clearly. Maybe for the first time.

That he is contemplating the idea of pursuing this charade of God's will is almost admirable.

You never know how somebody will react when faced with death.

People will give up their friends and family to save themselves. Mothers will choose between their children. Men will eat the other members of their sports team before starving on that mountain.

Most people just swear.

A famous last word.

I've never seen anybody ask for God.

'Okay, okay. I don't believe. It's all bullshit. Are you happy now?'

'Oh, Gary. That's worse.'

I lean forward because my body weight will help to push the drill through the front of his skull.

'Fuck,' he shouts, as the tip grinds through bone and into his soft, wet brain.

He makes a strange gargling sound in his throat and I pierce through again and again until his forehead looks like some kind of rudimentary colander.

I let go of the power and the drill comes to a stop. Everything is quiet. So quiet that I can hear the theme tune to the *Real Housewives* of some American city where they either have too much money or too many wives.

I take my glass from the side table, walk to the doorway and check my feet for blood so I don't walk anything down the hall carpet.

Clean up is the worst part of this.

It can wait half an hour while I watch six Botoxed women bitch about each other while arranging fundraising events to make themselves feel important.

And I could do with some dessert.

STEP **SIX**

'You are entirely ready to have God remove all these defects from you.'

Oh, Gary. If only I could tell you how much this one is not happening. I should skip straight to step seven.

Let's have a look at why I am not taking this shit:

1) – Some fifteen-minutes-of-fame priest, who is, apparently, a *friend* to Alcoholics Anonymous said, 'Step six really separates the men from the boys'. I hate that. Yes, it sounds a bit sexist but it's the fact that it's so outdated that really gets to me. Maybe it's my day job taking over my brain.

There are women who will be pissed off by that statement and it will derail them on their journey. If you are going use clichéd platitudes then stick with 'separating the wheat from the chaff'. It's just as crap and meaningless but at least it encompasses everybody.

The twelve steps book has sold millions of copies, next time it's due for a reprint, update it a little. There's no excuse in this digital age when you can alter the text for an e-reader version instantly and at negligible cost.

It's lazy.

It's also where religion falls down. You have to move with the times.

Edit.

Add a footnote that says the God stuff isn't real. This part is a parable, that part is a metaphor, it's a lesson or some guidelines. Say that Jesus was a real guy with some pretty funky ideas but wasn't really the son of God because a) that's fucking bonkers and b) in these times, it makes Jesus look like a cult leader.

While you're there, delete that stupid line about man not being able to lie with another man, or add something that explains it has more to do with farming practices and that it definitely doesn't mean we should be stoning gay people.

2) – You can't have this as a step and then tell addicts at meetings that God cannot clear *all* defects in character. Because if God is real, he could absolutely do that.

He can. He just won't.

That makes Him as judgemental as ever. And then, when you question this, the answer is that only God has the answer.

That's not going to fly.

3) – Alcohol is a weapon for those hell-bent on self-destruction. That's the rhetoric. It makes sense if you're trying to sell a solution. I get that. It's branding. It's making sure everybody stays on message. But then it's ruined by declaring that 'God did not design man to destroy himself with alcohol'.

Yes, Ephesians says, 'Do not get drunk on wine, which leads to debauchery.' But if you did a Bible update, then you could say, 'Don't get drunk on wine and take a stranger in your mouth, but it's okay to love somebody for one night if the booze is flowing and you appear to be getting on.'

Apparently, step six is all about attitude. Having the best attitude that you can in order to begin the lifetime commitment of remaining sober.

I don't have it.

I can see why it works for those who do but I can also understand why that chaff and the boys are separated from the men and that wheat. It's too much to ask somebody who is addicted, who loves something they should not, to give themselves over to something that is not there. It's easier to give yourself over to whisky and women because you can taste them and see them and feel them.

They taste good, they look good and they feel even better.

And they are really there.

I'm not quitting AA and I'm not quitting the wine. Or the occasional debauched moment. I'm just doing that thing where you are in a rush somewhere and take the steps two at a time. You miss a couple out on the way but you still get to the top.

I call Gary's mobile and leave him another message.

'Hi Gary, it's me. Maeve. Again. Look I don't know what you've been up to or if you've even listened to my last message. If you're listening to this one then you should just delete anything else I've sent you.'

I ramble on about how I'm doing much better recently and that I haven't been drinking for a few days. I keep my tone light, trying to sound like I'm trying to sound that way.

I tell him that it's not his fault that I fell off the wagon and that I am in no way blaming him.

'You can't be there every second of the day, waiting for me to call and put me right again. I get that. It's just that we had discussed that you would be the one to help me with my step five admissions.'

I go on to blow smoke up his arse and tell him that he's the only one I can trust and that I know I have to listen, too, and I am willing to do that.

'I've admitted my wrongs to myself. I want to admit them to you so that I can then admit them to God.' That should stick in my throat but I'm so removed from the emotion of these kinds of situations that it has no effect.

'If I don't hear from you, I guess I'll see you at the next Footprints In The Sand meeting. But I hope I do. I have work in the day but the nights are more difficult because I'm alone.' I trail off. 'Anyway, if you could call me back, that would be great. Thanks.'

I hang up the phone and place my bottles on the conveyor belt. I always think it's rude when people talk on their phone while packing their shopping at the supermarket.

A couple of days later, I'm watching *America's Next Top Model* with a bottle of Prosecco. These women are glamorous, so I'm being glamorous. Well, as glamorous as a Thursday evening on your own gets. Also, Prosecco is only eighty calories per glass, whereas a large glass of wine is 228 calories.

So I can drink more.

There's a knock at the door.

A man in a suit. He shows me his badge and tells me that he is a police detective and is wondering whether I could spare a few minutes of my time. When I agree, there's an awkward moment in which I feel he takes a step forward but I ask if we can do it on the doorstep because, 'While I believe that you are who you say you are, I am a woman who lives alone and feel more comfortable out here.'

'Yes. Of course. I wasn't...'

He's here about Gary. I know that before he even opens his mouth.

Gary, who is split fairly evenly between the freezer in the garage and the one in the kitchen. It's just easier to have him there while I decide what to do with him. I don't keep any food in there, so there's always room.

I am thinking of removing his glutes and giving them to the neighbours, telling them it's duck or venison – something gamey – that I'm not going to get around to eating and I don't want to waste them.

The detective asks me when I last saw Gary and I tell him it was at the last FITS meeting I went to.

He looks at the glass in my hand. I hold it up and say, 'Well, as you can detect, I'm not doing so well with this whole thing at the moment but I have been trying to get hold of my sponsor and he isn't picking up.'

'So that was last Tuesday? Was he not at the meeting two days ago?'

'That isn't always how it works. Sometimes, you're not doing so well, so you go to the nearest meeting to you at the closest time you can. It's not always the same people there, either. So, I did go on the Tuesday just gone but Gary wasn't there. He was last week, though, because we spoke for a bit afterwards.'

'And do you mind me asking what you spoke about?' He keeps scribbling notes into his pad.

'Well, it's a bit personal but he was going to help me with one of the steps. You have to say stuff out loud to someone and I asked if it could be him.' I take a drink and the detective looks at me. He's not judging, he just looks like he doesn't understand.

'Hey, I've started, so I might as well finish.'

I'm thinking about the top models. It's right near the end of the season and they are sent out into the real modelling world to try to book jobs. They go on interviews with fashion houses and designers. Except they don't call them interviews, they call them 'go sees'. Sounds like something the inventor of Footprints In The Sand would come up with.

I'm also near the end of my drink and I almost forget that I should be showing some concern.

'Is everything okay? I mean, has something happened to Gary? He's usually very good at calling me back but he also has his own things to deal with so I just thought it might be that.'

I think he buys it.

He tells me that it's just routine at the moment but a friend called in worried that he hadn't seen Gary in a week. This friend had an idea that Gary may have disappeared on a drinking spree but they don't usually last more than three days. So the police are now working through family, friends and the people that Gary was sponsoring.

'People?'

'Yes. Er, five that I've spoken to before you and another two when I'm done here, which I think I am.' He gives me his card and asks that I call if I hear or see anything.

I nod and shut the door.

People?

Five before me and two after?

I didn't even realise a sponsor could do that. I thought AA tried to encourage many different sponsors as a part of the process.

Eight of us?

It seems to me that little Gary had swapped one addiction for another.

I refill my glass. Tyra is disappointed that one of the models only booked one job. But the audience knows this is just for television; she's the one who always takes the best pictures. So what if she isn't great in the 'go sees'? She can't be expected to be strikingly beautiful and have a sparkling personality. She already has to walk and breathe at the same time.

STEP **SEVEN**

'Humbly ask Him to remove your shortcomings.'

Oh, God, will you just

fuck

off?

Why is this still about Him?

And how does this differ from the last step that I skipped? On the face of it, this seems to be almost a repetition. But at second glance I can see that the last step was like a primer, getting down a base coat before you add your coloured paint or your wallpaper.

The last step was about getting yourself ready to have your defects cleansed and this one is about getting it done. It's just packaged wrongly. Before, it was about sharing and saying the darkest things out loud so that another person can validate them. Now, it's really not about God, even though they always seem to lead with that – let Him be your anchor. It is about humility.

Step seven should say, 'Through true humility, you will find the strength of character to defeat your demons.'

But it doesn't.

It talks about God.

It reminds everyone that this is recruitment to the church through the back door. And that it's all well and good to embrace the AA community and refer to them as your higher power, but you have to come around to the idea of true faith otherwise you're screwed.

Maybe I'm missing something.

I should look into getting a new sponsor. Someone to make sense of this. Someone who won't disappear when we're only halfway through.

Alcoholics Anonymous hates desire.

I try the Finsbury Park Step meeting at lunchtime on Wednesday and the one thing I take away is that desires are no good. Also, that Mary is immaculate and clearly functioning at a level not too dissimilar to my own.

Maybe it's some kind of karma that the man leading the discussion is trying to drill this idea into my head.

'Humility is an ideal that is gravely misunderstood and, unfortunately, rarely seen in the world today.'

I would already like to humbly cut his heart out of his chest.

Apparently, it is the men of science who bring a quality of material blessings, thinking they have the power to make poverty disappear because they can create an abundance of the things that we desire.

Mary twitches uncomfortably in her skirt, which cost more than all the men's trousers put together.

He drones on. 'They believe that once our primary instincts are satisfied, there will be very little left for us to fight over and we will be left to focus on our conscience and our character.'

What's his beef with science? Without it, he wouldn't be able to fly overseas, he would still be at risk of catching tuberculosis and he wouldn't be able to twist a tap and drink the liquid that pours out.

He should also remember the women of science.

He should hate them equally.

I zone out for a moment as I take in the shape of Mary's calves. Exquisite. Truly. No way would you walk past her and think that she had any kind of dependency on a person or substance. She looks fucking regal at the very least.

You cannot look at somebody and possibly know the depths of them and what they are enduring in their life. Hell, you could be married to somebody for fifteen years and still not get that close.

'...they believe that intelligence and work can shape our destiny.'

I tune back in at something I can finally agree with.

'Alcoholics believe this the most.'

Oh, way to ruin it, Greg. I forget his name but he looks like a Greg.

Greg tells the group that we attain these base desires and then we drink so that we can dream even bigger ones. And if we don't attain them, there is always the option to drink for oblivion.

'For there is never enough of what we need.'

He's right about that part. It's endemic in our culture now. One hundred people like a picture we post on the internet and it's somehow validating. But if fifty only like the next one, that person feels like a failure. They want more. They want one hundred again. And then they want a thousand.

Somebody thanks their followers, humbly, of course, for reaching ten thousand.

'I don't know why you find pictures of my dogs and rants about my kids so entertaining but thank you,' they modestly brag.

But now they want to double it.

Or some fitness guru who made millions selling the idea of getting a six-pack and glowing skin by only working out for ninety seconds a day and eating avocado and lard sandwiches realises that they have fallen out of the public's consciousness. Nobody is talking about them any more. So they 'accidentally' post an image of themselves where their genitalia can be seen in the reflection of a window.

Oops.

Time for the release of the new workout video or cookbook.

All of this can be put down to one thing, a lack of humility. That's what Greg says.

To me, that's the same as blaming the next American school shooting on violent video games. Again.

There's probably a decent message somewhere in there, Greg, but it's wrapped up in crap like, 'Of myself I am nothing, the Father doth the work.'

You can't get people to break through by admitting they have become nothing and then keep reminding them of that. They need some desire. The desire to get themselves out of the pit, for a start.

But, to the Gregs of this world, humility is the desire to seek and do God's will.

That's the only thing we should desire.

Of course, character and spirit are essential, and perhaps he is right, if they come first then we will find it easier to attain our goals. They are the means rather than the ends. We do not get what we desire and then end with character and spirit.

But we cannot neglect the things that we desire. We should want.

And then something strange happens. At the same time, completely unchoreographed, both mine and Mary's chairs screech backwards, we stand up, look at one another, stifle a laugh and leave.

Her outfit is better than mine. And her legs.

Steps six and seven are too steeped in faith and the idea of handing oneself over to another's will.

You cannot remove desires and wants and wishes and lusts.

Somebody, whose name I forget, once wrote that 'the opposite of death is desire'.

And I desired Seth Beauman from the moment we met.

Thursday at work drags. I've booked a table at The Fellow and I'm hoping that Seth is not another DoTrue try-hard and that he is ready to drink and let loose a little.

Not as much as Jill, but he needs to put in a good innings.

I arrive first. There's no power play here. I don't want to turn up late and make him wait. I don't need to show him who's the boss. I don't want to play any games. I want to sit at my table and order a bottle of wine, just as I always do.

One of the hosts approaches.

'You are a little early but your table is ready if you'd like to sit down now?'

'Yes. Thanks.'

'And you're waiting for one other? Would you like a drink while you wait?'

He's very polite. That's what I need after dealing with the imbeciles I've had to deal with today. I agree and he tells me my waitress will be over right away.

I'm halfway through my first glass when I see a man enter and wait at the front to be seated. He says something to the host, who looks down his list and leads Seth towards my table. He's good-looking in a scruffy, not-quite-finished way. There's some kind of product in his hair but he uses it to make things messier. The top button of his shirt is undone and the tie is hanging low like it's the end of a wedding. And that suit jacket is just dying to come off so that he can roll up his sleeves and relax.

'Maeve.' He points a finger at me and half smiles. It's not a question.

'Seth.' I mimic him and hold my hand out. He shakes it, takes his jacket off and sits down. His shirt sleeves are already rolled up past his elbows.

The waitress pops up at the side of our table like a meerkat and asks Seth whether she can get him a drink.

'God, yes. I'd love a pint of lager and...' he looks at me '...is that your bottle or shall I grab another glass?'

Fuck, I like his style. That pint is for all the work he has done today and I don't think he'd judge me if I said that the bottle of wine was just for me but I tell him to get himself a glass and we can share.

Cue a minute or so of small talk. Did he find the place okay? Have I eaten in here before? He talks and I wonder how much he likes going down on women.

When the pint arrives he drinks half of it in one go.

'Aaaah. I needed that. Half my day on Tottenham Court Road selling laptops and monitors. Kill me now.'

Oh, Seth. I'm just getting to know you. It's not time to kill you yet.

The bottle of wine goes in no time with both of us going at it like it's a competition. We eat and we talk and we laugh. There's a little bit about business in there but we don't get into anything heavy.

I feel comfortable. Relaxed. My usual guard drops for a moment and I say, 'I'm glad you're leading the account now. That boss of yours is a grade-A tool.'

'Are you allowed to say that?'

This is where somebody with low psychopathy would get anxious and backtrack or feel embarrassed or guilty.

'I'm pretty sure I can say what the fuck I like.'

Drink.

'Can I?'

I wasn't expecting that response.

'I'm not your boss. Although I do think our dicks are about the same size.'

When he laughs, it seems genuine. It's part shock and part appreciation.

'I haven't been at DoTrue for long but I can see that he wants the company to do well. There is one issue, though, and it's that I fucking hate him.'

I smile. He's got some balls.

'I mean it. Just deplorable in every way. The best part about this job is that I can get out of the office when I need to.' He picks up the bottle of wine and shakes it. 'Looks like we're out.' Then Seth Beauman raises a hand to beckon the waitress back.

He talks to me first. 'You want more, right?'

'Only always.'

'Another bottle of this stuff, please. Don't bother bringing new glasses, there's no need for that.'

I like the way he's taking the initiative.

'You like gin, Maeve?'

'I like everything, Seth.'

'Great! Okay, so could we also get a couple of gin and tonics. Tanqueray, if you have it. Thanks.' The waitress leaves.

'Might as well settle in a bit.' He loosens his tie. 'I have to say, Maeve, this is the best Thursday night I've had in ages.'

~~I want to fuck him.~~

I want to share another bottle of wine with him, knock back the gins he's ordered, then get back to my place and take the rest of his suit off. I want to bite his chest and slap him around the face while I ride him hard.

The last sexual experience I had was pulling Gary's dick around and it didn't get me going at all. I was more turned on by the drilling. That really was something.

Messy.

Satisfying.

It is politely suggested by our waitress that we can settle up the bill for what we ate and drank at the table and move over towards the bar if we want to continue. I tell her to bring the bill.

'There is no way you are paying for this, Maeve.'

'It goes on the company credit card or my expenses, don't worry about it.'

'No way. I'll get it.'

'And expense it to DoTrue?'

'Damn straight.'

We clink our glasses together and laugh some more.

At the end of the night, Seth puts his jacket back on and we go outside to hail a cab.

'You take the first one,' he tells me.

I don't care much for chivalry.

'I thought we'd both get in the same taxi.'

'We could be going in opposite directions.'

'We're not going to the same place?'

'Oh, er, you want a nightcap? I've certainly got room left for more drinks if you know a place.'

'The place is my house, Seth. We can certainly have that nightcap but I thought we'd use our time wisely and get straight to having sex.'

There's a moment of silence while the statement registers.

'You are very different, Maeve. And I mean that in the best possible way.'

He pulls me in tight and kisses me.

I think I've found a new addiction.

PART TWO

LIST OF PEOPLE I HAVE (RECENTLY) HARMED

NOT JACK

HOBO #4

JILL

CAB DRIVER

GARY (SPONSOR)

STEP **EIGHT**

'Make a list of all persons you have harmed and become willing to make amends to them all.'

Finally, something practical. This is a step that I can really get on board with.

No mention of God.

And I like making lists.

It seems so obvious. Go back through your life and locate the moments where you were at fault for causing hurt of some kind. At this point, you should have already dredged up some of these instances when you made your admission to another person. The problem is, that was done in private whereas this will require doing so openly to the face of the actual person that it may concern.

That is not a problem for me. I do not identify with the emotions that would make other people feel scared or embarrassed.

Also, that admission session ended with Gary's name being put on this list.

I decide to start with some recent harm that I have caused. According to the programme, this can be a lengthy process, which can span months and years. I like to hit the ground running. I can cast my mind back further once I have made a more immediate list.

The only way that I can move forward is to survey the human wreckage I have left in my wake. I have undoubtedly forgotten some of the bodies.

What is meant by 'harm', though? I have certainly caused physical harm to people, especially men. There's spiritual harm. I'm not God's greatest advocate, and while I'm not preaching atheism, my words will plant seeds. It will cause people to question, perhaps become anxious as a result. And then there's emotional harm. I take work frustrations out on my subordinates. That could be easily rectified.

There's economic harm. I can't give a fiver to every homeless person I pass on the Embankment but I could make amends with the ones I have beaten around the head with a glass bottle.

And there's my favourite one of all, psychological harm. I have an addiction to the misery of others. The list will be considerable. I may need more paper.

I sit down on the sofa, *Married at First Sight* is playing quietly in the background. I have a Pinot Gris, a pad and a pencil. The contestants are in pods where they can't see the people they are talking to on the other side. At the end of the week, they have to choose one of them to propose to.

It's crazy.

Some of these people are already crying because they are so hopelessly in love.

Of course, there are no obese ginger people with adult acne. Nobody is going to be disgusted with their choice, which kind of goes against what the show says it's about. But it isn't about what it says, is it? It is about documenting human suffering and anguish and desperation and fornication.

I write down the names of five people that I have harmed in some way over recent weeks. Each with a different kind of damage.

I am willing to try to make amends.

And here's the best part: if I do this, it will, apparently, help me to forge relationships with the people I know, the people in my life now. To me, the people I know, the people in my life right now, are few. One, in fact.

Seth.

I'm going to forge a relationship with Seth.

STEP **NINE**

'Make direct amends to such people wherever possible, except when to do so will injure them or others.'

Steps eight and nine could easily be consolidated in the same way that steps six and seven should. We don't need to waste an entire step preparing or gaining the will to do something. A step can be, 'Think about something and then do it.'

I start with Jill.

I threatened her sobriety for my own amusement. I don't feel bad about it, we had an interesting night out. Expensive. Gin-drenched. And informative. That woman is filthy. Broken, I believe. I lured her in under false pretences. I guess that falls under psychological and economical harm. Though she didn't pay for one drink.

When I call her, she sounds pleased to hear from me.

'Ah, Maeve. It's been a while. I haven't seen you at a meeting recently. Have you heard about Gary?'

'What about him?'

'He's gone. Just disappeared. There's rumours that he went on a bit of a bender and walked into the sea, or something.'

This is perfect. Rumours can help muddle the truth.

'I heard he got drunk and fell in front of a train.' I stir. The next time Jill speaks to anyone, that story will morph into something else. He jumped off a building or he fell asleep with a cigarette in his hand and burnt his house down or choked on his own vomit.

It is so easy to disseminate false information now, with the internet and social media. Because it's done so regularly, people are developing an intolerance to bullshit, which means that they don't believe anything but continue to swallow everything.

I move the conversation on. I don't want to completely muddy the waters of Gary because I still have to make amends there, somehow. There's no sense in adding psychological harm to physical harm.

Jill tells me there's a new guy at FITS that makes Gary look like an atheist. 'It's all God this and God that...'

'How's the job hunt going, Jill?' I steer it back to the reason I am here.

Making amends wherever possible.

'I'm making ends meet.' She tries to shut me down.

'And what exactly does that mean?'

A supermarket. She is working nights at a supermarket. Stacking shelves. She says that she's working in the tins section, so it's a lot of heavy moving, which is making it feel like exercise, too. It means that she is tired in the day but can sleep while her kid is at school. Then she shocks me by saying, 'But it means I get to spend a bit more time with her, you know?'

Fuck. If I can't help her out financially then I don't know how to make amends.

'But it's nowhere near enough money, Maeve.'

And there it is.

She goes on to tell me that the benefit of working at night is that it stops her from drinking. She can't afford it, anyway, but by Friday she's dying for it. And the supermarket provides reduced price produce for staff. They get first choice on everything before it goes back out onto the shop floor with a yellow label across the barcode.

Jill picks up anything she can for cheap. Her favourite, red wine, but also beer, cider and some of the white-label spirits.

'You can kick a box of beer out the back, dent one can and they will give you the lot with seventy-five percent off.'

Turns out that she really needs the drink over the weekend. And not just because she is a raging alcoholic but because she is 'making ends meet'. Jill waits for her daughter to go upstairs to bed and then spends the next few hours on her back on the sofa, or bent over one of the arms, or on her knees. They pay her in cash and fuck off out the back door.

By Sunday morning, she feels red raw and has to soak herself in six inches of tepid water.

But she is paying her rent and her kid is clothed and goes to school every day with a packed lunch that contains fruit.

The men can come in her mouth but not on her face. They all have to wear a condom. And she doesn't do anal unless she has a bill to pay. The way she speaks about her lurid sexual exploits is so matter-of-fact. Like no woman I've ever known. Like no woman ever should. Like nobody should.

'So you're still drinking?' I don't want to focus on whoring herself out.

'Oh, Maeve, I wouldn't get through it otherwise.'

'I get that.' Of course, I don't get that, I can't empathise at all.

'Well, how would you like to see a little less of your daughter but not have to screw all the cheaters on your street?'

Jill tells me, first, that it's not just the bored husbands on the road, and that she screwed a guy from one of the meetings. He wouldn't tell her his name, thought it was cool to keep things anonymous. He paid her to be loud and keep telling him what a big dick he had. Eventually she asks me what I mean.

I tell her that I shouldn't have ordered the Gin Station when we went out the other week and that I'd like to sort her out with a position at my work that will pay her substantially better than shelf stacking and prostitution.

She gushes.

'How well do you type, Jill?'

'There are two things I'm good at in this life. One is drinking.'

'And the other is typing?'

'Sure. Let's go with that.'

I tell her that I'll come back to her before Friday so she can cancel the weekend appointments.

But I know that she won't.

There's a part of her that likes it.

She thinks she deserves it.

†

I can't fully rectify things with Jill just yet. But I can put some effort into the other side of my life. The part where I am supposed to engage more with the people that are currently in my life. I call Seth and ask him if he wants to come over for dinner.

It's Thursday again. Starting to feel like a routine.

Our day.

Raise your glass. For Thursdays.

Gary is still taking up all the space in the freezer but the fridge is well stocked with wine and food. Seth offered to cook for me but I don't want to risk him going to place something in the freezer and seeing what I have in there. That won't end well.

He doesn't ask me about staying over but I can tell he wants to. I don't mention it. It's fun to keep him on edge. But I absolutely want him to stay over.

We eat.

We drink.

We fuck.

I don't even have as many rules as Jill about that last part. Wherever it takes us. My only stipulation is that he doesn't have to pay for it.

He turns up in a pair of jeans. I hear his car on the gravel and go to meet him by the door. Some women would wait for him to knock or ring the bell so they didn't look desperate. I think of it differently. If he knows I've been waiting then he knows that I want him here.

The carrier bag clinks. I make out the shape of two bottles.

'You won't be able to drive after all that.' He pauses, not knowing what to say. 'I can drink for two, don't worry. It's just a shame that you didn't bring an overnight bag.' I don't smile. My face is showing exactly what is in my mind. That I want him.

'I did, actually.' Seth undoes the rear door and pulls out his bag. He feigns embarrassment.

'A little presumptuous, don't you think?'

He knows I'm playing but he also doesn't totally know. 'Well, I just thought that we'd have sex.' There's a moment of silence, then, 'Nope. I just can't pull that stuff off as well as you.'

That makes me smile.

~~Don't fall for him, Maeve.~~

Here's a way to spot someone that might be higher up on the psychopathy scale: when you're in a social situation and you laugh at something that isn't funny because you don't want that person to feel bad – a psychopath won't do that. You know how laughter is supposed to be contagious? Well, we are lacking in the empathy department that would force us into communal laughter – unless we did find something funny.

It's the same with yawning.

Seth makes me smile because it's real.

He kisses me and hands me the wine.

'Take a look,' he says, enthusiastically.

I pull out one of the bottles.

'Wine. Brilliant. Thanks. I do already have some but I can't think of a time where I've ever had too much wine.'

He looks hurt.

'What? What did I say?'

'Nothing. It's just that it's the wine we had at The Fellow. The same stuff. I hunted it down.'

'Oh, right. I didn't notice. Look, I'm not used to someone trying to be romantic or make gestures. So just tell me if I fuck up like that. It doesn't hurt my feelings.'

He thinks I've missed the point but he lets it go.

'Put your bag down.'

He does.

'Take your jacket off.'

He does.

'Now take down those jeans.'

He hesitates. Then he's unbuckling his belt. It's so light near the window, you can see everything. No hiding. As he starts to take down his trousers, I move in closer and kiss him again. One hand behind his head, the other moving down his body. I can feel that he's already getting hard.

Soon enough, his hands are on my back. We kiss and I push him against the wall. Almost immediately, I find myself being spun around so that he is in that dominant position.

He's pulling up my skirt and squeezing the tops of my legs. I don't even realise that he has hooked his fingers over my underwear on either side and he starts to lower himself to his knees, pulling down as he goes. I'm standing against the wall with my skirt around my waist, looking at the top of his head.

I want to kiss him again.

I want to grab hold of him.

He looks up at me and starts to kiss between my legs. I feel his tongue against me and squeeze my legs shut; I like the way that feels.

Seth continues with his mouth, stroking with his finger. And I'm lost for a moment before he stops, stands up and lifts me against the wall. I grab him and help him inside.

Holy shit. I'm fucking someone I've met twice and I'm sober. I can't remember the last time I had sex while sober.

My legs are wrapped tightly around his back. Mine hurts as it rubs against the wall each time he thrusts himself upwards. But it's the good pain. Each scratch is another release.

Seth steps back from the wall, holding up my entire weight. I had no idea he was this strong. With his hands beneath me, he lifts me up and down. Up and down. Fuck, I am turned on. It feels incredible but I think it's also something to do with his strength and masculinity and the control he has taken. It's rough but also tender somehow.

'Are your legs okay?' I ask.

'For now.' And he keeps lifting me up and down. Up and down.

Eventually, he lowers us both down to the floor. He never comes out of me. We finish in that same position. Seth is on top, doing all the work. I like it when he is close to me, his weight pressing down against me, making it harder to breathe. I don't know what is so different about this guy but the sex is blowing my mind.

It's as though we are connected.

We are both lying on our backs, staring at the ceiling, breathing heavily, when the smoke alarm sounds. Neither of us move.

'Well, looks like I've burnt the dinner.'

'I'm still letting the starter go down.'

We stay there for another minute. Smoke in the kitchen. The sound of the alarm beeping loudly. A couple of our senses trying to interrupt the feeling of our afterglow. But we won't let it. This is all part of the sex. Taking it in. Letting our heart rates lower naturally.

Seth gets up before I do. The second alarm upstairs starts blaring out that horrific noise. He jumps in a panic. His jeans are still around one of his ankles and he's only wearing one sock. He didn't quite have the flexibility to completely undress while still tending to me.

He runs into the kitchen and pulls the pan from the stove. I roll over and witness the carnage. Seth is in my kitchen, naked apart from one sock and a pair of jeans around his ankle. He is emphatically waving the smoke around with a tea-towel.

It's ridiculous.

But hilarious.

I'm glad he is here. I'm not saying that I want to take this any further than burnt food, beer and bondage. I'm not thinking about a relationship but I am thinking about having a better relationship with Seth.

I don't need him. I don't love him. But I do want him.

But, the feeling I have most right now is that I definitely don't want anybody else to have him.

Friday morning. Jill probably has her evening roster planned out.

Eight thirty, polish Len's cock.

Eight forty-five, give Cath's husband a quick tug before he heads out to play snooker with his mates.

Nine, cigarette break. Check your daughter is asleep.

Nine twenty, pretend Fat Aaron has a fat penis that fills you up real good.

Drink to forget Fat Aaron's fat tits.

Spread your legs for a couple of hours and pretend you like it.

Midnight, let Cath's husband watch you get fucked by the mate who beat him at snooker.

Repeat until death.

I can get her out of it. I can make amends.

Daisy brings a coffee into my office.

'This is not a caramel macchiato.' I glare at her.

'Sorry?'

'How fucking hard is it to get a damned cup of coffee right, Daisy. Jesus. It's Friday. It's caramel macchiato day.'

'I can go back and get you one. I just...'

'You just..?'

'I just ... I'll go back and get a macchiato.'

'And who answers the phone while you're gone? No. Just leave it. I'll drink this. Thank you Daisy.' The thank-you is not a thank-you, it's a get out of my office now, you imbecile.

I really don't care that much about the caramel macchiato. And Daisy is no imbecile. She's perfectly capable as assistants go. She's organised and efficient. She's probably a little too cheerful for my liking but that's it. She knows when to knock on my door and when to send me a message. But it's not the most difficult job in the world.

In fact, Jill could do it.

For the rest of the day, I pick up on every little thing that Daisy does. I shout at her. I fly off the handle about things that don't really matter. She looks sad at her desk. I don't care.

I call Daisy in to my office towards the end of the day.

'I'm not sure what's got into you lately, Daisy, but this really isn't working for me any more.' I look her dead in the eyes.

'Lately? What do you mean? I'm having a bad day, I realise that.'

'Yes. Well, as I said, it's just not working for me any more.'

'You're letting me go?'

'I'll speak with the agency and make sure you get a good reference.'

'Because I screwed up one coffee? You're joking.'

I explain that I'm not really one for jokes and that she needs to pack up her belongings and get out.

'This is ridiculous. I'm getting sacked for nothing.'

'We are parting ways before things get worse, Daisy. Calm down and don't blow your reference.'

'Screw the reference. And screw this place. I'll be alright.' She turns away from me and starts to head out of the office. It all happens so quickly that she doesn't have time to see me roll my eyes.

I call Jill right away and let her know the good news. She's my new assistant. Her new position begins on Monday at nine. She needs to dress appropriately and arrive ahead of time. And if she could learn to type over the weekend, that would be great, too.

She's grateful. Overly. She wants to quit the supermarket right away. I mention that she could quit all the ways she is making money but she brushes it off. ~~A girl's gotta eat.~~

Amends made.

That wasn't so difficult.

I can cross off Jill's name because I have been responsible for altering her fate.

I know that I am not supposed to injure the person that I am making amends to. And I realise that I am also not supposed to hurt others in the process. So, I add Daisy to my list.

LIST OF PEOPLE I HAVE (RECENTLY) HARMED

NOT JACK

HOBO #4

~~JILL~~

CAB DRIVER

GARY (SPONSOR)

DAISY

I open the door to the freezer in the garage.

Gary's head stares back at me.

'Look, you're a tricky one, Gaz. What can I say? You seemed okay, at first. You'd been there and done that, you knew the steps and you'd used them. I could see you inspiring people. Then you were talking about getting wrecked and blowing dudes, which is totally fine. But you can't say you're not gay and you especially can't say it because you're all into God, now. That's shit. That's not real. That's not what I was looking for. I don't want a sponsor like that.'

Gary's head says nothing.

Completely dead eyes.

'I know what you're thinking, does that really warrant being drugged and tied to a bed before some half-hearted masturbation and a drill through the brain? I'm guessing the majority would agree with your stance – that I went too far. I'm acknowledging that understanding but, still, I think I didn't go far enough. And I know I'm supposed to be making amends here, but I don't quite know how to do this just yet. So you'll have to hang in there while I figure something out.'

I shut the door.

Then I open it again.

'I have to say, I do prefer you dead. Honestly, the God stuff was getting too much.'

I close it once more and head back into the house. I've got the place to myself this Saturday. Seth had plans already but has agreed to come over tomorrow. I took one of those pills to help me sleep last night and didn't bother setting an alarm.

It's already lunchtime. I'm hungry. My mouth felt dry and off when I woke up. It made me wonder what Jill's tasted like after a night on the wine and some flavoured condoms bought from the machine at the snooker club.

I'm taking myself for lunch today near Primrose Hill. There's a Step and Tradition meeting later in the area. I'm staying close in case I feel the urge but my main priority is making amends. Today, my plan is to put things right with the cab driver that took Jill home after I had plied her with enough alcohol to kill a gorilla.

I'm still working out how I can get things right with Gary but the cab driver thing should be easy. I think a simple apology for suggesting that he was a rapist will suffice.

The next time I open the freezer door, Gary and the cab driver are staring back at me.

It did not go well.

He did fuck Jill. He told me that it wasn't rape. She wanted it. And when I talk to her, she says that she can't remember and, 'it doesn't matter, anyhow.'

This was when I first had the idea for bleach.

And this is why I need six bottles of it.

I still had the details of the cab driver from the picture I took of the licence he had displayed inside his car. Also, the app I used to book it with meant that I received a text with his name, details and number, anyway.

I called him. Not from my mobile phone, that would be reckless. At the Albert Road corner of Primrose Hill, there is still a working telephone box. Not one of those useless internet ones, either. An iconic red phone box. I arranged for him to pick me up at his earliest convenience, which gave me time for a quick lunch and a glass of Merlot, but meant that I would have to miss out on a meeting today.

Looks like the only misery I'll get to witness is my own.

When I get in the cab, it's evident that he does not remember me at all. Which makes me wonder how often he is accused of being a rapist and how oblivious he is to the world around him. My remarks, apparently, made no impact on him, yet here I am with some elaborate scheme to say a sorry that I don't even mean.

Fuck it. I figure I'm here, I'll get it out there and cross him off the list.

I put it off for part of the journey. He calls me 'love' three times in the first five minutes and I want to tape his mouth shut for the rest of the journey. I don't want to tell him what I've been up to today. I don't want to hear about his late night or his kids or his views on immigration. I want to put it out there that I was perhaps a little hasty in suggesting he was going to rape my friend.

I explain this to him.

'I'm guessing she didn't tell you that we had sex then?'

I don't say anything. I was not expecting that. If I'm quiet, he'll keep talking and showing off.

'Yeah. She was playing with my hair and kept touching me. Asked me if I'd let her off the fare if she ... well, you know.' He points down at his crotch and does some stupid whistling noise.

'I told her that you'd already given me the money so she asked if I just wanted to pull over and get in the back. You know, I thought I recognised you when you got in.'

He's disgusting. I don't care if Jill did do all that – I can imagine her saying it – but she was out of her mind on booze. In my books, that makes this guy a rapist and a simple sorry is not going to make amends.

'Of course she told me. Why do you think I ordered you specifically?' He looks at me in his rearview mirror. A slimy, cunty, rapey look. I throw back a coquettish grin.

'What are you saying, love?'

We're in Hampstead. The house is a couple of minutes away. I didn't give him my actual address because I don't want it on his records.

'I'm saying that we are almost at our destination. I can afford the cab fare, no problem, but I want you to pull into my driveway, kill the engine and unzip. Hell, I'll still pay you, I just want to see that thing.'

He checks the navigation on his screen so he knows how long until he's going to get his dick sucked. I open my bag, take a twenty out of my purse and my nail file from the zipped compartment.

Ninety seconds later, he pulls in, turns off the engine and I throw the money over his shoulder.

'Go on, then. Show me what I want.'

The fucking idiot unzips with his left hand and fishes around inside. While both his hands are busy, I stab him in the throat with the sharp end of my nail file. He panics and can't get his hand out of his pants. He tries to lash out with his left at first but then instinctively reaches for his throat.

The first few shanks get the job done. The next ten or fifteen are for my enjoyment. I can't help but laugh at his right arm, stuck down his trousers.

When he stops moving, I take out his eyes.

Just because I want to.

For the next forty minutes, I am rearranging things in the garage so that I can pull the rapist's car inside and get it out of view.

I check his mobile phone in case there is some kind of booking app but he's outdated, part of a fleet where you let the controller know if you are nearby for a pick-up, still dealing in cash, writing your miles into a notebook. Probably cooking the numbers.

~~Fine by me.~~

There's going to be DNA everywhere. Usually, I would give myself some time to clean everything up but I don't have that because Seth is coming over tomorrow. I know that I can cancel him but I don't want to. I can have all the things I want. I have to do this. I have to cross this bastard off my list so that I am ready to take things on fully with the Seth in my life.

The only thing going through my mind is that I have to get things clean. I have to erase myself from him. Then I can think about the car. The best way to get something clean and kill off any microbes of Maeve that might linger, is to use bleach.

I take the sticky plastic I used in my bedroom when I killed Gary and I wrap it around the cab driver's head, neck and shoulders so that no blood gets inside. Then I drag that attacker through my hallway and haul him upstairs to the bathroom.

I cut off his clothes, haul him into the bathtub and unwrap the plastic. Downstairs, underneath the sink, I look for bleach. There are six bottles. Two blue, two pink and two yellow. I don't remember buying this many but I'm still so angry that I take them all out.

Upstairs, I talk to the corpse like I talked to Gary's head this morning, pouring a bottle over his body until it is empty then reaching for the next. The second one, I am straight into the sockets where I have removed his eyes. Once all six are empty, I turn on the tap until he is covered and I leave him there.

This fucker is better off the way he is.

It can be my good deed for the day.

I can cross him off. ~~We're even.~~

The 'amends list' might look confusing to a non-psychopath but what am I supposed to do, write a list of 'people I am going to kill in order to restore balance'? Or 'people I have recently harmed and will now help, often through the act of killing them'? Feels a little wordy. Besides, it's a real list, somebody could find it.

I harmed the cab driver by inadvertently suggesting he was a rapist.

He was a rapist.

And now he is dead.

Amends made.

Atonement.

I have more than redeemed myself.

Perhaps I've made more amends with Jill without her even knowing.

I won't burn the dinner this time because Seth has told me that he will make it.

He never offered to do it at his place. I don't care, I like being in my home.

'Damn, it always smells so clean here,' he comments.

'I bleached the toilets. Very glamorous.'

What I've really been doing is bleaching a rapist cab driver. I stripped his body of colour. I burnt out any idea of contact with me. I bagged that piece of shit and stuffed him in my freezer with my former God-fearing sponsor. It was impulsive, yes, but necessary.

I will have to slow down a little with the murders, I'm running out of space for my ice-cubes. I need them for the gin and tonics.

In the garden, I have a burn barrel. It's just for twigs that come off trees and other wood. I set fire to some leaves, throw in a few small branches from the floor and drop the cabby's clothes on top. By the time Seth arrives, the only evidence is the two bodies in the freezer and the deceased driver's Toyota Prius taking up half of my garage. I've taken the number plates off.

'So, what are you cooking me and, more importantly, what wine shall I open to pair with it?'

'Well, there's sweet potatoes, broccoli, chicken, mushrooms and a mustardy sauce. Sound good?'

'Sounds great.'

'So what wine goes with that? I have no idea about that sort of thing.'

'Fridge wine.'

'Fridge wine?'

'Yes. Whatever wine I see when I open up the fridge.'

'Quite the connoisseur.' He cuts the sweet potatoes into wedges, oils, seasons and places them in the oven, then lights the flame on the hob to cook the chicken.

We drink. I watch Seth cook. He concentrates on what he is doing but talks to me as he chops and sears. This must be what couples do. He asks me what I've been up to and I tell him I went for a walk and had some lunch yesterday. I don't mention the meetings or the rapist.

'I watched the semi-final of *America's Next Top Model* and fell asleep on the sofa. A lazy day.'

'Oh, yeah. I can't wait to see the final.'

'You're fucking with me.' I drink. He doesn't say anything. I slap his arm and say, 'Don't fuck with me. You watch *ANTM*?'

'Oh, Maeve, it's *fierce.*' He laughs. Stirs. Looks at me. He can't tell if I'm amused or pissed off that he's screwing with me. I don't know, either. 'Okay,' he relents, 'I don't watch it. I know of it, of course, but it's not something that really ever appealed to me.'

'Until now.' I pick up my glass and head into the lounge.

'Maeve? Maeve, what are you doing?'

I switch on the television. It goes straight to the news. I panic that it will show something about some missing taxi driver, his wife and four kids would be making a plea to find him, neighbours would say he was a kind man. Six women he sexually abused still wouldn't come forward and tell their stories.

Ridiculous, of course. His body shouldn't even be cold yet. It is, because it's in the freezer, but he would not have been missing long enough for the police to be involved. It's just the tail end of a story about how a quarter of all known bees have not been seen since the nineties. One of those environmental pieces that people pretend to care about. Like that plastic straws campaign. Giving people the opportunity to make the smallest change to their lives in order to feel like they are making the biggest difference. They're not saving fish, they're just using a few less straws than they did before – how many straws do people ever really use in comparison to the fish they eat?

I press the button to get to my recordings. I haven't, actually, watched the semi-final yet. I just said that because it was better than starting a conversation about sawing through a grown-man's neck.

'Oh, God. Okay, but I am going to need a lot more wine.' Seth shakes his head in fake disgust. He turns his back on me and I smile at him. I don't know what this is. This is what people do when they're together. They compromise. They do things for the other person that they don't really want to do.

Who knows? He might even like it.

How long can it really last if he doesn't?

'A lot more? That's my favourite amount.' I follow him back into the kitchen.

We eat. We watch the show. I hold back my gasps at anything controversial because I'm supposed to have seen this before.

We drink.

We fuck. There's a worry that it wasn't fucking, it was something more emotional. Not quite making love, but certainly less animalistic than our hallway, up-against-the-wall session last time.

We sleep.

Tomorrow is a new week.

Jill starts tomorrow. I need to speak with her before she starts. And I need to get rid of a car.

LIST OF PEOPLE I HAVE (RECENTLY) HARMED

NOT JACK

HOBO #4

~~JILL~~

~~CAB DRIVER~~

GARY (SPONSOR)

DAISY

'Tell anybody how we met and I will fire you immediately, okay? Then I will kill you.'

Jill thinks I'm half joking.

She's right. I wouldn't bother firing her.

~~Don't ever laugh at me.~~

I don't want anybody to know me, they can think that they know me, like I'm some kind of hard-nosed, uptight ball buster, obsessed with her work. That's what they think. Because that's what I let them think.

Jill has scrubbed up well. She tells me that she didn't drink anything yesterday even though she was nervous about starting her new position. I let her know that, today, all she has to do is answer the phone. I show her how easy it is to put people on hold then check with me whether I want to speak to them. She also has to get me coffee.

'If anyone asks where Daisy is, tell them that you don't know and they can speak to me. If they ask how you got the job, you tell them through the agency. If they ask you which agency, tell them they are asking too many questions. Got it?'

'Got it. Don't know you. Never met. Agency sent me. Please leave a message and I'll get her to call you back.'

'Perfect. It's Monday morning, I'm going to need a black coffee. None of that instant crap. There's a machine in the kitchen area.' We leave my office. 'And this will be your desk. Andy will be up from tech in about ten minutes with your login information and I'll see you in about three with that coffee.'

'What should I do if I want a coffee?'

'It's not a prison, Jill. You can have whatever you like from the kitchen. Go nuts.'

She seems excited.

It won't last.

I can hear my mobile phone ringing in my office. It's Seth. I had to subtly force him out the door at the same time as me this morning. He has no reason to go looking through the freezers or wandering around the garage but there's no way I was going to leave him there alone.

'Did you forget something?' I don't even say hello.

'And good morning to you, too.'

'I already said good morning when I woke up.'

Silence.

'Okay, well, I'm actually calling about work.' It's pretty boring, run-rate stuff. Something to do with their distributors. He wants to use whoever worked the graphics for the last job. I'm as interested in this as he was in the *Top Model* semi-final. I tell him to email me what he wants.

He thanks me, says we'll speak soon, and it all feels more formal than the way we left it earlier in the morning.

Jill taps on my door and brings me my coffee, then sits at her desk and waits for Andy.

So do I. I want to see how she handles herself.

'So, you're Daisy's replacement?' That's his opener. He's tall and slim but does have that techy look about him.

'I guess so. I don't know who Daisy is.'

Well done, Jill.

'She was the last assistant. Lovely girl.'

I'm listening from behind the wall in my office. The 'lovely girl' comment makes me angry. I don't know why he would need to say that.

'So, you've answered your own question. Daisy was Maeve's last assistant and I'm the new one. I must be the replacement for that lovely girl.'

Jill is constantly pushed around by men, but I can hear that she probably doesn't always give them an easy ride. I bet she's gone down swinging a few times.

'Maeve? A friend of yours is she?'

'I met her this morning. The agency sent me in. Part of my job is remembering her name.'

Feisty. Maybe there is something behind this whole 'making amends' business.

I think Andy is impressed.

'I'm sure you'll do well here. You've already lasted longer than half the people who have been an assistant to that ballbreaker.' Andy thinks he's being funny. Jill does not laugh. I think about putting Andy on a future 'make amends' list.

'Look, Andy, you seem like a nice guy but can I just get my login details? I want to make a decent impression on my first day and slagging the boss off outside her office doesn't seem like the smartest move.'

I open my office door quickly and see that Andy jumps at the sound. I walk out without looking at either of them, leaving him to wonder whether or not I heard what he was saying. Taking my coffee with me, I walk over to one of the designers and let him know that I've got another quick polish for the DoTrue account. When I return, Andy is gone and Jill is tapping at her keyboard, reading the tech guy's ineligible handwriting he professionally wrote on a post-it note.

'Good work with Andy. Keep it like that.' I tap my knuckles on her desk.

'I've handled plenty of dicks in my time.'

She has no idea what she just said.

'Enough about the weekend work, eh, Jill. Let's keep it clean.'

She goes red.

I laugh.

And that's Monday.

By Thursday, I realise who I am going to make amends with next on my list.

Not Jack.

That rubbish alcoholic impersonator and cadaverous lay I met at a meeting a while back. The married guy who made the bed like a soldier on basic training. I remember him for all the wrong reasons.

And he just seems so much worse now that I have this connection with Seth.

And this passion I have with Seth.

And this need for more Seth.

~~I shouldn't need anybody.~~

Not Jack was the worst. I tend to go through life thinking that I have no regrets; the things I have done are the things I am supposed to do. But Not Jack does feel, not so much a mistake, but that I wasted some time and some Johnnie Walker Red.

But I definitely caused some psychological harm there by compounding insecurities about his sexual prowess. He had the emotional availability of a teenage virgin and was hung like one, too. I can't blame his wife for cheating on him in the first place.

I thought, 'How the fuck am I supposed to make amends to Mr Baby Dick and his lightweight drinking?' The idea behind the steps is that I talk to him and admit what I did was wrong out loud, then sit there and listen to his opinions and hopefully reach a state of accord.

Or perhaps this is one of those times when I should do nothing because my appearance in I'm-Alright-Jack's life would cause more damage than leaving that psychological trauma festering in his puny mind.

There's secret option number three where I find him at a meeting where he is preying on the vulnerable, give him a drink, fuck him again and tell him how great he is and how huge his cock is and how it fills me up and its magic adds years to my life.

And I'm an idiot.

I buzz Jill. 'Can you come into my office for a moment?'

She knocks, even though I know it's her and I tell her to come in.

'You need coffee?'

'No, Jill, come and take a seat.'

'You told me that one of these men ... these...' I lower my voice, '...Friday night men...'

It clicks in her mind what I am pointing towards and she nods.

I continue. 'One of these Friday night men was giving you money to overact and be loud as though you were really enjoying what he was doing.'

'That's right. Really wanted me to go on about how I could really feel him deep inside me. I know why he wanted that. You know? Because I couldn't.'

'And you met him at a meeting?'

'That's right. Why?'

'He told you his name?'

'That's the weird thing, he was playing this whole anonymous card. I think he thought it was sexy or brooding or whatever. I mean, he clearly doesn't know what he's doing. There might be something wrong with him. Like he's a social retard or something. What's ADHD, would that be something?'

'ADHD doesn't give an adult a penis like a toddler, Jill.'

I know the next question should be handled with some delicacy but I don't have time for that and Jill has been around the block a few hundred times, she can take it. I tell her that I assume she is still dabbling in some weekend work.

'I'm grateful, Maeve, I am. And I'm staying sober all week so I don't fuck anything up here. But I can't on the weekend. I want to have a drink and I've got nobody to spend time with unless someone comes over and pays me to tug them off with my feet.'

I explain that I'm not judging but do suggest that she could probably get a man to come over who wouldn't have to pay her for such things. She tells me that she's started saving that money.

'I've never had savings before.'

I'm bored of this part-time prostitute trying to act sweet. I tell her to text Anonymous and prompt him into a rendezvous by asking if he wants to come inside her tight hole this weekend. No teenage virgin could resist such an offer.

Here's the deal: Jill's daughter goes to bed. She may not even be asleep when the first man knocks on the door. He enters the family home and slips his streetwalker some money before they get into the act that has been agreed upon.

Jill isn't afraid to ask for it, either.

A first-time user who just wants to lose his virginity so the made-up stories he tells his friends have some basis in reality. It's like method acting. He's nervous when he enters.

Give me the money and I'll pretend that it's okay to last that long.

Or some married guy, who talks in hushes and whispers because he knows what he's doing is wrong in the eyes of God or matrimonial law.

No, you be quiet and give me my money.

Maybe some twenty-something bloke, raised on gonzo porn, strides in with swagger and bravado.

You want me to flick your balls and choke you just as you're about to come, put the goddamned money in my hand.

When they're done spraying their fluids around Jill's lounge, they pull up, zip up, and head straight out the back door that she has considerately left open for them.

At 20:20 on Friday night, Jill's daughter's bedroom light was still switched on and Not Jack passed Jill a few notes and said, 'You know what I want.'

'The same thing I want, baby.' Jill was a total pro. And, as it turns out, not a bad typist at all.

I'm in her kitchen. It's clean and organised and a little twee. Not what I expected. I came in the back door, which just happens to be what Not Jack is expecting. Jill tells me that she doesn't really offer that but that it's not bad with him because he's 'too small for the front, anyway'.

She has no filter.

I'm in her kitchen. Oak work surfaces and cookbooks and a small bowl on the side that seems dedicated to holding only lemons. I've double-checked and the sound is off. The flash is off. The camera is on.

The sound of a zip.

Jill's voice.

'Let me work you with my mouth, baby.'

Sounds like she's talking directly to his penis.

Not Jack's voice.

'Oh, fuck.'

Five more seconds.

'Fuuuck.'

I give him another twenty seconds or so to get his mind into it. I can see in the reflection of the glass on the door that he has his eyes closed and his hands behind his head. I capture him in the act on my phone. Three decent pictures where his face is easily identifiable.

He gets on top of her because he's excited. From the reflection, I can see him pumping up and down but I can't tell the woman he is trying to penetrate is not his wife.

Jill knows what to do.

I don't hear her say anything until she is on all fours with her hands resting on the arm of the sofa. My view is from the side but her back is facing me. Which means that Not Jack's back will be facing me.

I take a stream of photos as Not Jack squeezes his angry inch into my secretary's anus. It's less clear that it's him in the picture this time but is obvious when in the context of the blow-job portraits.

Sticking to a plan is not my thing. Even when I have made the plan. I was supposed to take the photos in secret and sneak out the back door without being noticed.

But I couldn't.

I held my phone against my jacket – both dark – and aimed it in their direction. I stepped into the room and held my finger on the button so it took twenty-four snaps a second until I let go.

'Oh, my God. Jill. I'm so sorry.' I feign covering my eyes to preserve everyone's modesty and run out the back door.

In my car, I leave the lights off and check through my camera roll. Lots to sift through but there are plenty I could use. There are three or four towards the end where they both turn to the side to view the commotion, remaining linked in the middle.

I wait outside for another eight minutes. Not Jack clearly wasn't put off and finished the task at hand. Jill has the skill to talk him around, I'm guessing.

He doesn't see me. Doesn't even look over his shoulder in paranoia as he is leaving.

The cocky little step-out.

I follow him for about ten miles, keeping my distance. He drives like a kid who has recently passed their test and has been given a car that is too powerful. I park across the road from the house whose driveway he blocks. He goes up to the front door and lets himself in with a key.

And now I know where he lives.

A few things worth knowing, should you ever find yourself acting impetuously and killing a person inside their car…

Never dump a body.

Never dump a car.

If you have a need to hurt somebody to the point of seeing their life drain away before you, if this sometimes makes you act out or perform impulsively, that is fine, as long as the spontaneity vanishes when the act is complete. Now, you have to be cautious.

Eat it, burn it, crush it up, dump it far and wide. Those are your best bets.

It's slightly harder with a Toyota Prius, but the principles are the same.

For both, you will need tools. A saw will always help with a body but a car will require an assortment of screwdrivers, wrenches and Allen keys.

I started by taking off the wheels. I knew how to do that, already. I don't need help if I get a blow-out on the motorway, I can change a flat tyre. An online video showed me exactly which parts to unscrew in order to take the seats out. The fabric and foam will burn. In fact, anything you can cut with a Stanley knife can generally burn.

The plastic parts can always be sawn into smaller pieces and put out with the rubbish. Sure, those blue bags are not supposed to contain plastics or bottles or even food, but the people who pick these things up and drive them to landfill do not love their jobs. They hear a couple of bottles clanking together, it's no skin off their nose. Throw it in the van. Crush it up. Bury it.

And those wheels can go to the recycling centre. There is a section for rubber and tyres but, if you'll leave them out and turn your back on them for a minute, somebody will have taken them by the time you turn back around.

Or you could throw them in to the landfill area. If you're a woman with two feet and a heartbeat, the workers there will often throw a blind eye.

What you're left with is a shell of metal and glass. The glass can be smashed. There are numbers in the windscreens and on the chassis that can identify a specific car, just as fingerprints are distinctive to each person.

You can take the engine apart piece by piece and throw it out week by week. You can take a door or two in the back of your own car and scrap it for money or throw it over the edge with a mattress and a bag of leaves.

There was no way I was getting rid of the rapist's car over the weekend but I did manage to get rid of three wheels, including the spare in the boot. A burly guy in his mid-thirties was throwing out a beaten-up washing line and some half-empty paint tubs. He asked me why I was getting rid of them when they looked so new. I told him my boyfriend cheated on me so I am throwing out all his stuff before he has time to come and collect it.

'Ouch!' he said, and laughed. And I laughed with him as I threw a bag over the edge onto the landfill pile. A bag that contained a mouldy tarpaulin and a cab driver's bleached-white head.

The muscly tyre-guy even helped me with the heavy torsos I was throwing out while I picked up the much lighter camping chairs that had been in the garage when I bought the place.

On the way home, I bought four bags of ice. I moved the remaining body parts to the outside freezer to be with Gary's head and the ice stayed in the kitchen. That way, Seth can make some of the gins when he turns up around dinner time.

That gives me the rest of the afternoon to attend a meeting and maybe update people on how well I'm doing with my steps, I need to finish making amends with Not Jack now that the photos are printed, and then watch the final of *America's Next Top Model.*

I suppose there's something to be said about taking time to plan a murder but that can take the fun out of it.

†

There are two envelopes. One has 'Not Jack' written on the front and the other says, 'Not Jack's wife'.

I'm waiting outside the house I followed him to last night. I have seen them both through the window. If I post them both, there is a chance that he will intercept them and prevent them being delivered to the intended parties.

I believe there would be the same outcome but I would not be as satisfied.

Not Jack's wife's envelope contains seven A4-size pictures of her husband hanging out the back of woman he has paid to fuck in the rectum. It is clearly the man she married.

The note inside reads:

This is your husband. I do not know his name. None of the women he has been picking up at AA meetings or paying for sex know his real name. He thinks it's sexy.

It is not. We call him 'Not Jack'.

You may have some arrangement that allows him to do this kind of thing, in which case, there is no need for you to look at the images. If he is the unscrupulous scumbag we expect him to be then it may give you some satisfaction to watch his face as he opens his own envelope.

Sincerely,
Alcoholics and whores.

I want it to sound like there are many of us that have got together to deliver this unsavoury news to her.

Two hours pass by. And nobody leaves the place. It's not Sunday. It's not a day to lounge around in your pyjamas, hungover and eating everything in sight. It's Saturday. People are supposed to get out on Saturday.

There are still a few hours until I need to leave and get myself home and ready for Seth's arrival. If it comes to it, I will make Jill call him repeatedly until he becomes so irritated that he has to leave the house to answer the call.

It doesn't come to that. The front door opens. Not Jack kisses Mrs Not Jack goodbye. He does the same to the small child she is holding in her arms and he pushes the happy dog back inside with his foot.

I don't know where he is going and I don't care.

Perhaps to the meeting I no longer have time to attend.

Making amends is really starting to take over my Saturdays.

Once he is out of sight, I take my envelopes across the street, place them down on the doorstep, ring the bell and run. I thought about posting them but figured I might have a chance to watch something unfold, to catch a little real misery.

Because I won't see any at the meeting I'll be missing and Seth seems to only bring me joy.

She looks confused. She picks up both envelopes – hers is on top – then looks around as though she might spot who posted them. She doesn't look anywhere near me.

I see her face. It's saying, 'It is illegal to open somebody else's mail but these are not stamped, they were hand-delivered and, even though the names are not correct, they were clearly meant for us, so I am going to open mine.'

This will be the last time she thinks of them as an 'us'.

She tears. She pulls out the paper. She reads. She drops to her knees. She cries. She stands. She wipes her eyes. She closes the door.

She is calm.

That's what Not Jack needs to be most worried about.

I want to stay and look through the window when he returns but I have Seth.

Seth is coming.

Seth is more important.

Perhaps Seth and I are almost an 'us'.

I can't wait around here for something interesting and miserable to happen. For Not Jack's future ex to kick him out or throw him through a window or stab him in the neck and not know what to do next until a stranger knocks on her door and helps her clear some freezer space.

She looked calm. I have to drive off and imagine.

I think of Not Jack coming home. Maybe he's been down the pub for a pint with a friend or he's watched the football somewhere. He could be at an AA meeting working that legendary anonymous charm of his. Perhaps he's at the Borehamwood Hotel Ibis, stroking some hooker the wrong way up as she pretends he's Errol Flynn.

It doesn't matter. He could be out picking up two pints of semi-skimmed milk, he is coming home to the end of his life.

In my head, she plays it cool. The kid is upstairs so it doesn't see everything unfold. Or she's had the foresight to shift the kid over to her mother's for the night. Either way, Mrs Not Jack is pottering about in the kitchen and happens to mention the package on the table labelled 'Not Jack'. Sure, she thought it was a bit weird but she left it for him as he's closer to being a Jack than she is.

He's intrigued. He tears the top of the envelope and takes out the eight pages. Seven photos and one letter.

God, wouldn't it feel poetic to really lay into the guy for his skulduggery? If ever there was a chance to do something witty and poetic and justified, it was in that moment. Some Oscar-winning voiceover monologue.

I opted for pithy, yet degenerate:

Hey, little baby dick.
She knows.
Not Audrey.

I take a large glass of Shiraz when I get home and I watch the final. Still, nobody has come close to Nicole Linkletter, who won cycle five of *ANTM*. They could have stopped the show there.

I think about the Not Whoever family and figure, as much as I hurt Not Jack's wife today, and I should never have fucked her husband, I somehow made amends for that without really trying.

I add her to the list then immediately cross her off.

~~I am good.~~

LIST OF PEOPLE I HAVE (RECENTLY) HARMED

~~NOT JACK~~

HOBO #4

~~JILL~~

~~CAB DRIVER~~

GARY (SPONSOR)

DAISY

~~NOT JACK'S WIFE~~

Seth stayed with me again on Saturday night. We fucked so much I felt raw. And numb. Like I could feel everything we had done between my legs but could also not feel anything as a result. We woke up and he was stroking his fingers across my stomach and I could feel his growing intentions against my hip, when I should have just got out of bed or said no because it was going to hurt – and not in the good way – I still did it.

I can't stop.

Drinking.

Fucking.

I can't stop.

Killing.

I can't stop.

Seth Beauman.

When he left after dinner on Sunday, I found myself aching for him. I didn't want him to leave. I wanted him with me. It's the same reason that my fridge will always have wine and my freezer will always have somebody's head inside and I will always put out, even if I have to grit my teeth through the chafing.

Monday morning in my office, I'm on a conference call, and I can still feel Seth inside me.

Jill is next to me taking notes on everything. I don't like to listen to these things. Daisy used to make great notes. She'd type them up and send to me after the meeting so I could recall what the hell went on. There's noise. I hear talking but it's just a hum. I'm in my own head, wondering where Not Jack slept on Saturday and whether the hobo made it after I hit him. I don't know how to make amends to Gary. These whirrings in my head all seem more important than the front cover of *Caravan Monthly* or the fact that some celebrity doesn't want to be airbrushed but her complexion is so pale, she'll never live it down.

It's hard to spot a psychopath these days. Before humans puked out every inane thought we had or took a picture of every meal we ate or attacked somebody we never met before from the safety of our home, hidden behind a screen and an avatar, people weren't worried about what they looked like to others at every moment of the day. They took twenty-four pictures of an entire holiday. They had an inner monologue. They could see other people walking in the streets or queueing for a train.

It was the psychopaths who went around thinking they lived in a world of one.

Stockbrokers and actors. Lawyers and surgeons. Journalists and priests.

Now everyone thinks they are being immortalised online. That they can do anything. They are invincible and can never die. Somehow, even politicians became celebrities.

This whole 'don't-airbrush-me-I-want-to-look-natural' stance is a stunt. Another bid for immortality or increased exposure. Or maybe this celebrity is sick of the way that women are portrayed in the media. It doesn't matter. Her skin is almost translucent, we will have to colour correct.

One of the old geezers from this magazine conglomerate pipes up and says his assistant is leaving. She got herself knocked up and is taking a year for maternity leave, 'But, between you and me, I don't think she'll come back once that baby is born.'

Between you and me.

There were twelve people on that call.

This was the only comment that managed to penetrate my own thoughts. I asked him whether he would stay on after the call had ended. When it did, I sent Jill out to type up her notes. Her first real test.

'Look, I'm going to save you a ton of money in recruiter fees and retainers, you don't even have to interview. I've got your next assistant. She is the best you'll ever have.'

I give that wealthy, white male Daisy's number and he agrees to call her. He thanks me, says he can't be bothered to go through the rigmarole and he trusts my judgement.

Three days later, I get a call from Daisy, which I ignore. I don't want to speak with her. I sorted her out. Amends were made. She leaves me a message saying that she doesn't understand why I would do that for her but that she has a new job. She adds that she still doesn't really understand why she was laid off in the first place. Then she tells me that I'm a bitch, and hangs up.

LIST OF PEOPLE I HAVE (RECENTLY) HARMED

~~NOT JACK~~

HOBO #4

~~JILL~~

~~CAB DRIVER~~

GARY (SPONSOR)

~~DAISY~~

~~NOT JACK'S WIFE~~

Two to go.

I can feel this step working. There's no talk of God's will, I am doing this. I am making amends. I am pushing myself into a place where a relationship is developing between myself and Seth. A dependence, perhaps.

Who knows what lies ahead.

But I must complete my list.

In the doorway of the old cinema, the one next to the camping shop, I see a mattress and dirty quilt. There's a box that has been flattened and a shopping bag filled with items wrapped in other shopping bags. It stinks. But there is nobody there.

I don't want to stand around and wait in this stench so I go across the road for a drink. It's cold out. I find a seat near a window that overlooks the road outside and nurse a double Ardbeg while I wait for that disgusting homeless animal to return from the skip he is raiding. Hell, I don't know what he does with his day, he could be at the library, he could be begging near a tube station so that he can buy a bottle of something to ease his pain.

Another Ardbeg.

Still nothing. What if that mattress has been there since I last saw him? He could have died in that street. He could have been taken to hospital and lives somewhere else. Some other street. Some other doorway. Grabbing some other woman's leg as she goes past.

He probably never even thinks about me. Only when he feels that pain in his head. The square dent that is the exact size of the base of a Johnnie Walker bottle.

Two more of those beautifully peaty whiskies, please, bartender. He gives me a look that says the drink doesn't suit me. I happen to think there's something sexy about a woman with a whisky.

I'm starting to get angry with this homeless person. What is he playing at? Why won't he just come home? Why won't he return to his piss-drenched mattress?

Then I see him. He's sitting between the two shops. The same spot he was in when he reached too high up my leg. I never looked there.

I was too busy looking at his bedroom when he was in the lounge. He could have been there all night.

I knock back my whisky. I don't like to do that with a drink that should be savoured. The glass remains in my hand. Part of me wanted to slam it down but it's best not to draw attention to myself.

I'm feeling impetuous again.

Gary's head is still there but I've gone through a bag and half of ice, which leaves room for another.

It's dark between the buildings and I don't understand why he likes it there when he's got a mattress and a quilt around the corner – even if they smell like three wet dogs had a pissing competition on them.

'Oh, lady. Can you help me out a little?'

The motherfucker doesn't even recognise me. I wait around all day and he can't remember who I am. Maybe I hit him on the right part of the brain to make him forget. Maybe I'm wasting my time trying to make amends with this guy.

'What do you need? Money? Booze?' I sound calm but I'm squeezing the whisky glass tighter with every passing whiff of his unwashed corduroys.

'The pain. I need something for the pain.' He rubs the dent in his head that I made.

'So, money or booze.'

'Make it go away.' I notice that he's slurring. Not a drunken slur. Half of his face has dropped slightly. He looks less like the man from that meeting who had punched his wife in the face, but that doesn't make me want to hurt him any less.

I've had enough by now. He's wasting my time. He doesn't even remember me. I don't entertain his ramblings any further. I crouch down and look at his sad face. I feel like I hate him. It's not about what he represents, it feels personal.

I'm boiling inside.

It's brewing.

'You are fucking scum.' I smash the glass I've been holding into his face. A triangle near the rim breaks lose, leaving me with a jagged edge. Two sharp teeth. I slash them across his eye and he makes a lazy noise, like he can't even be bothered to hurt. I cut his face to ribbons then thrust the sharp edges into his dent, knocking him to the ground. The glass is stuck in his head. I stamp down hard on it, pushing it into his skull a little before it shatters and I'm just stamping with all my force into his skull.

I want to hear it crack.

I want to feel it cave in.

He's definitely dead this time.

I took away his pain.

Cross him off.

We have achieved balance.

There's no need to get rid of the body or keep his head. Hookers and hobos can be left in the street.

LIST OF PEOPLE I HAVE (RECENTLY) HARMED

~~NOT JACK~~

~~HOBO #4~~

~~JILL~~

~~CAB DRIVER~~

GARY (SPONSOR)

~~DAISY~~

~~NOT JACK'S WIFE~~

'What am I going to do with you?'

Gary's head stares back at me like he doesn't care any more. It's the only part of anyone that I have left in the house. I'm still working on the Prius.

It is alleged that Ed Gein used a victim's skull as a liquorice bowl in his living room. Police even visited on one occasion to question him and ate from that bowl, made from the head of the person whose disappearance they were investigating.

I'm not sure that would be making amends with Gary as much as it would be upcycling him. Also, there are so many holes drilled into his forehead, I would have to attach a handle and use him as a colander. Every time the hot water drained through after boiling pasta, I would be reminded that God has an intricate plan that only He knows about and it involves an alcoholic sponsor doubling up as a kitchen utensil.

I would love to be around to see the outcome of this great scheme. What a story it will make. I'm sure He could nab himself a sizeable book deal.

The skull thing is a nice idea, like eating every part of an animal, nothing goes to waste, but it doesn't really fulfil the brief.

As far as I can remember from Gary's ramblings, he never mentioned any family. Alcoholics tend to alienate themselves. I never found out his full story so it may be that he does have family but they were estranged as a result of his addiction. Perhaps he leeched off a sibling or stole money from a parent to fund his habit. Gary didn't have a partner, he was still trying to find his way there. It could be another reason his family doesn't talk to him.

'Gary, did you not make amends with the people you had wronged?'

For me, this has been the best step. I definitely feel like I've got something out of this. If Gary couldn't do this, if he could not make amends with his family, maybe everything he said was a lie. He probably didn't even believe in God. (All part of the plan, I'm sure.)

There was a roommate or close friend, the police officer mentioned him when he knocked on my door. Perhaps there would be some sort of recompense if I put this person's mind at ease. I could let them know that Gary is no longer with us. Or I could lie and say that I have heard from him and he just wanted to get away, make a fresh start. Either way, it would probably end up bringing that detective back to my doorstep and the last thing I want is a narc in my life.

I could fill a sink with bleach and leave Gary's head to soak for a couple of days until all the Maeve was definitely off him, then drop it outside a police station or leave it in a park or with the peas at the supermarket.

'Why are you being so difficult?'

Nothing.

Dead eyes.

I check the time. Three minutes until the start of Australian *Love Island*.

'This atonement is proving illusive, Gary. I need to go because Seth is waiting in the lounge. You hold tight. I'll work it out.'

Seth is waiting on the two-seater sofa for me. I have a three-seater, too, but we sit on the smaller one together. The larger seat is redundant. Though I did lie down on it last week with Seth's head between my legs.

'This show is going to be a train wreck.' He hands me a drink.

'That's the beauty.'

'It's all abs and tits. Nobody is really there for love.'

'I know. It doesn't take long until they're all completely miserable and at each other's throats.'

'And that's what you like about it? The misery?'

~~Yes. Absolutely.~~

'It's not that. It's the moments, the very few moments, where they forget there are cameras on them and you spot when they are being genuine. It's when they stop the act and you see what is real.' I skip past Seth's question and give him a version of the truth.

And it's in these short tableaux where I don't have to think about whether I am projecting the right me. The cameras are off.

Seth puts a hand on my leg and strokes it lightly while we watch and drink and laugh and critique each character vying for their soulmate in the sun-drenched villa where young adults will argue and cry while parents at home hope their son or daughter is not like these people who fuck a stranger in a jacuzzi on national television.

I put my hand on Seth's hand.

I feel content. Happy, even.

Step nine works.

I decide then that the reason I can't find a way to make amends with Gary is that I never did anything wrong.

PART THREE

STEP **TEN**

'Continue to make a personal inventory, and when you are wrong, promptly admit it.'

Now, I'm supposed to become an accountant.

Muswell Hill: Sober Today. It's the first meeting I've been to in a while. I wouldn't usually come over this way but I'm avoiding some of the old haunts. Jill is there all day at work, I don't need to be seeing her during my lunch break at The Light Ahead in Euston or bump into her after hours at Wood Green Friends of Bill W. I would like to see if Not Jack is still doing the rounds, though. Jill says she hasn't heard from him.

She is still stroking dicks and egos on the weekends but looks and sounds healthier than ever at work. She says she's not drinking during the week now and I believe her.

When I first met Jill, she wasn't interesting to me. She sounded positive and like she was buying into the twelve steps. She's like that again now but I've seen her at her worst so it doesn't bother me in the same way.

But it does bother me.

It seems that getting to step ten is something of a milestone because everything before was preparation for a new life. Now, I am to put it to practical use.

The mood here is not sombre. The alcoholics at this meeting are well on their way to sobriety. It's boring as hell. They're acting so optimistically.

'Hangovers from drinking are rough but they are nothing compared to the emotional hangover caused by an excess of negative feeling.'

This kind of talk does nothing to curb my desire to kill somebody in this room.

My freezers are empty.

There's space for two.

So, here's the deal: I've stepped up. I've admitted I'm powerless over an addiction – in this case, alcohol, but that's the least of my issues – I've made my moral inventory. I've spoken out loud to someone. I've made amends. Now, I have to do the moral inventory thing again.

All the goddamned time.

Constant analysis.

A real buzz kill.

Basically, I am now expected to perform an hourly and daily analysis. And the real kicker is that I'm supposed to draw up a balance sheet. Praise myself for the things that I have done well but also be honest about the other things that are detrimental to my recovery.

Every day. Forever.

And it's often useful to come back to meetings every six months, apparently. Perhaps have an annual appraisal. A teetotal Care Bear, getting a blow job on Christmas morning at Disneyland would turn to the drink if forced to make these daily evaluations.

'And remember that we are sober by the Grace of God.'

Oh, not this again.

Don't say it. Please don't say it.

'...and it is more His success than ours, for it is His will.'

I have to leave. You can't tell a group of people to celebrate their successes then attribute it all to a bearded gas in the sky. It's counterintuitive. It's reductive. It's insulting. Maybe that's the idea. Bring people up then knock them back down and keep them coming back. These people are already weak.

I walk out. I don't want to be with these contradictory hippies any longer, and I certainly don't want to be in Muswell Hill if I don't absolutely have to be.

I went to a meeting to witness pain and left there being the only one who felt aggrieved. That's not what this is supposed to be about.

If you're looking for some revelation about why I seemingly hate God so much, there isn't going to be one. My parents weren't overly religious. I wasn't molested by the town vicar. Does it always have to be some deep-seated motivation? Can't a person be born good. Or evil. Or pissed off. Does something always have to go wrong somewhere in a person's history?

I lie a lot. But people don't know that. The whole God thing is so obviously untrue and people still buy into it. They let Him take the credit for their hard work. It's backwards.

~~Maybe I'm just jealous of how ingenious it is.~~

Seth is staying over again tonight. A midweek get-together. We haven't done that a lot. We have been a weekend couple – if what we are is a couple. I'm not labelling it. We drink. We fuck. We laugh. Of all the couples I've seen, that's not what they tend to do. I think things start to fade when the sex turns south. I can't imagine that ever happening with Seth.

He drinks whenever he is here. He never says no. But he's not an alcoholic. We share a bottle of wine, some pricey French red he brought over. I have to deliberately slow myself down because he seems to be savouring it and I don't want to quaff something that was not made to be devoured.

Red wine staining his teeth, Seth turns and kisses me. For no other reason than it seems to be something he wants to do. I haven't said or done anything that warrants affection. I kiss him back. Soon his lips are on my neck and I'm losing myself a little. Then he's on my breasts and the next time I open my eyes, I can see the top of his head as he kneels on the carpet and pecks lightly up the inside of my thighs.

When he's finished, he looks right into me, my stomach still shuddering in aftershock. He looks as though he is going to say something but holds back and takes another mouthful of his drink. Then he's sitting back next to me as I straighten out my skirt.

I put my hand on his thigh and look at him, my tongue touching my top teeth.

'I didn't do it for that, Maeve. I just felt an overwhelming need to do it.'

Fuck, how am I so connected to this man?

'Well, don't think you're getting away with it that easily.'

He has a look when I say that. A look that I think is probably the same as the one I gave him a moment ago.

I can hear the change in the sounds he is making as he gets closer. Then, as the tip of his penis swells against the roof of my mouth just before he comes, I think to myself, 'That's definitely going in the credit column of my balance sheet.'

STEP **ELEVEN**

'Seek through prayer and meditation to improve conscious contact with God (as you understand Him), praying only for knowledge of His will for us and the power to carry that out.'

Maeve, grant yourself the serenity to not strangle the man at the front of this room, for he cannot be changed. Be wise. ~~Follow him home and set fire to him as he sleeps.~~

I know that I have skipped certain parts of this programme, that I have bent and twisted them, and this is because it doesn't work. It is flawed. And for me, the flaw is God.

Making it about God.

Always bringing things back to that holy thread that stitches each step to the next.

I saw this coming. In the beginning, they draw you in with talk that it is a community, that you do not have to choose a deity as your 'higher power'; AA can be your higher power. The twelve-step plan can be your higher power. Yet, still, they weaved Him into everything. His plan. His unknown and unknowable plan. The first seven steps were creating the world. His next five, nobody knows.

Creating cancer.

Influencing war.

Famine.

Facebook.

It's ridiculous. Because they keep you going with the idea that you are becoming a better person and that it is because of God. His will, not yours.

I hate it and I love it.

I don't want it thrust in my face but I have learned a lot about what makes a successful support group, what keeps people coming and what a twelve-step programme should look like. I work in marketing, after all, I know how to polish something up to sell it, even if it is a pile of crap. Even if it is harmful. Even if it doesn't work.

The thing that doesn't work about this is that you get so far, to the point where you are making amends with people you have derailed in the past or have recently beaten across the head with a glass bottle, and then, just before the end, you are told that prayer and meditation are your conscious effort to have a dialogue with God.

And they mean a God. Because you don't need to pray or meditate to have a conversation with other AA members because you can see them or phone them or send them an email.

God created alcoholics. Why would anyone want to talk to Him?

I attended these meeting because I could see real pain, real people, real problems, real resolve. It was interesting. Sometimes it was fun and hilarious, but not now. They've taken things too far.

This is the final straw

God has ruined Alcoholics Anonymous for me.

I am no longer a friend of Bill W.

I quit.

I can do this better.

Not Jack is on the news when I get home.

The idiot went and jumped off a bridge.

With a rope around his neck.

It's not national news but it made the local segment after the main stories that have been playing on repeat for most of the day.

The last few men who are still alive that served in the First World War. That's national interest.

A royal pregnancy. Something to lift the spirits of an entire country.

Some twenty-something, bikini-clad, sub-mental boob job, whose job title is, apparently, 'influencer', went abroad, and nobody has seen a social-media post for half a day. She went for a walk and seemingly never came back. And we are supposed to give a fuck. All of us, apparently.

Then there's the Not Jack afterthought.

He was troubled. That's what they say. An addict. He had been attending Alcoholics Anonymous meetings to deal with his dependency on the bottle and had seen a therapist to examine some sexual issues. There were some family troubles regarding a recent divorce request and an impending custody battle.

Some talking head is pontificating about men's mental health and there has been a statement from Fathers 4 Justice.

And a note from Not Jack.

A whiny fucking note. He was a 'person of choice'. He 'found his courage'. And he 'chose not to fear'. The courage to hang himself from the railway bridge at Cannon Street.

I find this conclusion to his story deeply unsatisfying.

Instead of killing him, I allowed Not Jack to live. To stick his pathetic piece of gristle into Jill's arse, one last time. He was supposed to suffer for the things he had done. He was supposed to struggle with simple day-to-day tasks. He never had to deal with addiction because he had no tolerance for liquor and he wasn't overcome with the need to fuck any more than the next man, he just wanted to not feel small, to find a woman with a vagina that felt like it had almost been sewn shut, so that he could experience what it was like to touch the sides.

Isn't that how things are now? Everything is out there. We all want some kind of influence. It doesn't have to be half a million followers who are watching us sunshine in the Bahamas or two hundred ex school friends who are scrolling through our political rantings. Maybe there are twenty people who like our book reviews.

Nothing captures the imagination of onlookers like somebody who is having a rough time, somebody who feels shit about themselves. Somebody with a problem or three.

Nothing. Apart from pictures of dogs.

And demonstrating a life that is so much more amazing than the one we are living. That's why these 'influencers' are so popular, and Not Jack had nobody who was listening.

It's also why Not Jack had to kill himself and somebody else murders the influencers.

STEP **TWELVE**

'Having had a spiritual awakening as a result of these steps, try to carry the message to other alcoholics and continue to practise these principles in all your affairs.'

All newcomers are told that they do not have to accept or follow these steps in their entirety. But there comes a point when they are no longer new. They become oldcomers. And they are more than encouraged to open that door to the Lord.

I won't do that.

God only works for people like me when we are in court and we know we are going to jail for life or facing the electric chair and we think it's funny to say that He told us to do it.

'The coroner's report shows that the victim's head was removed before the mouth was raped.'

'I didn't want to do it that way. God told me to do it. He told me through my dog.'

And then you laugh.

Or, if you're a dumb fuck, you say something stupid, like 'Hail Satan'.

What a way to be immortalised.

This is how not to punctuate your fifteen minutes of fame.

I call Calvin.

'Hey, it's Maeve, we spoke a while back about the room in the community centre opposite the one where the Footprints In The Sand meeting happens. I just wondered whether it was still available. I want to take it. Would be great to commit to twelve weeks, to begin with. Please call me back.' I leave him my number. The room was still empty the last time I attended FITS. I think it's going to work out.

I can spread my message.

The cork breaks as I try to open a bottle of wine and Seth takes it out of my hands. I watch him as he delicately coaxes it out, millimetre by millimetre. Like it's something worth doing, even though there are more bottles in the fridge. He knows that it is important to me.

I drink in his image. He's trying to take care of me. He doesn't want control, he's gentle and thoughtful. And he's here. With me. He could be somewhere else, anywhere else, but Seth Beauman is spending more of his free time here. With me.

I don't want to hurt him.

I want to bite him, scratch him, pull his hair a little but I don't want to hurt him in a way that would force me into making amends.

This man, this kind and generous man, I believe, is the first that I have ever loved.

Now I have to figure out a way to make him stay.

PART FOUR

Seth tells me that I'm everything he's ever wanted. Next thing, Seth is standing on my doorstep and he looks as though he has been crying and maybe his collar is ripped and he's talking about how much he loves me and that he needs my help and I have to trust him and he takes me by the hand and is leading me out on to the drive towards his car and it's maybe the most exciting thing that has happened for weeks.

Maybe longer. I'm only on step eight of my new plan.

He's panicking, though. I haven't seen him like this. He's worried about Jill hearing because there are some things that should just be between the two of us. I tell Seth that Jill can't hear a fucking thing that's going on and that he needs to focus and stop worrying about that old, drunken whore.

He usually laughs when I say that.

Not tonight.

When you first meet somebody new and find that you have that immediate connection with them, everything is an explosion. You're interested in what they have to say and they want to listen to you.

Bang! Tell me more.

And, damn, they look hot. Straight after work, trousers creased around the top of the thighs. Hot. Top button of his shirt undone, tie hanging low. Hot. First thing in the morning. Stubble. Breath. Ruffled hair. Hot.

Bang! Fuck me. Give me more.

But flames extinguish and stars burn out and even suns implode and die. Is it really maintainable? Can love last forever? Can anything? (Apart from death.)

Seth and I have never had a down period, sexually. It's our constant. It's how we connect and show that we like the other person. But recently, he has seemed a little distant when we are together and we are not fucking.

I was thinking that maybe it was me. I've been spending too much time with the group and work has been demanding. He hasn't been as enamoured with my TV programmes as he was in the earlier days and I find that I've been drinking alone more and more.

The difficulty for me, and anyone who knows what it is to be an addict, is that I need Seth. I can't quit him. People call it love or infatuation or whatever but I know that he is a substance that I depend on now.

The difference between Seth and the alcohol or the sex is that I will always be able to get a bottle of wine and I can always find someone who wants to fuck me. But Seth could go. He could leave and take everything away. And, lately, I've been wondering how I could stop that from happening.

How can I make sure that I keep feeding this addiction?

Then the dolt turns up in the middle of the night on my doorstep when I'm supposed to be here with Jill, six bottles of Malbec and a Sangiovese. And he's on his knee, crunching it against the gravel of my driveway, asking if I will marry him.

Perhaps that's why he looks so nervous and emotional.

'What? What is this? What do you want me to say?' I don't go in for the grand gestures and I don't think that marriage is the way to keep hold of Seth.

He looks pathetic down on the ground, pale, dishevelled, his eyes look as though he isn't sleeping well. Nobody in their right mind would say yes to this desperation. But not everybody is right of mind and it could easily be a bottle of Cloudy Bay lying in my driveway or a sex toy I haven't tried.

It's all so difficult to say no to.

'I want you to say yes. Because I love you. I've loved you from the beginning and I'll love you until the end.'

I don't say anything to that because I don't know how much I appreciate the sentiment. So I wait. He will get awkward and try to fill the void.

'And because, if you don't say yes, if I don't know that you are completely with me, I can't show you what I have in the car.'

STEP **ONE**

'Admit that you are powerless over your psychopathy and that you don't care.'

Months before Seth got down on one knee in my driveway I'd hired the room at the community centre opposite Footsteps In The Sand, which was still there and was being run by some guy in a loose cardigan.

Calvin had allowed me to advertise on the noticeboard next to the knitters and chess players and Pilates enthusiasts. I was very careful with the way that I worded the poster, suggesting that the group was for those who find that they 'think differently to others'. I made it sound more like a mental-health group.

I wrote a few questions on there that would lead someone to believe they are exhibiting elements of psychopathy. Obvious things that any reader would understand to be traits of a psychopath.

Do you find yourself lying more than you think you should?
Have you ever been described by others as manipulative?
Do you act against society's rules and 'normal' behaviours?
Is it difficult for you to show remorse?

These seem like the kinds of questions that could trigger a response and are certainly more oblique than:

Have you ever killed anyone?
How did you feel afterwards?
What do you do with the bodies?

We can get to that.

I didn't want to put my name or contact details on there like the Zumba instructor or piano tutor. This was mainly going to be men turning up – if anyone did – and I didn't want to keep them away by showing that the sessions would be run by a woman. It may have enticed more women had I been more honest but I have always preferred the company of the opposite sex.

And they're my favourite group to fuck with and kill.

I stand outside the FITS room and watch as people slowly filter inside and take their seats. The cardigan at the front is trying to catch my eye to see whether I want to join the Bible bashers. I don't. I've done that. I'm just waiting to see whether anyone is crazy enough to turn up to my room.

A man enters. Early thirties. Attractive. But awkward. He looks at me, smiles shyly, reads my poster on the board, checks that the room on the sheet matches the room he is heading towards and moves his way to the door.

There seems to be a lack of confidence there. He appears anxious. That might tip him more towards sociopathy but he might also be faking it to get a read on the room.

'You're the first one here. Go in and take a seat, I'll be along in a couple of minutes.'

He does as I request.

I wait another five minutes. The FITS session is about to start and Mr Cardigan beckons me in with a sign-language question. I shake my head and point across the hall to the room that cost me eleven pounds. There are six people sitting in there, two of whom are talking. All men. It's not a sold-out stadium but it's enough to get started.

I bid them all a good evening and welcome them to the first meeting of Psychopaths Anonymous. And I launch straight in.

'People who have mistreated you. Your enemies. Winning the lottery. Success in something that you have put almost no effort into attaining. Nobody to find out the bad thing you did. Your favourite sports team to win the next game. Finding a parking spot. These...' I pause, '...these are the top things that people pray for.'

I have their attention.

They did not expect me to talk about God but that is what every twelve-step scheme comes around to. I want to get it out of the way early.

'Imagine praying to a God who let the Holocaust happen and thinking that He gives a fuck about whether or not you get a speeding ticket through the post.'

I want to see if any of them feel uncomfortable at what I said so that I can kick them out.

None of them seem to.

I left the door open and I'm speaking loud enough that my voice should carry into the FITS meeting. Hopefully it will give them something to think about.

'There's another mantra which starts "God, grant me the serenity to accept the things I can't change, the courage to change the things I can and the wisdom to know the difference. Thy will, not mine, be done." There will be none of that here.'

The sound of chairs scraping across the floor from the room opposite, followed by the clunk of their door shutting.

'This is not a group that will trick you into having faith in anything other than yourself. This is about acceptance. You think a certain way and you act a certain way, and it sometimes flies in the face of what society deems as proper. We cannot help the way we are and we will not apologise for it. And, hell, if it's true, if we are all psychopathic in some way, then we just don't need to care.'

~~Can I get an Amen?~~

They nod in complete agreement and I think to myself that this is how easy it must be to start a cult.

Like-minded people in the same room.

That's all you need.

Nothing nefarious here.

'There's only one rule. If this is your first meeting, you have to talk.'

It seems only fair that I should go first, so they know what to expect. To a certain degree I'm winging it but I have researched this kind of thing by going through the AA programme and coming out the other side as a fully aware and awakened functioning drunk.

I tell my group of six men that being psychopathic does not mean you are the next version of Ted Bundy. That things don't have to manifest themselves in violence and a string of bodies across the local university campus.

'A lot of people who are successful in business demonstrate traits of psychopathy. Look at someone like Steve Jobs. Hailed as a visionary. But, if you delve a little deeper, you find he was incredibly assertive in pushing his own ideas through, and displayed almost no association with risky decision-making. Probably due to a low sensitivity to punishment. So you can be a psycho and change the world without having to kill everyone in it.'

We discuss Bill Gates and decide whether he, too, shows traits. He is highly successful and captivating. But, later in life, has become overtly philanthropic. Perhaps this is just because he can. Maybe he had more money than he knew what to do with. If he somehow felt guilty about his success then it rules him out of our club. I prefer to think he did it to make himself feel good.

'You look at somebody like Donald Trump, listen to the way that he speaks, and you know that he is too stupid to be a psychopath. It's pure narcissism with that guy. He's the kind of idiot that would run for president. He'd pretend it was a joke but deep down he'd feel that he deserved it. That he was the best man for the job. That he'd be the greatest president of all time. The real psychos are the ones who would vote for him.'

They laugh.

They're comfortable.

And now they have to talk.

I let them know that I'm turning things over to them now. That it is everybody's first meeting so they have to speak. They don't have to say their name if they don't want and nobody is to pass judgement but I want to know why they are here.

One of them raises his hand and asks whether things are confidential. Can he say something in this room and know that it will not be uttered outside of these walls?

I tell him that is the case. Unless he divulges that he stabbed the referee of his Sunday-morning football match for showing him a red card.

I have to say this. Because they won't all be violent. It would be easier if everyone was going around and chopping people up, we could swap stories, but it's doubtful that's the case.

As he's already on the edge of his seat, I tell him that he can go first.

BOB

For a start, I do not believe his name is Bob. He doesn't look like a Bob. Robert, maybe. Perhaps Rob, but he's probably only just tipping into his forties, his clothes fit perfectly and there's something about those dark, brown eyes that could even be black.

I tell him that he's not a Bob and that I will call him Bobby at the very most.

He tells me, tells us all, why he thinks he belongs in that room.

So, Bobby met a woman. She was married. That made her more interesting, something of a challenge. He's got the looks. He's got the moves. He knows all the lyrics. She's not happy. Yada yada yada. Never going to leave him.

Yawn. Sigh. Spit.

He gets her into bed.

Of course he does.

And it's amazing. She's fucking him like his dick is adding years to her life and, soon enough, they are making excuses to see each other whenever possible.

'Months go by and I'm falling hard for this woman. Is that even possible? If I'm psychopathic or whatever, can I feel love? There's a lot that I don't feel.'

They're all looking to me for an answer.

I think of Seth. Beautiful, warm, thoughtful, funny Seth Beauman. It sounds like our story. A physical, sexual connection that developed into something more. Is it love? Or do I just not want anyone else to have him.

'Do you believe that what you were feeling was love?'

'Yes. I do.'

'Then that's what it was.'

And maybe that's what I have with Seth.

Robert Bobby Bob met her and couldn't stop himself from divulging these feelings. She was still married. Still adamant that she could never leave but he was convinced that she would. For him. Because she loved him, too.

But she said that she didn't. She said that she couldn't. It could have broken him but he was confident. Again, that low sensitivity to punishment. He explains how he manipulated her into feeling the same way. To admitting her love for him. The sex changed. Something new. Something better.

Then she broke it off.

And he knew it must have been love that he had been feeling because the result was his utter heartbreak.

Yet, Bobby Robert Robertson would not give up. First he had to get good and drunk – always a good plan – then he screwed a couple of strangers. Then he picked a couple of fights and let them beat him up so that he could feel some other kind of pain.

Then he got her back. Full charm offensive. Every trick in the book to win her over, admit her love again and eventually leave the man she had been unhappily married to for half a decade.

Doesn't sound so psychopathic. It was, perhaps, even romantic. Bobby loved her, inordinately. But this love was equal to his hatred of her for what she had done to him. She had given up on them. He couldn't let it go.

He opened up her heart and her legs. She rediscovered love and freedom and, most importantly, passion. Everything that had been lost in her marriage. It was natural for them to move in together and he eventually proposed.

Though shy, she had prepared a speech to give at the reception in front of their family and closest friends. Not one for public declarations, she was going to make an exception.

But it didn't get to the reception.

Bobby ditched her at the altar. He didn't just stand her up. He didn't get cold feet. He announced that he could not spend the rest of his life with this woman. He could not spend another moment with her. And he never wanted to see her again.

Bobby dedicated himself to her downfall. He took years away from his own life in order to ruin hers. It had to be this grand, public gesture of distaste.

He had to break her the way she had broken him. Only more.

When he had finished his story I couldn't help but think back to what he had said about loving her but hating her just as much. That final act showed just how much he loathed the woman who had broken his heart but if his statement was true, it meant his affection for her equalled that bitterness.

But he stopped and shrugged his shoulders like it was nothing.

Bobby belonged.

CLYDE HARPER

Clyde did not belong.

He gave his full name. Whether it was real or not, I don't know. I don't care. After he spoke, I figured he was going for the single-syllable first name and double-syllable surname. Like Charles Manson or Ted Bundy to John Gacy. Clyde Harper would achieve no such notoriety.

He was a cliché. Talking about how he didn't care about anybody.

He was numb. He lies a lot. He's been in trouble with the police several times. He remembers being a kid and using a magnifying glass to set fire to a line of ants. He killed his grandmother's cat just to see what it would look like.

I can't let him continue.

He sounds idiotic.

He does everything but call himself 'nefarious'.

'Clyde. Stop.'

'What? What's wrong? You didn't stop Bob.'

'That is correct. I did not.' Bobby looks at me in a way that I'm sure has worked on many women in the past but I am not here for that. 'I believe that you have trouble with your lying. You are lying right now.'

'What?'

I don't let him speak.

'It sounds like you have gone on to the internet and looked up what violent psychopaths are like. Killing animals as a kid? Come on, Clyde.'

'What happened to no judgement?'

'I'm not going to judge somebody who comes here for a real discussion. If you come here and lie, you're insulting all of us. Do you understand that? What you have done is come into a den of psychopaths and insulted them all. By pretending you are a deranged killer.' I find myself playing to the crowd a little here with subtle off-stage looks.

He stands up. 'Well, how do you know I'm not a deranged killer?'

I laugh and so do two of the others who haven't spoken yet. Clyde looks uncomfortable.

'Because you wouldn't stand there and say that. Because you exude no confidence at all in what you are saying, even now. Because I can smell the bullshit.'

Because I know what it feels like to kill somebody, a lot of somebodies. And I know what it means to go through your entire life not telling anyone anything about it.

I can see that he wants to say something. He's thinking it. 'Maybe

I should kill you, you bitch.' I can read his mind. But he knows he's outnumbered, outmanned. Surely he's not that stupid.

'I think it's probably best that you just leave, Clyde.'

He doesn't move.

Bobby pipes up. 'Come on, buddy. Time to go, eh?'

Clyde listens to Bobby. Because he's a man, I assume. The rest of us stay silent as he shuffles towards the door, mumbling. I give my supporters another look.

Clyde turns back when he gets to the door and looks at me, embarrassed cheeks and venomous eyes. He says, 'You'd better watch your back, lady.'

Before I even have time to laugh, one of the five remaining psychos jumps out of his seat and bolts to the door. Clyde runs but the unknown man goes after him.

We all wait, looking at the door.

Nothing happens.

While we wait, I add Clyde to my make-amends list.

Three minutes pass before a dark figure rounds the doorway and comes back into the room.

It's not Clyde.

'Everything okay. You left in quite a hurry?'

He explains that he wanted to catch up with Clyde and 'have a word'.

'The idiot wasn't listening, was he? I know you chided him a little but I thought you were pretty restrained, actually. If he'd have heard what you said, he would have left here quietly with his tail between his legs.'

He sits back down in his seat.

'Should I expect him to fly back in here in a minute?'

'No. I told him that he shouldn't just throw threats out there like that and that he shouldn't try to intimidate women. I wanted to explain that it's ridiculous to do something like that when you don't know who you are talking to and what they are capable of doing.'

'You don't know Clyde and what he is capable of doing.'

'Sure, but I know enough about who I am.'

'And who are you?'

'My name is Eames.'

'Did you kill him?'

'Not yet.'

EAMES

I liked him straight away. And that was enough to tell me that he was in the right place. I didn't need him to stand up for me, mine and Clyde's paths are destined to cross again at some point. But I still appreciated his instant response.

Eames didn't say much about himself. He didn't have an amazing tale of heartbreak and revenge like Bobby. But he had been seeing a married woman. The wife of a police detective. Clearly got off on the risk of it but certainly didn't feel love for the woman.

He was honest. He just wanted to see what the group was all about. Part of him thought it would be filled with idiots like Clyde but he was pleasantly surprised.

'I know you probably wanted more people to show up but I think I prefer that it's more exclusive.'

He was charismatic as hell in the most understated way. And if he was lying, I couldn't tell.

And if he had killed Clyde, I didn't know.

And if he wanted to fuck, I probably would.

There were three left. Eames and Bobby were a little older. The remaining men were all around my age.

EDDIE

A hotshot. Young surgeon. Says he has the ability to completely separate himself from the situation. That's what makes him so good. This is Hampstead, so I expected to see some high-functioning professionals.

His chat would undoubtedly come across as arrogant to anyone that wasn't in the room but to me he was self-assured as a result of his achievements. He would take on patients where the risk of death during procedure was high and wouldn't even break sweat. Some of the older surgeons played classical music while they worked but Eddie liked rap. The surgical assistants did not. But Eddie didn't care.

Because he was the star. And he was psychopathic.

I liked the guy.

He looked like he hadn't slept for days but he held himself well. And, in a room filled with alpha males, I would expect him to try to be the ultimate, but they were all respectful of one another. They listened.

JAKE KILLEY

'I know, I know. Killey. The amount of times people have asked me if I'm feeling a bit "kill-y"...' He trails off as he rolls his eyes. 'Honestly, I never realised that I could feel kill-y until the hundredth fucking person asked me that.' He smiles a cheeky smile where only half of his mouth turns upwards.

'I'm not a killer. Let me get that straight. I'm not like Clyde. I'm not here to brag but I certainly don't feeeeel anything when I contemplate doing that. It's just your normal road rage, though.'

He says he's here because he feels separate from the world. Misunderstood perhaps. Against the grain.

'When people talk about psychopathy, they talk of being anti-social. But it's not about having no social skills, as you know, it's exactly what you are saying, Jake, it's about swimming upstream. It's about been set against social norms.' I return his half-smile.

The fact that he said he's not a killer has me thinking that he just might be.

NO NAME #1

There's always one who takes the anonymity stance. No Name #1 is also the youngest. I realise that this group of men, all alpha males, presented themselves in order of age, starting with the eldest, Bob. I don't think they were aware of this. I believe it came naturally because they all knew they had to speak, they all wanted to, but, rather than vying for top spot, fell into some manly respect-your-elders sense of propriety.

He's a DJ. Works the club scene. As soon as he tells us this, he looks like a DJ, to me. And seems even younger and more naive than I initially expected.

No Name #1 says he does dabble with substances. 'Part of the lifestyle, you know?' But he has that feeling of invincibility without having to snort anything. There is nothing that comes across as a risk. He screws around. 'I'm not boasting but if I told you the number of women I've been with it would turn your pubic hair grey. I was thinking of going to a meeting for sex addicts but I saw the poster for this and thought it might be more my thing. You know?'

He says, 'You know?' at the end of his sentences. He says it a lot.

The first part of any of these programmes is acceptance.

Accept that you are powerless over alcohol.

Accept that you are a slave to your libido.

Accept that you are aware of fruit and vegetables but they just aren't processed enough or packed enough with sugar or coated in enough MSG for the warped pleasure centre of your brain to register.

Just stand up in front of a bunch of strangers and state your name and your addiction. Immediately feel the weight of the world lifted from your shoulders. Know that you are in a place of safety, of people that are exactly like you.

They can drink an entire bottle of vodka.

They understand the panic you can only feel when the amount of anal beads you pull out is not equal to the amount that went in.

They can see the figures the government have produced concerning the average recommended daily calorie intake but know that they have become so out of shape that if they can only eat three times that magic number, it will be enough for them to drop a few pounds.

You don't have to act right now. Just accept who you are.

Hi, I'm Bob, I devastated a woman by jilting her with my open hatred on our wedding day and I don't feel an ounce of guilt. I'm a psychopath.

I'm Eames. I've fucking a detective's wife and will probably taunt him about it because I'm a psycho. A beautiful, brooding psycho.

I'm No Name #1. I'm a psychopath and I'm definitely going to live forever. You know?

We are who we are and we don't care what you think.

Footprints In The Sand is still in full sombre swing when we leave the room I booked for our first meeting. I always thought those sessions were a labour and went on far too long.

The door is shut and I can't hear them but I know they are in full God-fearing mode now. He will help them through their most difficult times – as long as they completely give themselves over to His will.

Four of my psychos head out of the door ahead of me. Eames stays behind to make a call on his mobile phone. It's cold out but I don't mind. The men have dispersed across the park in different directions and I take the path that cuts straight through the middle and will take me towards my tube station.

I'm a hundred yards from the building when Clyde emerges from behind a tree. He looks even more dishevelled than when he arrived at the group and I wonder whether he has been drinking. That thought alone sparks the need for wine.

'Hey, bitch.'

It's supposed to be simple and threatening but it's so unimaginative every part of my body rolls its eyes.

'What do you want, Clyde?' I'm not scared of him. I know where the keys are inside my bag. There are keys for the house, the garage, my car, there are keys for the garden gate and the back door. And there's a key that isn't a key. It doesn't open anything. I've just sharpened it enough that if I need to, I could open up a hole in Clyde's neck if he tries anything.

'Where's your bodyguard, eh?' He raises a hand to his cheek. He doesn't look bruised or cut but I imagine that Eames probably slapped him about a bit earlier.

'Is there a point to this, Clyde, or are you just trying to scare me? I don't have a bodyguard and I don't need one.'

'You made me look like a fool.'

There is no sense in debating with this moron. Any normal person would brush it off and walk away, go in the opposite direction, maybe even walk back to the safety of the building.

I'm not normal, though.

'You made yourself look like a fool, Clyde.' I keep using his name to punctuate my sentences, to take away his anonymity. That way he fits neither the psychopathic element nor the anonymous element of my club. 'What are you doing hiding behind that tree, biting the heads off squirrels?'

I can't help but laugh and it riles him.

'I'm gonna show you exactly what a fool looks like.' He takes a step forward and my hand instinctively reaches into my bag for the keys. I'm going to cut a bright crimson smile across his fucking throat.

'Everything okay, here?' A voice from behind.

Eames.

My bodyguard, apparently.

'Yes. Everything is fine. Clyde and I were just catching up on old times, weren't we, Clyde?' My right hand is still gripped around the keys in my bag. I've singled out the weapon.

'Fuck you, lady.' He turns and paces off.

'A real charmer, that guy,' Eames jokes. 'I'll walk you to your car, or the tube.'

'There's really no need. I've known worse than Clyde.' I let go of the keys and hoist my bag back onto my shoulder.

'I'll do it anyway.'

We walk together back to the car. He tells me that he enjoyed the group. He's not sure what he'll get out of it other than piquing his own interest but he'll definitely be back.

To be honest, I'm not sure what I was hoping to get out of it, either.

'Maybe we could go for a drink after the meeting sometime? Not that any of us need loosening up...' He lets it hang in the air.

I look at my watch. Seth is coming over tonight but I have time.

'I've got half an hour to kill now, if you like.'

I've known him for an hour but my adrenaline is pumping due to Clyde's near-death experience moments ago.

He looks at his watch.

'Ah, shit. You know, I would, I just ... You'll think it's sounds ridiculous but ... fuck it, I'm going to a show.'

'I forgot to mention that a love for the theatre is a classic psychopathic trait.'

'It's not the West End or anything. It's a tiny space. An unused room in the upstairs of a pub. Every few weeks they have magicians try out their acts. They've got some young kid who does tricks really close up. I can't figure him out. Look, it's kind of a fascination of mine. I like the discipline of it.'

'You like trying to work out how they do it.'

'That, too.' He smiles that smile.

We arrive at my car.

'Let's do a rain check on the drinks tonight, then. Enjoy yourself with Penn and Teller and I'll see you next week.' I keep it calm and casual as I slip into the car.

Door shut. Seatbelt on. Car starts. Pull forward. Change gear. All in that instant. One movement and I'm out of there. Just the mention of a drink and I'm salivating at the prospect of some cold Chardonnay.

With Eames behind me I thrust my intentions forward towards wine and Seth.

There are no bodies in my freezer and three days ago I left the remaining couple of wheels from the taxi in my driveway. I gave them out for free to somebody local who was working on an upcycling project. He told me that he was going to wrap each one in rope to make garden seats.

I didn't ask him what he was going to do with them. I didn't care. People are less reluctant to hold information in these days. They feel like they have to constantly be saying something.

Free speech never had it so bad.

What that means is that Seth is free to roam the house now. There's nothing that I'm hiding. Nothing physical. Mentally, I'm freely admitting my obsession with crap television, and sexually, I'm freer than I've ever been. But I'm not letting on that I've killed people and cut them up or that I went to AA or that I've started my own group for psychopaths. He thinks I go to a Pilates class. He will ask me how it was and I will tell him that I feel stretched and relaxed and he will think about how he is going to push my legs wide apart later to test my flexibility before plunging himself deep inside me.

When Seth gets to the house, I am two glasses into my evening. We kiss. He asks me about my class. I know what he's thinking. I pour him a drink and the doorbell rings. I'm not expecting anyone but my mind flits to Eames for some reason.

'Who could that be?' Seth wonders.

'You sit down in the lounge, I'll check.'

I take my glass with me and open the door a few centimetres.

He looks me in the eyes, then down at my glass, and back to my face.

The same detective as before.

The same look as before.

It doesn't matter what time of day he turns up, I'll be drinking. But he already thinks I'm an alcoholic because he's here to follow up about my ex-sponsor, Gary. I thought the investigation was as dead as he is.

'Sorry to disturb.' I don't appreciate his bite and judgement. If he is questioning everybody Gary knew, he must be coming into contact with some real lowlife drunks. How dare he come to my home and give me that look.

I want to be rude. I want to tell him where to go. But I don't want Seth to come out here.

So I bite my tongue.

~~Don't you dare fuck this up for me.~~

'Not a problem. How can I help?' I swig some wine. My way of demonstrating rebellion and apathy. I smile as I swallow it down.

'I'm following up on the inquiry into the disappearance of your sponsor, Gary.'

'Ex sponsor.'

'Well, yes. I've spoken to a few of the other people he was sponsoring and some members of the ... group, and they say that you haven't been to a meeting for weeks. Since Gary seemingly went missing, in fact.'

'I quit.'

He looks at my glass again.

I roll my eyes.

'Not the booze, detective. I quit AA. It wasn't working for me.'

'Clearly.'

I let it hang, uncomfortably. For him. Not me.

I don't care.

'I was doing okay until my sponsor stopped helping me. I tried to get hold of him. I went back to the meetings. But he never answered and he never showed. I tried different meetings in the area but didn't find one that fit quite as well as Gary's.'

He scribbles something onto a notepad.

'The last day anybody saw Gary he was apparently coming to see you in the evening.'

I want to ask him who gave that information, so that I can add them to my list.

'He was. That's right. But the fucker never turned up. I probably left him six voicemails.' I know that it was four and I am sure they have a record of the calls and the fact that I left him several messages of desperation. Two while he was passed out and two after I'd drilled through his skull.

'You realise he is still missing?'

'The fact that you are here tells me that. I stopped looking.'

'And I'm not sure it's appropriate to refer to him in that way. We don't know what happened to him.'

I had no idea the detective was so proper.

'And I don't think it's appropriate to abandon someone you're sponsoring when they are only on step seven of a twelve-step plan. But Gary did. Is there anything in particular that I can help you with this evening?'

'I'm just doing the rounds, following up on new information.'

'I'm sure his family are worried.'

'There's not much family out there, it seems. It's the church. Gary did some great work for them and they're not letting go of things.' He reaches into his pocket. 'I know I gave you my details last time but I'll just give them again. If you hear anything…'

I take the card. 'Sure. And when you find Gary, tell him he's a piece of shit, from me.' I take another mouthful of my drink and shut the door.

If I knew anything about Gary's disappearance then it would be foolish to stand on my own doorstep and call the guy a piece of shit. Perhaps the detective will realise the double bluff. That's fine, I'm happy to do a dance with him, they're not going to find Gary. 'Who was that?' Seth asks.

'Sorry?'

'At the door.'

'Well, apparently, there is a real government in Heaven that will replace our human governments to accomplish God's purpose.' He stares at me. 'These are the last days.'

I raise an eyebrow and drink. I don't want him to ask me any more, so I move over to where he is sitting and straddle his legs.

'Jehovah's Witnesses? You didn't just tell them to go away?'

'No. Everyone tells them they're not interested. I like to get them to explain things to me before doing that, fuck with them a bit.' I kiss Seth and bite his bottom lip.

'You are naughty, Maeve.'

'You have no idea.'

STEP **TWO**

'There is no power greater than ourselves.'

I tell them a story, an experience I had at one of my AA meetings. I can't remember which one. Could have been Cricklewood Reflections or Highbury Newcomers or Archway Sobriety or Holborn Keep It Simple, it doesn't matter. It was well attended. We were in a large circle and a thin, sickly-looking man stood up and told his tale.

He had been a firefighter straight out of school. Trained up. Volunteered for a while. Then got himself a permanent position. He loved it. He loved it all. Whether he was tackling an inferno, getting a cat down from a tree or cutting a person out of their car after a crash, it was his calling.

He didn't look like a firefighter. He looked like he was dying from some mysterious wasting disease. I tried to imagine him with a more muscular physique.

One shift, he is called to a burning building. A friend on the squad took the lead and this guy backed him up. You can imagine the lead guy saying something like, 'There's no better man to have behind you on the hose.' It's all so wholesome and brave.

The floorboards were burnt and brittle and the lead guy fell through to the floor below – a basement where the fire started due to an overloaded socket sparking. Our withering alcoholic friend is left on the floor above, trying to control an errant hose while his friend calls out to him.

The smoke is thick and he's thankful for his mask so that his eyes don't get burnt out of his head. He's shouting down to his friend to check he's okay, to see whether he can get hold of the hose and help to push the flames back.

Smoke thick.

Flames loud.

He's shouting down, still. He could leave him down there, save himself, but the thought never occurs to him.

The guy downstairs is in Hell, his face mask is cracked and his ankle is twisted but he gets hold of the hose and they work together to push the fire backwards and eventually put it out.

They're both hailed as heroic but our alcoholic more so because his partner who fell through the floor wouldn't have made it if that future drunk hadn't stayed around.

He's so grateful to the dipso. He owes his life to his friend. At the hospital, where he is taken as routine because the broken mask meant he inhaled a lot of smoke, a wife and two children hug the formerly muscular torso of our skinny storyteller.

His friend, just a sprained ankle, is kept in overnight to be monitored but dies of a heart attack brought on by his body's inability to filter the poisonous gases he had ingested during battle.

Then the nightmares came.

Followed by the drinking.

'And that's not all,' I say. 'Our hero has a wife and a daughter.'

My audience is hooked. They want to know what this has to do with the reason we are here.

Pretty soon, this guy is burying his friend, who he stayed to save and is wondering why he even bothered because the night terrors are getting worse and the drinking isn't helping him forget enough to get to sleep.

He hardly eats any more and all that muscle mass is in a rapid state of atrophy. The skin on his face has become red and blotchy and he's even experienced a couple of seizures.

His daughter is sixteen and hates watching him do this to himself so gives him an ultimatum: either he stops the drinking or she moves out and goes back to her birth mother. His wife thinks that this is the shock he needs to quit the booze, that finally he has hit rock bottom.

He hasn't.

Now he has lost his friend, his daughter, his personal health, he can't do his job properly, perhaps the answers are further down the bottle than he has been looking.

He says that he often thinks that things might have been different if he had just let his friend die in that fire because nothing he did helped in the end. But he came to the conclusion that doing that would still have led him to the bottle. Like it was fate for him to end up looking like a half-dead, scurvy-ridden stowaway whose family had all but given up on him.

The short story is that his wife eventually said that she was not getting what she needed from the relationship and she would go and get it elsewhere if he didn't at least try to pull himself from the pit.

'That's how he ended up at that meeting.'

'What happened to him?' asks Eddie.

'I'll get to that.'

Once the firefighter reached the end of his tale of woe, the room went silent for a moment as another twenty alcoholics digested the information to see whether they felt sympathetic towards the brave hero or whether they were left questioning themselves. What reason did they have to be drinking when they had been through only half as much as this man?

'It's the only time I've ever seen some kind of ovation at one of these things, they're usually so sombre. Well, apart from Bobby's revenge story last week.'

Bobby smiles.

'My question is, what do you think to that story? How does it make you feel?'

Bobby is straight in. 'Look, I get why they all applauded the guy, people like firemen because of their apparent courage. I'm just not sure what's so valiant about him reacting the way he did. If you're having bad dreams, take a pill, see a psychiatrist, have a week where you let loose but don't drag it on and lose everything because you should have just jumped in the fire with your mate.'

'So you don't care?' There's no barb or bite to my question, I just want to know.

'I'm saying that I can understand why people do ... but, no, I don't.'

'Maybe you can't.'

'What happened to him?' Eddie, again. Maybe he cares. Maybe he's intrigued. Maybe he likes a good story. Maybe something about being a surgeon means he needs an end product.

'He blew his brains out, after finishing a bottle of Jim Beam at his best friend's grave ... I'm joking. It was worse than that. The motherfucker found God.'

'That's worse?' Eames, this time. Surprisingly.

'It is.' I confirm. 'He gave himself away. Yes, he is still alive and he no longer drinks and he's packing on the bulk and his daughter lives with him again, but he's not him. He is not the brave man who walked into fire. He gave himself over when he surrendered his will to God. What he has done benefits everyone around him but he is not himself. He's diluted. He hasn't dealt with what happened, he's let God in. But where will God be when he walks into another fire and freezes up?'

'Do you care?' No Name #1.

'No. I don't know the guy. The AA are not my community, they can walk into the fires of Hell for all I care, what I want to get across is this: there is no power greater than ourselves.'

'And you think we don't already know that?'

'So my big, poignant story was a waste of time?'

They all nod.

'Well, fuck you, psychos.' We laugh. Something we never did at FITS.

I drink some water and take a seat in front of Eames. There's no circle here.

'Okay, new guy. There's only one rule here. This is your first week. What's your story?'

The kid was weird but passionate. He got me wondering just what the hell I am doing and what I am hoping to achieve with this group. What is the point? Do I just want to grab a few people like me, sit around talking about the traits we share until someone antes up and confesses to an act of violence?

Then we could really start to share.

This isn't like a normal twelve-step programme; I don't want them to stop being psychopathic. I don't want them to quit and let God guide them. This is about owning it. This is about not shying away. We are not oppressed. This has nothing to do with race, gender or sexual preference but it is about having to hide who we are.

Well, that's what I thought until our newest member stood up and spoke.

SAM RAMIREZ

Tall and wiry. His age is a bit of a mystery. Soft, sun-kissed skin but dark holes for eyes. Cheekbones that could cut glass, but long hair that obscures his face. I could imagine him walking down the corridor of some American high school, head dropped, not making eye contact with anyone until he gets to class and opens fire on every pupil that had called him strange or knocked his books out of his hands and laughed like they'd overheard Joan Rivers talking about divorce.

I ask him if he is any relation to Richard Ramirez.

He says he doesn't know who that is and I don't think I believe him.

The level of contempt he has for the world is astounding. He hates everything and everyone for what they are or are not doing. But there's no focus.

He doesn't understand the need for the royal family other than the money they bring in from tourism. And he wonders whether that even covers what they earn each year.

He's bored of political scandal. Somehow leaders are forced into resignation for infidelity in their personal lives but are allowed to remain in power despite flouting the responsibilities, going against the rules they championed and not following through on the things they promised in order to gain their positions in the first place.

He's sick of big business but can't justify the prices of independent retailers. Tax dodgers are on his ladder of lunacy, one rung underneath paedophiles but one above estate agents. And the Church is so rich but expects its congregation to foot the bill when one of their buildings has a leaky roof.

Sam Ramirez is all over the place. He's angry about things but doesn't know why and I can smell the violence on him from here.

'You can call me Sam Ram,' he says, like everyone calls him that but I think it's just something he's trying on for size.

After his cool tirade about every possible group in a more privileged position than his own, Sam Ram fizzles out and sits back down in his seat. He lets us all know that he has been in trouble with the police on more than one occasion. The latest was for biting a guy's ear when a peaceful protest bubbled into agitation.

The problem was that the judge expected Sam Ram to display remorse for what he had done. Rather than explain his psychopathy he told the judge that he had sworn on the Bible and could not, in good conscience, tell a lie about an emotion he did not feel.

He felt no remorse.

He never had.

Never would.

Sam Ram was in the right place. I knew he was the violent type. The others in the group looked wary of him but not intimidated. He had energy and an ego but he also gave me the idea that we need to *do* something.

Step three at AA would be the first call to action and that's exactly what I wanted for Psychopaths Anonymous. Without all that crap about God.

Jill is waiting outside the FITS room. I first met Jill at one of the newcomers' meetings in Kilburn. She tends to stay in that part of town. But she has been to FITS before. I should have expected her to show up at some point but I see her every day at work, which means that she completely slips my mind.

I ask her what she's doing outside of the meeting. She tells me that she's had enough of it, feels like she has things under control, she hardly has anything to drink during the week then uses excessively on the weekend. She's still fucking local Neanderthals for extra cash even though she's earning enough as my assistant.

She wants to know what I am doing in the room across the hall. I point to the poster behind her. I say it's a mental-health thing. 'Friends of Maeve.'

She laughs.

All of these support groups have those kinds of names. Addicts don't always want to admit that they have a problem with whisky or dildos or Black Forest gateaux, so the groups are obscured by being called 'Friends of whichever person started the organisation'.

Friends of Bill = alcoholics

Friends of Jimmy = drug addicts

You'll find a friend for overeaters, clutterers, debtors and workaholics.

'Oh, you are funny, Jill. Thank you.'

'You could be on to something. Mental health is all the rage right now, isn't it?' I know she means well but the ease at which Jill can make herself sound unboundedly stupid is something to behold.

'Read the small print.'

Jill bends over to get closer to my advert.

'Psychopaths Anonymous?'

'Catchy, huh?'

'Sounds a little more up my street, Maeve.'

'Come along next week. And, as usual, not a word to anyone.'

Jill is worried about the dynamic in the group when I tell her: 'It's about time we got some female blood in there, keep things in order.'

I know that she's more than capable of taking on two men at the same time but there are five in there.

I'm not worried about Jill.

And it's another person I've taken away from the God recruitment group.

I'm feeling pleased with myself. That's when the man with the silver hair and dog collar enters the building.

A priest, a whore and a psychopath walk into a Hampstead community centre.

It's not a joke.

'Good evening, ladies. Are you waiting to go into the meeting?' He has a soft voice, sounds as though he cares.

'God, no.' I don't hide my disgust. He looks at me.

'Then what, may I ask, are you doing outside the door? This is a private group, it's not for eavesdropping.'

'We're not listening in, Father.' Jill cowers. I don't like the way she refers to him. 'In fact, we were just leaving. Weren't we, Maeve?'

I see something spark behind the old man's eyes. Like he's heard about a Maeve.

'Not Gary's Maeve?' It seems an odd way to phrase the question.

'Nobody's Maeve.' I bite. Though I know that I am Seth's. All day and all sex-fuelled, booze-drenched evening.

The priest apologises for his turn of phrase and discerns that Gary was my sponsor.

'Such a shame. He really was one of the best we've had here. So strange for him to just disappear like that without letting any of us know.'

'Well, you know what they say, "You're only one drink away from a relapse."'

'They say that?'

'I don't know. But they should.'

'You haven't heard from him?'

'No. Not a word. I told the police the same.'

Jill looks at me, worried.

'He left me when I needed him the most. And this guy,' I point through the window in the door, 'he's a joke. As inspirational as "Amazing Grace".'

He wants to be hurt but knows deep down that he hates that hymn and how it has affected every worship song since its inception, turning Sunday mornings into a ninety-minute drone fest.

Jill feels uncomfortable. She wants to leave. She gives me a look and moves her head towards outside.

I stand my ground.

'I see you've started your own group across the corridor.' His voice changes. The frail and affable priest has transformed into the image of his capricious and damning God. 'Psychopaths.' He scoffs. Then leans in and speaks quietly, 'I told the police that they should be looking into you. Gary told me things. And now it turns out you're a self-confessed psychopath. I'm sure the police will be thrilled to hear that.' He turns and smiles over his shoulder at Jill, who has made her way closer to the exit.

I speak at a normal volume so that Jill can hear.

'It's a mental-health group, Vicar. Trying to break the stigma that comes with that word you so beautifully spat out. Please feel free to come along to a session and see what we discuss so that you can understand better what we do.' ~~You might learn something.~~

Then I lean in.

'I don't know if you're brave or stupid but you just called me a psycho and then threatened me. What kind of fool does that?'

He's trying not to look afraid. And I'm trying not to look angry.

The God-lover can't admonish me for being threatening because he just did the same himself. An eye for an eye. And, if he does ask if I am making a threat, I can tell him that I only make promises.

He just looks at me. But I want the last word, so I look over to Jill and say, 'Let's get out of here,' and, as she leaves, I take one last jab at that holy piece of shit: 'I look forward to seeing what God's plan is for you, Father.'

Outside, Jill has her arms folded across her chest as though it's the middle of winter.

'Fuck.' I'm infuriated. 'That guy is a real piece of work.'

'What did he say to you? What did you say to him? The guy's a priest, could it really be that bad?'

'You're not being brainwashed at AA any more, Jill, you don't have to buy in to those snake-oil salesmen any more.'

Poor Jill. She believes in God. A god. Not in a devout way. Not in the way the programme wants her to. She can't give herself over completely. She just wants to feel like there is something more because her life has been a cesspit. Deadbeat men. A kid she's not even sure she wants. Spreading her legs for anyone with a couple of pennies to rub together because she feels like she should be kept down, she doesn't deserve to break free.

I don't understand how this would provide anyone with solace. You live a shit existence and then you die but if there's a God and He is forgiving, your death will be a time of wonder and prosperity. It's ridiculous. I'm more inclined to believe that we are all already in Hell. That would make more sense.

I suggest that we go for a drink. Jill says her sister is taking care of the kid while she is out at a meeting.

So it can only be a quick one.

Jill has work in the morning and she is taking her position seriously, so we could share a bottle of something and go our separate ways. She could buy a packet of mints to disguise the smell from her sister and I can have a more interesting drive home.

Jill is still a raging alcoholic, so there is also the possibility that she could end the night in a fisting contest.

I leave my car parked and we walk to the nearest bar. A real dive.

I order a bottle of Prosecco with two glasses. It arrives at the table and it is Frisante. Hardly any fizz, tastes like acid and burns the throat with every gulp. We finish it quickly to get it out of the way and I make sure I get what I order the next time.

Most of our time is spent with me ranting about the priest, the Church and my abhorrence for organised religion. Even disorganised religion. I'm talking like Sam Ramirez. Then I'm talking about Sam Ramirez. Jill is nodding along as she sips down drink like it's ambrosia.

If I was handed Psychopaths Anonymous at work I'd want to know exactly who they were, what they stand for and what their overarching message is.

Initially it was something to do, something to oppose AA, somewhere for likeminded people to meet. A club rather than a cult. Then Sam Ram set my mind whirring and Father Interference pissed me off and I'm wondering whether our plight should be to take down the Church. I'm dreaming of Psychopaths Anonymous groups showing up wherever there is an AA meeting with the purpose of derailing proceedings and pulling these desperate folk away from their Lord.

I click back into reality and Jill is talking at me. I haven't heard a word of it. But she is shaking her empty glass and appears expectant.

'Grab your coat. Let's get out of here.'

I'm not buying another bottle, the drive is going to be treacherous enough with the amount of alcohol I've already had. And I'm not going to drive Jill across town. She can take the tube.

The air outside hits my face and feels refreshing. There's always the danger that it will speed up inebriation but it's giving me a gentle buzz that will put me in good stead to handle the car all the way home without a scrape.

Jill and I part ways outside the pub. Her sister will know right away that she has been drinking and Jill will have to take another lecture about being a responsible mother. And it will make her want to drink more.

When I get back to my car, all the other vehicles that were parked around it have gone. I don't feel like we have been out that long but all the lights in the community centre are out and my car is half in darkness with the street lamp only illuminating the corner closest to the building. And, if he hadn't been smoking a cigarette, I probably wouldn't have noticed the man sitting on my bonnet.

When I get home, Seth is waiting for me in his car on the drive.

I'm late.

Couldn't be helped.

I had to kill Clyde.

It wasn't a drawn-out affair. This isn't a movie. You don't always get to perform your Oscar-worthy monologue before you kill someone or get caught by the cops. Sometimes, you just have to get the job done.

That fucking clown was relaxing on my car. He was sitting on the bonnet, leaning back against the windscreen and staring at the stars while filling his lungs with smoke. That is not the posture of somebody waiting to have a conversation, perhaps offer an apology. Clyde wanted to intimidate. He wanted to let me know that he could get to me, that he knew where I was and when I would be alone.

He wanted to scare me.

I think a part of me was frightened. There was nobody around and it was dark. I didn't have Eames with me this time to add some extra muscle. Clyde wasn't a psychopath but he was clearly unstable and unpredictable.

So, no speeches. No conversations. No witty banter. I had to take away the unpredictability by predicting its inevitability.

I reached into my bag for my car keys. There was the possibility that I could click the car open, jump inside, lock it and start the engine before Clyde could hoist himself off the bonnet. But I didn't want possibilities. I wanted certainty.

I found the sharpened key among the bunch and squeezed it tightly in my hand, walked up to the driver's door and, before Clyde could say anything or sit up from my windscreen, I jabbed that sharp metal into his throat. It must have been three times before he even realised what was happening and the cigarette fell from his mouth.

Another two jabs and he starts to do what everyone does when blood starts shooting out of their neck, he grabs at his own throat. That takes his hands out of action. He can't swing for me now because he's trying to keep the blood inside his body.

I turn the key around in my hand so that I no longer thrust it forward in a poking motion but bring the sharp point downwards like a hammer. I pierce his stomach twice, then, on the third blow, I leave the piece of metal inside his body and pull back, scraping through his skin and opening him up.

Clyde falls off my car and onto the floor.

He's still alive.

I don't want the possibility that he could get out of this.

Only certainty.

Those first eight stabs were for Clyde. To start him on his journey towards death. The next sixty-two were for me. I hammered down so many times into his throat that I thought his head might come off.

It didn't.

Even when I wound his hair around my hand and dragged him by the head from the car park, across the grass and into a bush behind an overflowing dog waste bin. Somebody would find him in the morning.

My right hand was covered in Clyde's blood. I had some tissues and a bottle of water in my bag. I got a lot out but it would need more. I couldn't go home like that with Seth waiting for me. He had already messaged a couple of times asking where I was. I told him I had been with Jill and was on my way.

At the petrol station on the way back, I purposefully spilled some on my hands before filling the car to get the last bit of red off my skin, then scrubbed them with soap in the public restroom. I paid for my fuel, a packet of gum and another bottle of water, before running through the car wash on its most basic cycle and driving towards where Seth was waiting.

The drive was not as tricky as I had anticipated after leaving the pub.

Murder has such a sobering effect.

'There you are.' Seth gets out of his car as soon as I pull in. He's parked in my space and I'm annoyed but I don't show it.

'Yeah, just ran over a bit with Jill. Some boring work stuff to sort this week. We had some wine to ease the pain.' I smile. He smiles back.

'You know what would make this kind of thing easier?'

'What kind of thing?'

'Me, waiting around.'

'I don't know, a comfortable cushion?'

'A key.'

A sharpened key to the throat can solve a lot of problems.

I wonder whether I've cleaned all the blood off my weapon.

'A key?'

'Yes. So that I could let myself in if ever you are late. I could get the dinner started. That sort of thing.'

I know that he is taking a risk here, putting himself out there but I can't concentrate on what he is saying because he is stood next to me and I don't want him to see blood. I open my hand a little to see if there's any red on my skin. It looks okay.

I open the front door and kick off my shoes.

Seth wants his own key to the house. Is he thinking about moving in? Already?

Does that mean that I have him? Seth is mine?

No. Of course not. Not yet. It's a key. Just a key. A piece of metal.

~~Idiot.~~
I can't have him here all the time, surely. I need to be able to come and go, freely. If he's here more, he'll notice how often I drink. But I do want him here. But I can't. It would be like moving house to an apartment above a bar. I can't have Seth here like that. I can't have the thing I want around me all the time. That doesn't work.

It's only a key, though. He doesn't have his own wardrobe or coffee mug, I'm not doing his washing. Perhaps it is more logistical than emotional.

I don't respond to his question. I can see him hankering for an answer. I do what I always do when I get home from work, I walk to the fridge, take out a bottle of wine, open the drawer next to the fridge, pull out the opener, get the cork out and pour myself a large glass.

This time, I put the opener back in the drawer, rummage around through the utensils I hardly ever use, there's a screwdriver that has never screwed anything and a metal straw that's still sticky on the inside. Then I find it.

'Maeve.' Seth is behind me. I haven't spoken to him since he suggested having his own way of accessing my home.

I turn around.

'This is my spare key.'

He looks shocked but gives me a smile that says, 'I love you, you big psycho'.

'You can have it. But it's not for you to come over here while I'm not in so that you can rearrange my cupboards or go through my underwear. Equally, I don't want to come home one day and you are already here cooking dinner. I don't want to be surprised. Okay?'

He nods.

'It's for this exact situation. If I'm late, I don't want you waiting out in the cold.'

There's nobody in the freezer or wrapped in plastic. There's half a car that I could explain away if he ever ventures into the garage.

'You're a big romantic, Maeve.' He moves in closer.

'Oh, shut up.' I slap his chest.

He keeps coming.

Then I'm sitting on the kitchen counter, trying to take a mouthful of wine as Seth kisses my neck, before I start to lose myself. And then he's standing there and fucking me and I pull him deep into me with my legs around his back, trapping him so that he has to come inside me.

He's breathing heavily.

'Shit. We shouldn't have done that.'

He wants his own key but he doesn't want kids. Got it.

'It'll be fine. I'm a couple of days away from my period.' He doesn't look convinced. 'Besides, my cold, dark insides will kill your sperm before it can do any lasting damage.'

STEP **THREE**

'Make a fearless, honest moral inventory.'

I'm not pregnant.

A couple of days go by and my set-your-watch-to-it period arrives. I leave the box of tampons on the shelf in the downstairs toilet so that Seth will notice that I'm plugged up this week. That way he knows not to worry about the load he left in me last time he was here, and if he wants some action, he will have to lay down a towel and deal with the consequences.

I'm tired after dinner and drinking and a crappy day in the office. Seth and I watch TV for a bit and I move myself over to the other sofa so that I can lie down.

I drift off for a while. Too deep to dream. I wake up some time after that and the television is still kicking out the sound of some obnoxious American reality show contestant but my head feels too heavy to turn and see which one it is. I don't turn around to see whether Seth is still watching either because I know that he's not. I can hear him in the hallway, talking on his mobile phone.

There's still a lot of wine in my system and I'm groggy from sleep, so I can't hear exactly what he is saying or guess who he may be talking to but there's enough from the tone to suggest that he is being quiet, not because he doesn't want to wake me, but because he doesn't want to be heard.

It's different.

It feels conspiratorial. I don't like it. But I don't move. I don't want the sofa to make a noise and obscure any part of his conversation. I want to catch a word here or there, perhaps a name. What I don't want is to hear a woman's name. I don't want to feel suspicious of Seth. I don't want him to turn out to be a rat bastard that I will have to gut and bury.

Because I like spending time with him, being near him, having him inside me.

I don't know if this is love because I don't know what love is. I also like spending time with wine and being near vodka and having tequila inside of me. Do I love alcohol? Or do I love the feeling?

Seth won't raise his voice. All I can hear is a conversation between two Beverley Hills housewives and the fundraiser they want to arrange that they don't want Janet to be involved with because she was a real bitch at lunch the other day.

'Can you believe she said that?'

'I. Can't. Even.'

Shut up. I'm trying to listen to my boyfriend having a late-night conversation on the phone.

Shit. My boyfriend? That doesn't sound right.

Maybe I'm hearing things, seeing things, imagining things.

I want to move. Maybe I should spring up and catch him in the act, just have it out with him. Maybe it's nothing. Maybe I'm paranoid because I care. Maybe I just don't want anyone else to have him. Maybe I need to know that he is mine and mine only. Maybe I'm getting soft. Maybe this is love. Maybe this is jealousy. Fear. Possession.

Maybe.

Maybe.

Maybe.

Seth walks back into the lounge and I close my eyes. Somehow, I try to make myself more still, even though I am not moving at all. He comes over to me, bends down and kisses me on the head.

Not a guilty kiss. I can feel that. It's affection.

It was probably a work call. I know his boss, he is a prize dick. Of course he would call him in the middle of the night.

Seth goes back to the other sofa. I hear him take a drink, settle back in his seat and continue with the programme. He doesn't switch channels or flick through the on-demand movies. He sticks it out.

Maybe he likes it. Maybe he doesn't want to turn it over in case I wake up. Maybe he is taking notice so that he can tell me what I've missed.

Maybe.
It's alright. Seth is mine.
I keep my eyes closed and go back to sleep.

†

I say, 'Abstinence is not the answer. Priests abstain from sex and end up fucking altar boys.'

That's when Father Jessop enters our meeting.

He took me up on my offer.

Of course he did.

'Good evening,' he says in his soft Irish lilt. Everyone looks confused. Sam Ramirez looks angry. He always looks angry. I was hoping to take some of his passion to ignite a fire in the others. A call to action. To solidify what we are about at Psychopaths Anonymous.

Now I'm working on the fly.

'Come and take a seat, we were just getting started.' I give the members a look and they stifle their laughter, knowing what I said just before the dog collar walked in.

I explain that our esteemed guest is here to better understand what we do at Psychopaths Anonymous. He is a patron of the group across the hall – because it's a recruitment room – and he is interested in all aspects of mental health and diversity.

The priest nods but his eyes tell me that he hates me.

I don't like being put on the spot. I like to plan. I like to be prepared. I am regimental with my day job and I prefer my murders to be premeditated. I'm sick of God and all of his employees.

So I copy.

I take something that I know and I adapt it to fit my needs.

'What are your liabilities?' I ask. It's not the way I usually talk in these meetings so they all know I'm putting on a show. All but the man of God, who sits forward on his chair, as if edging two inches closer will mean that my words get to him quicker.

'I need you to think about how your mindset has affected others.'

Mindset. I'm watering it down, which goes against the very reason we are here.

'How have aspects of your psychopathy, your psychopathic behaviour been detrimental to yourself and others.' I use the term twice in one sentence to make up for my initial failing. 'We call this "making a fearless and honest moral inventory". It's not always a nice thing to do but it is necessary.'

In AA, you do this after surrendering your will to your higher power.

Horse shit.

We are our own power.

I don't remind them of that but I will when the holy idiot leaves.

'For me, I had trouble when I was younger at school because it constantly came across that I didn't care about what I was doing. That wasn't the case with my schoolwork. I was very focussed. Sometimes it was suggested that I was too laid back, and that wasn't the case, either.'

Just because someone isn't smiling, it doesn't mean they are not happy.

The opposite is also true of people who smile all the time.

Everyone is hidden.

'That is obviously a very tame example. I want you to dig a lot deeper. Make a list of everything. Think hard. You may have hurt somebody else. It may have caused you to act out in some way, do something that you know you shouldn't have done.'

I look around and I can see I've lost the crowd. They don't know what they should be doing. Sam Ram can't stop staring at the religious gatecrasher and the others are either deep in thought or dreaming of being somewhere else.

The priest puts his hand up.

'Yes?'

'Could you give us an example of something deeper?'

I don't like that he used 'us', like he is part of what we do, who we are.

'For example, someone close to you might tell you that their parent has died. You understand why they are upset but your lack of ability to empathise comes across as apathy, upsetting them further. And you don't understand why you don't feel bad about it.'

'Yes, yes. That is a slightly worse scenario but what I meant was could you perhaps call on something that you have done. The leader of the group across the hall was an alcoholic and he uses his own experiences to draw the best from the people in his group. He isn't afraid to get his hands dirty, so to speak.'

He sits back in his chair like he has defeated me.

You can point a sharp stick at a cornered lion, it doesn't make you king of the jungle.

'First of all, he is still an alcoholic, even if he doesn't drink any more. That's what they teach you.'

'Ooooooh,' says Sam Ram, like he's a guest on some comedy roasting.

'When Gary told me that he got drunk and took another man in his mouth, it didn't make me want to open up about my own failings. But let's give it a try.' I shift my body slightly so that Jessop knows that I am facing towards my people and away from him. 'I'm driving home from work one day and some idiot beeps his horn to alert me that he is about to cut me up. Now, that noise alone is enough to get me going, but I was enraged. I hit my own horn in anger.'

Sam Ram is completely enthralled.

'He wound down his window, stuck his hand out and made a gesture that suggested I enjoy masturbating men.'

Cue laughter.

'Most people would have left it. Some would shout obscenities in the safety of their own vehicle. Occasionally, you would see somebody get out of their car, walk up to his car and punch the window in. I did nothing of the sort. I went calm. My schoolteachers would have looked at me and thought that I still did not care. But I cared.'

I feel the priest's eyes on me.

'It seemed stupid to put myself in a position of danger by confronting the man, I didn't know who he was or what he was capable of. He was clearly aggressive and couldn't manage his anger. But then I thought, he doesn't know who I am. He doesn't know what I am capable of. He has no idea that I am capable of controlling my anger and focussing it on an end goal.'

Aside: 'Feel free to endorse me on LinkedIn.'

Another chuckle.

'What did you do ... with that anger?' Sam Ram looks as though this is turning him on. He's excitable. Young. Probably not young enough for the visiting clergyman.

'I tailed him. Followed him all the way back to his house. I sat on the opposite side of the road and watched as he entered. I was annoyed by his swagger. But I waited. I watched. Eventually the lights went out all over the house. I waited another hour, to be sure. Then I took the petrol can from my boot, poured it all over his front door and set fire to it.'

'This is outrageous.' The holy man stands up, his chair squeaking against the floor as he pushes it back.

I just look at him.

We all do.

'You can't admit to committing a crime and be so blasé about it. What happened to the poor man? Did you stay to see if he was hurt? Was his entire house burned to the ground? This is outrageous.' He repeats himself, shuffling from side to side.

The room is silent. Six psychopaths, staring at an ageing, unconfirmed child-fucker.

Eames laughs.

Everyone follows suit.

'What? Why are you ...? Oh, you're joking. That is not funny.'

'But you believed it instantly because of the stigma that surrounds the word "psychopath". This is what we are working with. We are as soul-searching as that group across the hall. We are making our moral inventory. The group knows my background and troubles, I do not need to be put on trial about my qualification to lead these discussions.'

He looks at me as though deep in thought. I don't know what he is thinking. He may be contemplating forgiveness, he may have realised he was wrong in some way.

'You are here by invitation and I think you have seen everything you need to see. We have work to do now, so if you would kindly leave and allow us to resume our discussion so that the group is comfortable to talk freely...' I point an open hand towards the door.

~~Kindly, fuck off and die.~~

He mumbles a thank-you and lowers his head as he walks.

I turn to the group, 'Thanks for going along with that.'

More mumbles. 'Oh, yeah. "Going along with it". Sure, sure. Wink, wink.'

Nothing more is said.

I imagine the way I want to kill the priest.

It makes me smile.

He looks sullen and defeated as he leaves.

I should really make amends with him at some point.

LIST OF PEOPLE I HAVE (RECENTLY) HARMED

THE PRIEST
CLYDE

A text says that Seth won't be coming over this evening.

My mind whirs.

Something is going on.

That surreptitious slink into the hallway last week replays in my mind. Why is he ducking out to make a late-night call? He is thoughtful and considerate but that felt private. Secretive. It wasn't that he didn't want to disturb me, it's that he didn't want me to hear.

Unless I'm seeing things that way. Something that isn't there.

~~What if it isn't there?~~

I want to ask him what he is doing instead, what is more important than seeing me, spending time with me, drinking with me, fucking me. But I don't want to appear desperate. I don't want him to think that I need him.

I do need him.

He's mine.

I head the marketing for the company he works for, so I know when they have a drive or he's up against it and DoTrue are not a priority for me, right now. I could ask him whether it's a work thing. If he says that it is, I will know he is lying.

Then what? Go to his house? Follow him? See where he's really going? Confirm whether he is cheating on me?

I can't resist. I have to send a message back:

Okay. No worries. I'm the understanding partner. I'm breezy. I have my own life. *Shame, though...* Of course I'm a little disgruntled because, *I wanted to make you dinner tonight and I bought some Pinot Noir.* It's not different to any other night apart from the fact that you won't be here. *I'll have to start the new season of Project Runway without you.* I could add a smiley face to show that I am joking around. But I'm not a child. It's obviously light-hearted, and he will see it that way if he's not feeling guilty about doing something behind my back. *The dessert I had in mind was for two but I guess I can do that by myself.* Look what you're missing out on.

What I really want to write is, *Why aren't you coming over? What are you doing that's more important?*

I may be a psychopath but I'm not crazy.

I hit send and then I sweat.

...

He's typing.

Ha! Look, I just need to help someone out. I'll explain when I see you, it's too long for over the phone. I'll keep you posted. Reckon I might, actually, make it in time for dessert. He finishes with a winking face and I shudder.

Great. Now I have to buy a bottle of Pinot Noir on the way home and think of a dinner to cook.

'So, are we really supposed to make this mental imagery thing?' Sam Ramirez. Young, enthusiastic, angry Sam Ramirez.

'Not a mental imagery, a moral inventory. And, yes. I think it's useful. I have done it and it's eye-opening. Have you ever watched these programmes on television where a morbidly obese person is trying to lose weight and the doctor tells them to keep a food diary for a week?' I have because I watch all of those types of things. 'They are frightfully unaware of what they are putting into their body on a weekly, daily or hourly basis until they see it written down. That's the point. We all think we are self-aware, and the people in this room probably think it more than other people, but sometimes you just have to get the poison out.'

There's a discussion about how far it should go and what they should put down on their list. I can see a couple of them baulk and I know they've done something awful or unlawful but I expected as much.

They are wondering whether this is just an exercise for themselves, so that they can see how the way their brain works has an effect on others. I can see the nervous energy over in the corner that 'Son of Sam' Ram occupies. The guy is pure electricity in his calmest moments and I'm guessing he keeps his mother's body in the basement and her head has been hollowed out to be used as a fruit bowl.

'Look, you don't have an addiction. You are not trying to overcome anything, you are just trying to be at ease with it, to understand it and accept it. But at some point, there has to be a call to action.'

'Yes.' Sam Ram pumps his fist.

'Ordinarily, you write these things down for you and then you have to say them out loud to another person. And that makes it more real, or something. I don't know, my sponsor left me at that point.' And I tell them, 'I don't give a fuck what you write down. I don't want to know. I don't care.'

I want them to rise up. Like any oppressed group. We need to push back against the people like that priest, whose views are so predictable and narrow.

'So, that's what I want you to do. I want you to write this shit down and I want you to say it out loud to somebody. But not just anybody. Him. That condescending piece of shit who walked out of here with his chin on his chest and his tail between his legs. Get in a box and confess to him. Make him listen. Form a queue and torment him.'

My call to action is juvenile perhaps but beautiful in its simplicity.

We are going after God.

Tim Gunn arrives at the artists' residence, first thing in the morning, and tells them that their challenge is to make an outfit out of the pyjamas they are wearing and one bed sheet. They are provided with some dyes and trims and zips. I consider myself a creative person but what these designers come up with is fascinating. Often because it's magical, but a lot of the time it is due to those at the bottom making an absolute fool of themselves.

I eat a microwaved meal and swill around the expensive red wine between the laughter at what Raphael has produced on *Project Runway*.

The trousers are awful. He promised they would be 'camel-toe free' and not only can I read the model's lips, I think I'm learning Braille from between her legs. The waistcoat looks like scraps of bed sheet.

This guy is gone. I'm sure of it. I don't even need to see what the other designers have stitched together.

The doorbell rings.

I pause the episode and pick up my glass of wine to take with me, just in case it's that persistent detective again. I wouldn't want to disappoint my audience.

'Good evening,' I smile, opening the door.

'Not too late for dessert, am I?'

'Seth, you have a key.'

'I know, but there are so many rules about how and when I can and cannot use it that I figure it's always best to ring the bell unless I am instructed otherwise.'

'You are a good boy.' I kiss him, forgetting for just a moment that I'm possibly pissed at him for cheating on me and ditching me for his mistress. 'Come in, tell me where the fuck you have been all night, then we will consider dessert.'

For someone seemingly respecting my privacy, Seth makes himself at home by kicking off his shoes in the hallway, going into the kitchen to grab himself a glass for the wine and then taking a seat in front of my paused programme.

He picks up the container for my soggy lasagne.

'Wow, I'm so gutted I missed this dinner, you must have been slaving away for minutes.'

I give him a look.

He gestures at the wine. Less than half a bottle remains.

'Go for it. I have more.'

He reads the label. Pinot Noir. My story checks out. Now for his.

Seth gulps down his first glass with impressive gusto. He's showing me that he is exasperated by his day or his evening. Then he explains. His friend, Olly, has been kicked out of the marital home. Odd because it was his wife who did the cheating. But he's a nice guy, a pushover, really, so he has left her in the house and packed a few bags.

'He's on my couch right now. I've already had a few beers while we talked about what he did wrong and how he pushed her away. I'm definitely over the driving limit but I wanted to come and see you. I explained that he didn't force her into the arms or the bed of another man and that he's an idiot for not kicking *her* out. But he's a bit of a sap and he doesn't want to hurt her even though she has broken him.'

He's saying all the right things. Like he has disdain for this adulterous harlot who betrayed his friend. Like it's not a way that he would behave.

'You just left him at your place?'

'Not much more I could do, Maeve. He was knocking back the drinks. He got some shit out of his system and I threw a blanket over him on the sofa. He's not suicidal, he's homeless.'

He takes down some more of my Pinot Noir and puts a hand on my leg.

'Besides, I wanted to come here and see you.' He repeats, and moves it up my thigh.

'Okay, I'll buy it. But you're going to have to wait for your dessert.' I click the button on the remote and my programme continues. Christina Ricci is a guest judge. She looks incredible. Bert's design wins. Rafael is rightly eliminated.

We get right to dessert on the sofa. Straight-up missionary. Seth hooks his arms underneath my shoulders so that his weight pushes the air out of me. I love that closeness but also that sense of strangulation, it seems to heighten the sensation.

I feel myself getting closer and I ask Seth to put his hands around my neck. He pauses for a microsecond but obliges.

'Tighter. Don't be afraid.'

I can feel.

He's not afraid.

He likes it.

Forcing himself into me harder and faster, it's not what I want but I go with it. I'm no longer in control. He pulls out and finishes himself off with his right hand, his left stays firm around my throat. I love watching his face in this moment.

When he is lost.

And I take back the control.

I don't want it to end, but if it ever does, I can already see that it will end just like this.

People are stupid.

Psychopaths are not. Usually.

The idea of taking another human being's life is so unfathomable to most people, that they will believe anything you say if you decide to give them a motive.

If a violent psychopath is caught by the police, often, it is not because the detectives have outwitted the killer. The cat has not swatted the mouse. It is because the killer wants to stop. Or the killer is bored. Or the killer has nowhere else to go; there is no way to obtain the high of the previous thrill.

They kill fifteen prostitutes and they say that their mother was a whore who beat them and put cigarettes out on their skin. The public do not sympathise but they feel as though they can understand why somebody would go that way.

A popular one is that Satan played a part. That He communicated a message calling for blood. Some psychopaths prefer to say that it was a direct discourse while others blame the neighbour's dog for being a conduit of the message.

And stupid people lap it up.

Because you would have to be that mad to shoot people through their car windows at random. You would have to believe that the

Lord of the Underworld was speaking in your head to chop up half a university hockey team. Of course, nobody would kill a woman, cut off her breast and use it as a paperweight unless their mother chastised them as a child for dressing up in girls' clothing. Suddenly, it all makes sense.

It doesn't.

It isn't always because Uncle Larry touched us in our special place. It's because nobody misses a whore or a bum and it's funny to watch people believe the occult crap. They're bored of life and its lack of challenge. So they find a new hobby. Taunting the police. Telling tales in court. Starving themselves in prison. Offering an interview with the press after years of incarceration.

You can be psychopathic without killing people. You can be psychopathic without hurting people. You can be psychopathic and nobody would ever know.

But you can be psychopathic and kill people and hurt people. And nobody would ever know. And you are not doing it because of some childhood trauma or mental breakdown or abuse or neglect, you are just doing it. It's who you are. You understand right and wrong. You know what evil is. You know how to be good. But you are who you are.

~~We are who we are.~~

Psychopaths could be everywhere. Just walking among 'normal' people.

~~We are everywhere. We are your brother, your mother your babysitter, dog walker, solicitor, doctor. We got you your job and sold you your car and delivered your newspaper.~~

For the intelligent psychopath, life can get pretty boring.

Even the killing gets monotonous.

But it is a compulsion. An obsession.

An addiction.

And it's so much harder to kick than the drugs or the pornography or the bottle.

When a psychopath gets caught, it's their way of saying that they want to quit. No rehab. No twelve-step plan. Cold turkey.

That's not me.

But recently, since Seth, I guess, since it got more serious, I've been wondering whether I could slow things down, whether I want to. Can I keep both things going?

Do I have to choose?

Could I stop for love?

STEP **FOUR**

'Admit to yourself the exact nature of your wrongs. Then admit to another person. Make that person a priest.'

It doesn't have to be a priest. It can be your rabbi or guru or village elder. It just has to be somebody who believes there is a higher power than themselves and that they are connected to this power through their faith or prayer.

We know there is no God – and if there is, He hates us all – but talking to your local holy man covers things off if the big guy decides to come out of retirement and clear up the shit show He created on our sick and dying planet.

This is our first call to action. For our group to do something with our shared psychopathy. We are not heading out on a killing spree. Not all psychopathy is violent – look at the high-achievers, the class clowns, read some Sherlock Holmes. Just because psychopaths have traits that make them more likely to be violent, does not mean that they definitely will be. But for any group that feels marginalised or misunderstood, anarchy is an effective use of time and collective energy.

No God could hate me as much as I hate Him. I have a focus. And that focus is disruption and mayhem. We can do something useful with our nihilism.

We have talked.

We have listened.

We have looked within ourselves at our failures.

Now we want poke the hornets' nest.

Jill is not at her desk when I arrive at work. She's a different person to the initial wine-drenched, crudded-up, double-penetration-loving, mother of the year who bleated out her pathetic history at Camden Newcomers – or wherever it was I was crashing. She's got a hold on her life.

She's not clean but she's also not drunk all the time. She spending time with her daughter. She's earning her own way. Sure, she still makes a little extra tax-free on the weekends and she's definitely not banking that anywhere – my guess is underneath her mattress – but she looks presentable, she works hard, does as she is asked and she is always here when I arrive.

But not today.

I'm not worried about her, but I am wondering where she is.

I take a quick look at my phone but there are no messages.

'Has anyone seen Jill this morning?' I ask the bank of creatives. A few shake their heads but I see a number of them making a face that says, 'Who is Jill?' They're caught up in their own worlds. Why would they need to get to know a secretary or an assistant?

I walk away.

~~They don't see Jill but I do.~~

A voice behind me mumbles, 'A bit too early for the pub to be open.' And then a couple of others laugh.

Jill means nothing to me. She types up my notes and gets me my coffee and occasionally I prod her out of sobriety because she can drink like a giant and she's amusing. So I could keep walking to my office and leave it alone.

'Who said that?' I don't turn around at first. I let them look at one another. They can determine just how close they are. They have a split second to work out their loyalties and whether they will throw a colleague under the bus to save themselves.

I turn. They all look at me. I fold my arms and wait.

'Sorry. It was me. It was stupid.'

He's younger than me. Attractive. Though I don't like his long hair. I can't think what he is called, he must be new.

'Remind me of your name.'

'Keach. Jamie Keach.'

'And what did you do here, Jamie?'

'Did?'

'My bad. What do you currently do at this company, Jamie?'

'I'm a junior designer.'

'Well, I suggest you spend a little more time designing and leave the bitching about single mothers to the HR department or the ladies in accounting. Sound like a good idea?'

'Sounds perfect. Sorry.'

A smile at some of the others as Jamie Keach gets his head down.

I add him to my make-amends list even though I think I've scared him into a state of perpetual terror that I'm going to take away his job. It's just that the list is short, at the moment, and it's nice to have something to look forward to.

There doesn't always have to be a reason.

And I don't think anyone would miss Jamie Keach.

LIST OF PEOPLE I HAVE (RECENTLY) HARMED

THE PRIEST
CLYDE
JAMIE KEACH

It's lunchtime and I still haven't heard from Jill. She's not picking up her phone. I haven't had so much as a text or email from her. It's odd. I know how committed she is to this job. For some reason, she may even like it. The only other thing I've seen her this invested in is Cabernet Sauvignon.

I divert my office phone straight to my mobile, pick up my bag and my coffee and head out. If I ever leave the office for lunch, the only person I tell is Jill but she isn't here so I decide to tell Jamie Keach that I'm leaving for a bit but that I will be back. It will give him a little respite before he starts worrying that I have returned without him noticing.

I drive to Jill's.

She doesn't answer the door at first.

'Jill, I know you're in there.' I don't. 'It's Maeve'. It is. 'I'm worried about you.' I'm not.

Eventually I see her slumped silhouette through the glass. Two bolts shift heavily and she removes the chain before opening the door enough to peek her left eye at me.

'Can I come in?'

'Now is not a great time, Maeve, to be honest. I...'

'Do you even know what time it is, Jill, because you were supposed to be at work three hours ago?' I push my way in.

She doesn't even put up a fight.

Her lounge is disgusting. The last time I was here, it was tidy and Not Jack was pounding his angry inch into her from behind. But at least it was clean. There are bottles and cans tipped over on the carpet and a mirror on the coffee table.

'Looks like someone had a party. Where's your daughter, Jill? Tell me she's not here in this fucking mess.'

Her head is hanging and I hear her mumble something about her sister.

'You should have called me.' I understand what went on here. Drink. Drugs. Disgusting sex. But I'm not being understanding. She can do what she wants in her own time but this is my time she's fucking with.

That's when she lifts her head and I see her face.

Her eyes are red and bloodshot. One of them is swollen. Her lip is cut. As is one of her cheeks. She's chipped a tooth.

'What the fuck happened here, Jill? Who did this to you?'

'It doesn't matter. It happens sometimes. They get a bit rough.'

'They get a bit rough? Is that what you're telling me? That this is normal. You just let these animals do this to you?'

Jill cries and I want to slap some sense into her.

She tells me what happened. There were three of them. Two brothers and their father. The Maynards. A filthy bunch of local hoodlums with ideas beyond their station. Think they are the Krays or the Corleones. They'd show up at Jill's from time to time with a crate of beer, a bag of powder, balls ready to burst.

It wasn't like her weekend, extracurricular activity, this was like the Gambinos or Genevoses taking their monthly rent from struggling shopkeepers. They ran a few of the local girls and Jill's weekend work was taking a chunk out of their pockets but they would let it slide because once every few weeks, they got to take a chunk out of Jill.

She had a respectful job now. A decent wage for a first-time assistant, she didn't have to spread her legs for every limp-dicked, Irish-cursed construction worker in town.

I think she likes it.

Jill believes she deserves to be treated like shit, so welcomes the opportunity for further humiliation. Maybe she gets off on it in some way.

Another addiction.

She can't feel anything unless she is feeling awful about herself.

They drank and snorted and drank some more. Then they lined up, this family, pulled their dicks out in front of each other and Jill knelt down and fluffed them all up like a twitching sea lion.

The Maynards didn't take it in turns, they all found somewhere to put their dicks and went to town. The two brothers pounding Jill and trying desperately not to accidentally slap their balls together.

The father stayed in her mouth. They know it's not normal but they've seen it so many times before with their free porn access and their search for *Gangbang Brothers*.

'The boys slapped my arse and my breasts, their dad hit me in the face. That's how he likes it. Rough.'

Degrading.

~~The boys? Sounds affectionate.~~

And Jill tells me that each of them finished on her face, spraying the Maynard glue into her eyes. That's why they are so red, she says. She couldn't come into the office like this. And she didn't know how to tell me.

Men, no woman wants this.

I know who I am. I know what I am. And I know what I do. But history will not look back on what I have done, what I have achieved and look at it with the same degree of disdain that they will for their generation of man.

What we have now is bad enough but these kids, raised on easy, instant access to infinite pornography, who think that women want to be beaten and gang-banged. Who believe that we like to be fucked in the mouth so hard it makes us gag, who think that spitting in their own hand and rubbing it between our legs counts as foreplay. What are they being taught? They think anal sex is de rigueur.

They think a slap is okay. A mean word is okay. An unsolicited advance is okay.

It's not okay, boys.

Someone will have to teach you about respect.

'You could have called and said you were sick or hungover and had a relapse. I know your story, Jill. You can have a day off, for crying out loud.'

'Okay. I'm sorry.'

Damn it, I am bored of people apologising to me, today.

'Take a couple of days off until your eye goes down. You're sick, okay? You still get paid.'

'Thank you, Maeve.'

'You can thank me by telling me a bit more about this Maynard family. Where do they live? What do they actually do around here?'

'What are you going to do? You don't want to get mixed up with that lot.'

'I'm not going to do anything, I just want to know a bit more about what we are dealing with, here. I'd rather you not have two days off every month, but if you do, I'd like to know why.'

I'm lying, of course.

Jill tells me what I need to know.

It's Jamie Keach's lucky day because I bump him off the list. He's already been punished enough by my ridicule and the anxiety of possibly losing his job.

I replace him with The Maynards.

If I hadn't given Jill the job that helped her clean up her act, then she probably wouldn't have the confidence to fuck her local neighbourhood for extra money, therefore taking a chunk of change from The Maynards' pimp commission.

It seems that I have wronged the family in some way.

I will have to make amends.

LIST OF PEOPLE I HAVE (RECENTLY) HARMED

THE PRIEST

CLYDE

JAMIE KEACH

THE MAYNARDS

We line up outside the confession booth.

A queue of psychopaths.

Eames goes in first. I think he wants to get it out the way and make a quick exit. No idea what kind of information he is going to impart to torment our favourite priest but I'm sure it will be juicy enough to get the ball rolling.

Before this field trip session, Eames took me aside to let me know that he won't be at any meeting for a while as he has an important project coming up that he has to focus his time and efforts on. He may have to go away for a while. He says that he appreciates it and that it has been enjoyable and he likes the direction that things are turning now that we have more of a purpose.

He seems averse to risk, to me. Like he wants to lie low.

You don't have to have every trait of psychopathy to be considered a part of the group. Not everyone likes to brag. Not every murder is solved. Not everyone is caught. Not all psychos kill.

Perhaps we will never see Eames again. I think about adding him to my list, just to make sure I get one last chance. Maybe I shouldn't take it so personally when somebody wants to leave.

He's inside that wooden box for ten minutes or so. He's smirking as he exits. We had a deal that the next in line would jump straight into the hot seat so as not to give the priest a second to take stock of what he was hearing.

Don't let him breathe.

The person next in the queue blocks the priest's exit.

Bob is up next. He is in there for a long time. I assume he is regaling the priest with his tale of warped love, obsession and revenge. It's a great story that I think no amount of Hail Marys could possibly cover.

'Great listener,' Bob says as he walks out of church. A wink in his voice.

Eddie jumps straight in. I bet he's already mentioned that he's a surgeon. Anyone who has known Eddie for more than eighteen seconds knows what he does for a living. He is more proud of himself than anyone could be of him.

He's out.

Jake is in.

He's the most enigmatic member of the group. Too nice to not be a maniac. He smells like a killer to me. He's too calm to not be violent. Too thought-out to not be impulsive. Sam Ram is on the brink of explosion at any moment but it's Jake Killey who I feel could do the most damage.

Out.

No Name #1 in.

The guy is so unapologetically promiscuous and open about his sexual activity he's probably turning on the unsuspecting vicar. He'll be heading straight to the altar boys' changing area with a bottle of sacramental wine and chloroform-drenched flannel.

But not before Sam Ramirez gets to spit some vitriol through the confession booth partition while admitting some of his deepest, darkest troubles.

I'm quickly inside the box but I notice how entertained and fulfilled Sam Ram seems as we cross over.

'Oh, child. I was about to take a break.'

'I'm the last one. I've been waiting.'

'Okay, okay.' He sounds exasperated. Perfect.

'I've never been to confession before.'

'Well it usually starts with "Forgive me father for I have sinned" and then you tell me how long it has been since your last confession.'

'What if I'm planning on committing a sin? Can I get some pre-forgiveness for that?'

'That's not really how it works.'

'So, I should go out and commit the sin first then come back and get the forgiveness?'

'Ideally, you wouldn't commit the transgression at all. This isn't a get-out-of-jail-free card. What is it that you have done or feel you will do? Would you like to talk about it?' He's exhausted.

'Well, there's a slight problem. You see, the six men that you spoke with before I entered this place, they're bad.' I say this coyly, almost childlike.

'What do you mean by that?' I hear him shuffle on his seat. He's uncomfortable.

'The things they told you, the things they confessed. Awful things. Inhumane things. Vengeful things—' I was planning on continuing my list but the priest interrupts.

'How can you possibly know what the people before you were confessing?'

'I heard them talking together,' I lie. 'They wanted to torment you. They want to hurt you, Father.' That last word sticks in my throat but I need to appear soft so that my bite has more venom.

'Hurt me with their words?' I can hear him sweating.

'I think they already did that, didn't they? Were they repentant about their sexual activity or euthanasia or destroying relationships? Did you absolve them? Did your God let them get away with murder?'

'I—'

'Because they were laughing afterwards.'

'Why are you telling me this?'

'I'm confessing.'

'Confessing what?' He agitated.

'That I was eavesdropping on a conversation.'

'The church is empty and quiet, you cannot help what you heard.'

'I'm confessing that they want to hurt you.'

'That's not for you to confess. You have done nothing wrong.'

'Well, that's why I asked the question about getting forgiveness before you have done something wrong.'

'You're not making any sense.'

'One of those men is going to kill you, Father.'

'What? What are you talking about now? It's not funny to play games like this. Did you actually hear them say that? Are you just trying to cause trouble?'

I say nothing.

The air is so uncomfortable I find myself getting excited.

'Hello? Are you still there?' He is trying to collect himself, sound calm.

I give it another beat.

'You've got me. I have to confess. I am a liar. I find it hard to tell the truth. I don't know why I do it. Just the way I am, I guess. My grandmother always said I had the Devil in me when I was a child.'

A wait again but he is allowing me to speak.

'Am I supposed to ask for forgiveness for saying something that was not true?'

'It's okay. You are forgiven. It was a misunderstanding.'

He breathes.

I let him.

'Is there anything else you would like to discuss?'

I want to ask him some questions. Whether he has been moved around to different parishes. Whether he is attracted to young boys. Who he confesses to when he sins. Is it God? Does God always forgive? But I don't ask him anything.

I am in control.

'Well, you have already said that I can't confess prior to the misdemeanour but there's no way to ask you for forgiveness if you're dead. To be honest, for once, I don't really want it. I don't need it.'

'You said—'

'I know what I said but I'm a liar. I told you that. But let me tell you the truth, old man. Those men were here to tease you. They're not going to hurt you. They're not going to kill you. I am. Not now. Not tonight. But at some point. I just have to. You're on the list.'

I stop talking and he says nothing.

Perhaps he still doesn't believe me. Maybe he thinks it's another one of my ill-conceived jokes. Maybe he's having a heart attack. I don't know. I've already left the box and run out of the church before my words have had time to register in his feeble, old, God-fearing mind.

Our group has purpose.

The fun part comes when you get to make amends.

STEP **FIVE**

'Make a list of people that have harmed you.'

There's nothing. No sign whatsoever in the media that anyone I have killed has been found or reported. The homeless man bludgeoned in an alley across the road from a busy bar. That detective appears to have given up on ever finding Gary. The rapist cab driver. Clyde the wannabe psycho. Nothing. I mean, fuck, I just left Clyde near a bush. A bunch of lazy dogs being walked around that park, I tell you.

It's as though someone is following me around and cleaning up after me.

This lack of attention is the kind of thing that could make someone believe they are invincible, that they could stab a priest on Oxford Street and not get paid a second look.

It would be an issue if I was one of those psychopaths who wanted to be noticed. I'm happy to be getting this much luck.

I want to be careful.

I have Seth now.

I should stop.

But there's a list.

~~And I don't want to stop.~~

The Maynards are cleaning up in their area but, by God, are they stupid sons of bitches. Any whore giving them a cut of their hard-earned money deserves a dose of something pernicious or a week of pink eye.

You would think that anybody who considered themselves a gangster would want to keep that quiet. There's something so menacing about a quiet authority. No way should a career criminal have a social-media presence. If they have an account at all, it should be locked and visible only by family members that they trust.

Not The Maynards.

Hell, no.

Videos of them drinking, swearing, fucking about on the street. Fighting. Drinking more. Fondling women who don't want to be fondled. Acting like Al fucking Capone.

But here's the most stupid thing they have ever done: they fucked my friend in every hole and emptied their inbred, halfwit seed over her face and slapped her about for good measure. Then they posted where they are right now, which is eight minutes from where I am.

And here's something even more stupid: I've been doing this shit for longer than I can remember and I haven't been caught. So my plan is to find the two Maynard boys, cut off their dicks and stuff them in the father's mouth.

The next day, Jill is back at work. She's clearly still tender and there's some bruising around her eye but I think she has done an adequate job in covering it up with make-up.

'Morning, Maeve, you have a ten-thirty interview today. A replacement in the PR team.' She is very professional.

A pro.

I want to tell her that she should stop the weekend whoring. Maybe I could find some money to give her a pay rise. I don't think she'd quit. I don't think she can fully quit everything. Part of me wants to say that she doesn't have to worry about those Maynard idiots any more but that would be stupid; I don't want to draw any attention to myself.

I shake the travel mug I brought from home this morning.

'I'll bring your coffee in a moment. It'll be there before your computer has even booted up.'

'Thanks, Jill. Good to have you back.'

I'd forgotten about the interview because I didn't have Jill here to remind me. It's a PR position. Probably going to be someone straight out of university who doesn't really know what they want to do with themselves yet but they get on with people and they're positive and enthusiastic and they consider themselves to be creative.

The girl is what I expected. Blonde. Pretty enough. Wholesome-looking. With a name like Blair Conroy, you expect her to come from money but she's from some small backwater town that I've never heard of. She seems average. Run of the mill. Then she says, 'If I can be honest, I want to be in the city. I want to get away from my dead-end, Christian hometown and start living.'

I respect that. She has a huge bag with her. I ask her what she's carrying around and she says she snuck out and got changed on the train on the way. And that she would have to do the same on the way home. Her parents think she is meeting a university friend for lunch.

I don't know why she confides this in me and I don't care. She's sick of being surrounded by God-lovers and that seals the deal for me. She can start next week.

'You might have to commute for a while,' I tell her, screwing my face up at the prospect.

'Nope. I've already found somewhere to stay.' She smiles like her life is about to start.

I shake her hand and tell Jill to inform human resources.

'Not a problem.' She obliges.

I turn back to my office.

'Maeve, can I have a word?' She looks so small in her chair, I feel like I am towering above her.

'Of course. Go ahead.'

'In there.' She nods her head in the direction of my office.

'Okay.' I'm wondering whether she is thinking of handing her notice in, it has all got too much for her.

I sit behind my desk and offer the chair on the other side to Jill. She doesn't want to leave. She wants to join my group. Jill says she has had enough of AA and that she has a handle on her drinking – as much as an alcoholic can – and that she isn't getting anything from the groups any more.

'Can I come along to the next meeting of Psychopaths Anonymous?'

I'm sure I have already invited her but I have a lot to think about and a lot to drink, so I sometimes think things that I want to say and say things that I want to think.

'You want to join us on a Tuesday night, Huh?'

She nods.

'Well, of course you can, Jill. You're just about the craziest fucking person I know.'

†

Something strange happened last night. We followed our usual routine of eating, drinking, watching mindless television, drinking, fucking, drinking, but, when I wanted to go to bed, Seth didn't come with me. We always go up together.

He said he wasn't tired. He was going to stay up a while longer and maybe throw a film on. He opened a bottle of beer. And his laptop. Said he just wanted to clear his inbox, it had been a crazy day in the office.

And that's fine.

If it's true.

The problem is, it was different and it rattled me. So I couldn't sleep. I laid in bed with my eyes open and my ear strained to hear the sounds coming from the living room. Seth was watching a film. Lots of gunfire, so assume war or action. I could also hear his fingers tapping the keys on his laptop. He's very deliberate when he types, like he is pressing down the keys on an old typewriter, making sure they push as much ink as possible into the paper.

Then I thought I heard him speaking. It sounded like he said his own name.

'It's Seth.'

But who would he be speaking to at this time of night?

Was I hearing things?

I could go back down there. Sneak down. Remembering that the fifth step creaks. I could catch him in the act. But maybe it isn't anything sinister. He could deny it. It might be work-related, he's speaking to an overseas supplier – their machines are built in China – and I'd look like a crazy, jealous girlfriend.

I don't want to be lied to.

I don't want the uncertainty.

I don't want to feel gaslighted.

I need to know what is real and what isn't. Because, if I let things fester, I imagine the worst. And the result of that thinking is Seth ending up on my list. I don't ever want Seth on my list. I've never felt this close with anyone before.

I need him.

~~I love him.~~

I want his unconditional love and obedience in return.

Dennis Nilsen had Bleep.

Dahmer had Frisky.

I have Seth.

It's her first meeting, so she has to talk.

'Hi, I'm Jill ... and I'm an alcoholic.'

The psychos laugh. Jill is used to this part being a lot heavier. She continues.

'I'm also probably a sex addict. And according to Maeve here, I may well also be a psychopath.'

She sits down.

'That's it?' Sam Ramirez. Can't keep his mouth shut. Always so angry.

'It's her first week, Sam. Give her a break.'

I explain to Jill that this isn't like the meetings she's used to. It's not about feeling bad about who you are or giving yourself over to a God or the rest of the group. It's about realisation and empowerment and owning yourself.

Her face beams in a way I have never seen before.

'The group just wants to hear something about you. Something that might suggest that you belong here. Maybe you felt nothing when a parent died but locked yourself away for a week crying and listening to Joni Mitchell's *Blue* album on repeat when your dog had to be put down.'

Jill takes a moment to think. Then she stands up again.

'I don't know if this counts but ... I was a kid, maybe eight or nine. Maybe a bit older. I was on holiday with my parents and my sister. We were walking into the sea. I was on my own while my parents held my sister's hands because she is younger than I am. I remember taking a step and dropping under the water. I came up once but went back under and then I don't really remember much but it was green and cloudy and, even though there wasn't really any sound under there, it felt so noisy.'

I have no idea where she is going with this.

'The next thing I know, I am lying on the sand and the sun is in my eyes and there's air in my lungs and a male lifeguard with long, curly hair kneeling over me. And I used that air to laugh. I didn't thank God or the guy who had breathed life into me, I laughed. My parents always thought that was a strange reaction. And I don't know why I did it. I think that maybe it made me realise that I didn't fear death. Maybe it was that lack of fear that led me to make some of the stupid, risky decisions I made later in life. But I still feel that way.'

She waits.

'Is that the kind of thing you mean?' She looks at me for affirmation.

'Welcome to the group, Jill.'

'You're a friend of Maeve,' Sam Ram says to Jill and smiles.

'Well, I don't know about that, she's my boss, really.'

'Ha! No, that's what we call ourselves. Like the dolts across the hall call themselves "a friend of Bill".'

'Oh. I get you. Then, yes. I guess I am a friend of Maeve.'

'Right. All present and accounted for. Everyone is acquainted. Let's get on shall we?'

I tell them in Alcoholics Anonymous or any other twelve-step plan there is a very important part of the process where one has to take responsibility for the hurt that they have caused others as a result of their addictive behaviour. After making your searching moral inventory and pulling out your worst moments, you then have to attach those moments to the people that were affected.

You have to make a list of all the people that you have wronged because you wanted a fix of whatever it was that you craved. Maybe you stole money or got wasted and said hurtful things that you would never have said in a sober state. Maybe you were violent.

'And I'm sure that you all know the step that follows. You would have heard about it or seen it in movies or whatever, but I don't want us to jump ahead. Because I am not asking you to make a list of the people you have harmed.'

I tell them all that they don't have to apologise for who they are.

'I want you to make a list of the people who have harmed you. I'm guessing it won't be too difficult. When you're done, you need to speak with these people and make amends.'

He's usually the angriest guy in the room but, after I say this, I've never seen Sam Ramirez happier.

There's a colleague of Seth's, some sales guy from DoTrue, James. I don't know him but our paths have crossed a few times. Or maybe I just feel that way because Seth talks about him. It turns out that James is having a birthday party and has invited his friends. His neighbours. And some people from the office.

Seth had sucker-punched me with 'our' invite a month ago and I had reluctantly agreed, knowing I could get out of it nearer the time. But it meant so little to me and I wasn't looking forward to it at all, so I forgot.

'Are you sure you want to go to James's party, I know you don't really like him?'

This was Seth's attempt to guilt me into doing something I didn't want to do.

The only problem with this is that I don't feel guilt.

But I am forced to explain why I am reacting the way that I am. Because people don't understand a psychopathic mind.

'It's not that I don't like him, it's that I don't care for him. He doesn't mean anything to me. I'm happy to go to a party and drink and dance or whatever the plan is but I'm not going there for James, I'm going for you. James could drop down dead tomorrow and it wouldn't affect me in any way. I don't care about James.'

'Jesus, Maeve, it was all going so well until that last part.'

The problem is, the last part is the most important. That is the way I feel. Seth is going to the party so I might as well go because it means I get to spend time with him. But I don't care if I never see James again ever. He's not in my life. He's not a part of anything I do. And I don't see why it is unreasonable to explain it the way that I have.

'I mean, if Jill was having a party and asked us both, you'd want me to come. You'd want me to want to come.' He's trying to make a point.

'You wouldn't want to go to a party that Jill had put together, trust me. You'd need to get a tetanus shot beforehand.'

'I'm serious, Maeve. Look, you like Jill, so I have to make the effort with her. That's the deal, right?'

'I do like Jill. She's a bit screwed up but she's genuine and she means well. But I wouldn't give a fuck if she died, either. She's nice but what consequence does her life or death have on my existence? I'm the same either way. I could find another assistant. Besides, I already said that I would go to the stupid party.'

I did it again. I had him until the last part. He thinks I'm cold. I can see it. I chose the death explanation because I thought it best described the way I think about things. It's not meant in an evil way,

I just know how to remain detached from things that aren't important.

People go through lives thinking that their jobs are important or what other people think of them and say behind their backs is important. I don't.

'And what about me? What if I just died tomorrow? Would you miss me? Would you be upset?' He's getting emotional.

I had to go over to him and show him that I cared, lay a hand on his chest, look him in the eyes.

'Oh, Seth. You are different to everybody. I need you.'

He took it. He dropped the conversation.

I never actually said 'yes'.

This is why I don't like explaining myself.

And I don't like being pushed.

But it looks as though I am going to James's damn party.

The priest seems unfazed by his verbal waterboarding at confessional the other night. He's outside the door and peeking in through the window to see what's going on. To spy on us. It's quiet in here, though. Sedate. Everyone is writing names down on a piece of paper.

Sam Ramirez is acting like the enthusiastic swot in an exam, raising his hand every few minutes and asking for more paper. A lot of people have crossed him, it seems. I see the pleasure in his eyes. The guy wants havoc, mayhem and blood.

I have to respect his passion.

The priest doesn't look at me. He's scouring the room. His finger is wagging like he is counting the people in here. Perhaps he has a theory about who was involved in confessiongate. I told him the number of men who went in before me and his finger points at each man in our room, one by one.

There's no Eames here tonight. The maths doesn't work. It won't add up. He obviously didn't realise it was me because he does seem to be the feisty type. He would confront me or call the police. Maybe he's taking a look at Jill. He doesn't recognise her. It could have been her throwing threats through the partition.

I'm not sure how to play it. I could invite him in, ask him what he is doing. Keep it pleasant.

I don't want him to hear my voice.

So I ignore the old louse.

This is quite a baptism of fire for Jill. She's coming off the back of recent humiliation at the hands and fists and dicks of the Maynards so added them to her list. But it scares her to write their names down.

'I don't really know how to confront them about what they did, Maeve. You know the type of guy. Neanderthals. Real knuckle-draggers. I don't think there's any reasoning with people like that.'

I explain in no subtle way that amends cannot always be made with words, that she is right and you can't reason with the unreasonable.

'They scare you, Jill. I understand. Here. Look. Cross them off.'

'But doesn't that defeat the purpose of—'

'You've got plenty of other names on there.' I scan her sheet to make sure I don't see my own. 'Besides, I've got those pieces of shit on my own list. I'll cross them off for you. Kill three birds with one stone, so to speak.' I laugh.

Jill laughs.

She belongs here.

And Seth was right, I do like her.

Social media is the greatest and worst creation of all time.

You can see and hear people getting dumber by the minute.

It's the biggest legally addictive substance on the planet. I think I could clean up if I had a group called Social Media Anonymous (a frightfully accurate oxymoron). My group of six psychopaths would pale in comparison to the numbers I would provoke from a generation who lie about how happy their family is on Facebook or spend thirty minutes taking the perfect picture of their nourish-bowl lunch for Instagram or set up a separate trolling account on Twitter to hurl abuse at anyone ready to be offended by a faceless stranger.

Just by using your mobile phone as your alarm, you are ensuring that it is the first thing you see when you wake up in the morning and the last thing you see before you go to sleep. Temptation to scroll is always there. That is the same as an alcoholic sleeping with a bottle of vodka on the bedside table.

If you don't think it's addictive, try taking a phone away from a fifteen-year-old for two minutes and let them hear the notification tone of all the Snapchat messages they are missing. Now lock a heroin addict in an empty room and tell me the reaction is not the same. Only, it's much faster with the phone. Because these kids have to have everything instantly, even withdrawal symptoms.

Sure, there are people who have found lost relatives or old friends they have fallen out of touch with or they speak with their family more and that is a positive for most people.

Not me.

The one encouraging thing is that people have forgotten what thoughts are. They share everything. There's no filter, any more – unless it's being used to smooth out your wrinkles in a photograph or add a dog's tongue to that 'cheeky selfie'.

And this is how I find the Maynards.

Every feature of social media can be turned off. You can lock your account or you can shut down elements.

Want people to see your profile picture but none of your photos? Shut it down.

Want to update your 'friends' with some exciting news but not allow that bitch, Hazel, from secondary school, who you only accepted because you were curious about her weight gain but now can't delete because you want the higher ground? Shut it the hell down.

Want to beat up and degrade a struggling, single mother then go out on a pub crawl in the middle of the week and video yourself downing shots and talking crap about women and how good you are at fucking? Be born into the Maynard family.

Fuck, they are idiots.

I can see their pictures, their dates of birth, their relationship statuses, their location and their job titles of 'Thirsty Gangsters'.

They are making it too easy to find them and even easier to hate them.

The Good Mixer is a pub in Camden, known for its lively music and livelier atmosphere. I wonder whether they go there because it's loud and people can't hear that they're talking about illegal matters over a few pints. Although their recent post shows three shots on the table, including one with a flame on top.

I could sit here, on my sofa, and know almost everything about their evening but I want to get closer to them. I want to hear them speak. I want to see how they move. Do people in the pub know them? Are they scared? Are these two thirsty gangsters as much of a low-level joke as they seem online.

Nobody puts their real self online, do they?

The music is loud when I arrive. Ska music. The worst. I see they have a different band here every night of the week from a poster out the front.

The Maynards have no idea who I am or that I know Jill. I don't want to get too close to them because they seem like the type to letch over a woman on her own. I put my safety at risk by coming here in the first place, I understand that, but I'm not going to blow the long game.

They're inside at the bar. I move myself near them so that I can get a drink. They don't notice me. They are talking about a woman that one of them had sex with and it doesn't sound pleasant; I don't think both parties are reminiscing in the same way. It's so rammed in here, I could probably sink a screwdriver into one of the Maynards' kidneys and walk outside to finish my drink before anyone noticed.

It's tempting but I don't have a screwdriver with me.

I take the large wine I have ordered outside. There's a row of tables. I can see a space next to a young couple and assume they'll be okay with me perching on the end and pretending to look at my phone.

The Maynard boys are animals. They're bouncing around inside to the music. They're certainly not using the volume of the saxophone as a classic espionage trick to cover their devious plan for insider trading.

They are physically much larger than I am and no doubt stronger but it still doesn't feel like much of a challenge. Like a comedian playing to a crowd of stoners. Where's the pay off?

Nobody is treating them like local royalty. They just seem like a couple of young, ill-educated ruffians, drinking heavily and dancing hard on a weeknight.

But the atmosphere changes.

I see the old man walking in my direction. There's a swagger. He nods towards people as though greeting them, even if they haven't acknowledged him. He walks through the front door and the sea of people parts like he is Moses.

The boys stop jumping around and stand to attention. He gives them each an affectionate hug and a drink appears in his hand from somewhere. They clink glasses. The old man steps towards the nearest booth, I'm not even sure he says anything but the people sitting there all get up and the Maynards sit down.

It's confirmed.

The father is the one I want.

Cut the head off the monster.

Seth seems distracted tonight. Like he's not really here with me.

He smiled when he arrived and he kissed me. He rubbed his hands down my back in that way that he does, too. We ate – he ordered from a local fish restaurant that has recently started doing home deliveries.

The food was great.

The wine was great.

We didn't fuck, even though the meal came with a dozen oysters on ice in a polystyrene container. We don't need help with our libidos but aren't those things supposed to give it a kick-start?

For whatever reason, we sat on the floor. It was what people would describe as romantic. God, some might even call it 'cute'. But it worked and it was a bit different and it was comfortable.

Now I feel like he is waiting for me to either go to bed without him again or fall asleep on the sofa. He's edgy. I know that I sound paranoid, but I'm not imagining this. Something is off.

I wonder whether it has something to do with our argument over James's party. But he was so sweet all night until now. It's like he doesn't want to get too close. And I don't want to bring it up again because I'll end up saying something he doesn't understand; I'll inadvertently tell him that I wouldn't cancel my lunch plans if I found out my mum had hanged herself, or something.

I'm always content with taking risks but raking that up is just idiotic.

I decide to start an entirely different argument.

'What's going on, Seth?'

'Nothing.'

'You do this lovely thing of ordering in a delicious meal. We drink wine and laugh and now you are gone. You're somewhere else.'

'Why do you think I got that meal?'

'I don't know, because you're nice and thoughtful?' Another part of me thinks it's because he feels guilty about something but I keep that inside for now.

'I wanted to do something special.'

'Yes. That's what I said.'

'For our anniversary.'

'What?'

'You forgot?'

Here's the problem with that question, I drink alcohol every day. I can't quite put my finger on the moment that it all began but I do go through the wine. And I have done for a while. Two things that happen when you drink as much as I do: firstly, it makes you fucking paranoid. It can just be that you're a little more suspicious but it can develop into full delusions.

That's not me.

Secondly, it screws your memory. Short-term and long-term. You can stop drinking for a year and you might get some of that brain function back but if you keep going at it in a heavy manner, those things can get lost forever.

'I know that you probably think that women are all over that sort of thing but I'm really not that kind of woman. It's doesn't matter how long it's been, to me, just that you're here. I remember the time before you and I didn't like it as much, but I can't tell you exactly how long ago things changed.'

'Nine months.' He looks crestfallen. Of course he didn't focus on the important part of what I said, the bit about life being better with him in it.

I have a gift for making bad things worse.

'Nine months? That's not even an anniversary, Seth. I thought it might have been a year or something. Why would I think you were doing something special for nine months?'

'Why would you think it had been a year, Maeve?'

It feels like I'm losing him. And I don't want that.

But I won't apologise.

I put my hands on his legs because I can see that he wants to stand up, maybe just to cool off, but if I think he is trying to leave, I can't predict how that might make me act.

So I play the game. I hush him with some sweet words about what a lovely gesture it had been. I repeat the part about life being better now that we are together, hoping he hears it this time.

He stops twitching.

I kiss him.

He says, 'You're getting a bit forgetful in your old age, Maeve. This and James's party in the same week.'

He's masking what he feels with a very thin veil of humour. I want to tell him that I didn't forget about the damn party because of my memory, I deliberately pushed it out of my thoughts because I don't want to go.

I bite my tongue.

'I'm such an old lady.'

I bite his lip. Masking my own annoyance with flirtation and playfulness.

Seth doesn't brush off my advances. Things heat up. I know he wants it on the sofa again. And I'm sure he wants to put his hand around my neck. He loved it. He'd love it more tonight because he's definitely still upset with me for missing a made-up day.

'No. Come on. Let's go upstairs.' I take him by the hand and lead him to the bedroom. My bedroom. Which I hope will, one day, become our bedroom.

There's no choking or slapping. Seth stays on top of me the whole time. I like the way he looks when he's in that position, holding his weight up with his hands so that I can see his face and chest. He likes to look down at himself going inside of me.

I wrap my legs around his lower back and my arms around his shoulders to keep him pressed against me. He kisses my neck and pushes deeper into me. This is how I like it. He's not going anywhere. I have him.

Seth rolls to his side of the bed. I know that look. He's not going anywhere. No late-night calls tonight. He won't even be going back downstairs. He's hungry again but he wants to sleep and that's exactly what he does.

I lie and stare at him for a while. Innocent and pale.

Maybe I'd be less paranoid and forgetful if I stopped drinking all the time...

There's more chance of me quitting the killing.

STEP **SIX**

'Be truly willing to make amends with all the people whom you have harmed and have caused harm to you.'

It's Friday night, work has been difficult this week, and now I am getting ready to go to James's party. I have a glass of wine in my hand and three outfits laid out on the bed that I can't choose between. I'll ask Seth which one he likes best and flip a coin for one of the remaining two.

'I don't even know what the party is for. Is it his birthday? Did he get a promotion?'

~~Is it his nine-month anniversary party?~~

'It's nothing. That's the beauty of it. James and his wife throw a party every year for no reason. It's not on a specific date. They get a DJ and catering. There's booze but you're expected to bring something, too. They just think that there shouldn't always be a reason or event for people to get together and have a good time.' He seems genuinely excited.

'Wow. They're so crazy.' It's obviously sarcastic and Seth gives a light-hearted look that says, 'Don't start that'.

He sprays himself with some aftershave and pulls on his jeans. Clearly a smart-casual affair. I toss the black dress to the side.

'Oh, no. I love you in that.'

'I'm not sure it's that kind of non-event.' I settle on some tight jeans myself and appease Seth with a black vest top that I'm sure he likes because every time I wear it he comments on how amazing my arms look.

'Oh, that's not fair.' He wants me now.

'What do you mean?' I know what he means.

'You fucking know I love that look. How long until we need to leave?'

'Not long enough, you.' I'm playing the coquettish partner. I could easily unbutton my jeans, bend myself over the bed and let Seth take me quickly. We have time for a knee-trembler but I want to make him wait. I want to leave the house with him wanting me. I want to be at the party with him dying to get home for some drunken sex. He can fall asleep again straight after.

Not go downstairs.

Not use his phone.

I can control him.

The cab is eight minutes late. I manage to squeeze in another glass of Chenin Blanc and Seth downs a beer.

'Looks like we would have had time. Bastard cab driver.'

'Calm down, horn dog, we'll get there.'

James and his wife look like they have real-life Instagram filters. Soft, smooth, tanned skin and firm bodies. She is definitely one of the five percent of women who does not have a stretch mark or cellulite of any kind. I can't believe they drink because I think they hit twenty-five and stopped ageing.

They smile. White, straight teeth. Of course.

I hated them before I even arrived. I bet they're overly friendly.

'Seth, so glad you could make it.' James shakes Seth's hand. Music blares behind him. There's a hubbub of people. We are the fashionably late ones, it seems. 'And this must be Maeve.' He comes in for a kiss on the cheek. Just the one, which I wasn't expecting, they seem like the double-kiss kind.

'We've heard so much about you,' his gloriously stunning wife adds. I'm guessing her name is Chastity or Patience or Temperance or ... 'I'm Anna. James's wife.'

Anna? How dull.

I hand her a bottle of Champagne.

'That is very kind of you, Maeve. Thank you. James.' She presents the bottle for his perusal.

'Very kind,' he agrees. And they show us inside.

The decor is your classic 'live, love, laugh' aesthetic. Lots of individual pieces that everyone seems to have now. But the layout is perfect. The lounge leads straight into the kitchen and you can see out into the back garden in one straight line.

Beautiful people are drinking colourful drinks and not-as-beautiful people are conversing in corners with beer straight from the bottle. That's the camp that Seth and I seem to fall into.

Boring, beautiful Anna asks what we would like to drink. Seth asks for lager and I ask if there's any Champagne going around. I don't want to bring a decent bottle and get lumbered with some cheapskate's Prosecco or Cava.

Anna seems put out. Like she was saving that bottle for herself. She's waiting for me to show that I'm joking. But I'm not. So I don't.

'Sure. Of course. I'll be right back.'

I see cracks in the veneer.

And then, across the lounge, through the kitchen, out into the garden, under a shelter by the DJ booth, I see No Name #1.

†

I set fire to a few trees when I was fourteen years old. And that night, I wet the bed.

My father grounded me for a month because of the fire. And he was right to. You can't just go around setting fire to stuff as a kid. He shouted at me. But he didn't hit me. He didn't lock me in my room or make me sleep in the cellar with the rats and the tormenting sound of the boiler every time the heating clicked on or off.

He wasn't around that much because he worked hard, so my mother was left at home with me. But I didn't feel neglected. I didn't hate my father. I wasn't scared of him. From what I could understand, looking at other kids around me, it was a pretty normal set-up. The dad worked, the mum was at home with the kids, the dad would get home in time for dinner. On the weekends, you would have one day as a family and another where the dad played golf or went drinking with male friends. Sometimes, we'd all go out and he would drink with his friends.

What I am trying to express is that home life was normal. We weren't a happy family but we weren't struggling to pay the bills or anything, either.

The fire wasn't a retaliation of any kind.

I wasn't trying to release some pressure or pent-up anger.

There was no feeling of helplessness as a consequence of parental humiliation.

Four of us had a box of matches. Three of them wanted to use them to light cigarettes and see what it was like to smoke. I didn't care what it was like to smoke. Smoking was idiotic. It was unhealthy and it made you smell. I was happy to use my matches to set fire to leaves and twigs and old crisp packets.

We were crouched behind a bush, next to the park in front of my house. The smokers thought they looked cool but I had lost interest in them before they even started. I'd burned a few of the dry, brown leaves. I had a small twig alight and watched closely as an ant ran away from the encroaching heat.

There was an empty bird's nest on the floor that went up in flames quicker than I had expected. It set light to the bottom of the bush. That spread to the tree behind, which spread to another two trees. The fire brigade had to be called.

I owned up.

I don't know what happened with the bedwetting thing. I had my dinner in my room that night and my father said I wasn't allowed out – Mother was drinking in the kitchen, I think – so I stayed in my bedroom. I did as I was told. I was being punished for things that I had done.

It was fair.

A two- or three-year-old wets the bed and you understand it; they're learning, there are hiccups along the way. I had a few incidents when I was nine, and again when I was ten, but nothing since. So, at fourteen, in the wake of the fire, you'd be forgiven for thinking that it was something to do with feeling helpless or humiliated for getting myself into trouble.

Maybe it would be the start of a cycle where I would act out about the bedwetting by starting more fires.

But I didn't.

It was a one-off.

Left in my room all night, not even wanting to venture out to the toilet. Things must have built up.

The problem is, you get some armchair psychologist come up with a theory like the Macdonald triad and it seems to fit.

Three signs that your child is going to grow up to become a serial killer:

1) Persistent bedwetting after the age of five.

2) Fire-setting.

3) Animal cruelty.

It's ridiculous, really. All of those things seem more indicative of an unhappy home life, of abuse and rejection. I didn't have any of that.

I wasn't a violent child. I didn't cut up the neighbour's cat. I didn't experiment on my hamster or burn ants with a magnifying glass and the light from the sun. I just made a mistake while experimenting, as all kids do.

People are so quick to look for psychological indicators that a child may grow into a violent psychopath, that these things can be prevented if the signs and patterns are spotted early enough.

~~Idiots. Nobody can help being born.~~

But this assumes that killers are made.

Childhood was fine.

I'm just like this.

I never harmed a living thing until I was an adult.

I also didn't have my first drink until I was eighteen.

No Name #1 hasn't seen me yet and I wonder whether he will adhere to our code of anonymity. I don't want Seth to know about Psychopaths Anonymous but I also want to test its strength.

Where the fuck is perfect Anna with my drink?

'What do you want to do? Mingle? Dance?' I ask Seth. I know he will need a few drinks before he starts showing his best moves but No Name #1 is outside and I want to get out there.

'Shall we have a few drinks first? Loosen up the legs a bit.'

He puts his hand around my waist and pulls me into him. He kisses me and whispers something into my ear about how much he wants me. It's hot. Maybe he is marking his territory in a room full of salubrious youngsters, quaffing their gin and juice, but I don't care about that. He can show me off. He can piss in a circle around me, if he likes. Just don't leave me alone with wrinkle-free Anna and her Ken Doll husband.

She returns with Champagne in a bowl glass rather than a flute. Greater volume. My respect for her inches up a notch.

'I've put your bottle in the fridge. I'm sure we'll get to it.'

I hate that. You turn up to a party with a bottle of something expensive and the host palms off their crap onto you, leaving your quality Pinot Noir for themselves while offering you some supermarket own-brand Merlot.

I want to say something witty and cutting but Seth interrupts.

'Oh, don't you worry, Maeve will get through anything you've got. She may be petite but she can handle herself with the fizz. Last woman standing. I guarantee.' And he winks.

There's so much wrong with this.

Firstly, he's acting like I'm some kind of lush, when I'm not. I'm a drinker. There's a difference. In the same way there is a difference between a mum and a mother or an author and a writer.

I've never thought of myself as petite, either. I have curves. I am womanly. I'm guessing he was avoiding the word 'small'.

Seth, never say fizz. Ever again. It might help you fit in at some of the bars in Hampstead but not in my home.

Still, he was right. I will get to that Champagne and I will be the last one standing. And I'm pleased he used 'woman' rather than 'person' or even 'man', in an ironic way.

I down the contents of my glass.

'Whew. Just a bit parched from the journey over here.' Then an obvious aside, 'Little fella couldn't keep his hands off me.'

I hold out my empty glass towards vaginally rejuvenated Anna.

'You want to just show me where the fridge is? This could take all the fun out of your night, otherwise.'

I know this couple is fake. And Seth is putting on some kind of act, too – though I find his less offensive – I'm guessing he just feels anxious or awkward. So I am playing up a bit, but I also want them to know that I'm on to them. Hopefully they'll just avoid me now, and Seth and I won't get invited over for dinner or anything in the future.

'Of course. Follow me.' The genetically flawless Anna doesn't break character. I purse my lips towards Seth in a jokey 'fuck you, I'm off' and he responds with a playful roll of the eyes before starting up a conversation with James.

There are groups of people hanging around in the kitchen. White granite worktops, white slab cupboards with stainless-steel handles, white tiles, white walls. Soulless. Sterile. Fitting.

Anna's manicured hand with French polished nail tugs at the giant, stainless-steel door of the double-sized refrigerator.

'So, that side is beers and mixers and this side is wine and bubbles.'

Oh, God. Bubbles. Please, let's go back to fizz. I don't want to kill anyone tonight.

'Now, I can't remember exactly which bottle is yours but there's plenty to work through.' She shows me her porcelain gravestone teeth, so white they make her kitchen seem dull.

There are maybe eight or ten bottles of Champagne in there that are the same as the one I brought to the party.

Well played, Anna.

I thank her, take a bottle that is open already and fill my glass.

She tells me to just help myself to whatever and totters off, back to the living room with her thigh gap and bleached anus.

There's about half a bottle left once I have poured myself

another glass. I contemplate putting it back in the fridge but just hold it by the neck in my right hand, glass in the left, and I kick the door shut.

As it closes, I am greeted by some smarmy singleton on the prowl. Too much product in his hair. His T-shirt has no creases. He's too confident.

'So, who do we have here?' That's his opener. Talking to me like he is browsing for something on a used car lot.

I stare at him, say nothing, and take long a swig from the glass. Then I top up what I've taken out from the bottle.

'Ooooh. Party girl, eh? Me likey.'

'Are you fucking kidding me? Does this shit ever actually work?'

'I'm just trying to be friendly.'

'You're coming across as a pest.'

'That's a good note.'

Damn. It was quick response and I have to hold back a laugh.

'You're beautiful when you smile, you know that?'

'Oh, God. And you were doing so well.' I roll my eyes dramatically.

'Are you going to tell me your name or not?'

I think about saying, 'not', and walking off.

'Tell me your name, motherfucker.' So I can put you on my list.

'Hey. Hey. I'm sorry. I was just nervous about meeting you. I'm a friend. Really. I'm a friend of Maeve.'

I'm rooted to the spot. He turns and leaves.

How did he know about that? How has he heard about being a 'friend of Maeve'? It must be someone from the group. It could be Eames. He has left. He could be talking to anybody. Everybody.

He's on the list.

It won't be Jill. I could text her and ask if she has said anything. It's the paranoia thing again. Fuck.

Did that just happen?

I drink.

I top it up.

I don't know how to get in contact with Sam Ram or Bob or Jake

Killey. I know that Eddie is a surgeon but there are hundreds of hospitals he could work at. Hell, he could be lying.

But there is somebody I can speak to. He's outside this very building. And he's the only one from the group whose name I do not know.

You hear about the Black Panthers and you probably think of Huey Newton or Bobby Seale.

If somebody talks about the Nation of Islam, some might recall Elijah Muhammed but most people will think of Malcolm X.

I say Branch Davidians, you say David Koresh.

FBI. J. Edgar Hoover.

Suffragettes. Emmeline Pankhurst.

They had a leader. A visible head of their organisation.

I like the idea that Psychopaths Anonymous could generate a much larger following but the anonymity is important. It's all well and good to have the 'friend of Maeve' in joke but I don't want groups to spring up that use it as their name.

I don't want Bristol Friends of Maeve.

I don't want Windsor Lack of Empathy or Swindon Risk/Reward or Ilford Manipulation Management.

It was disconcerting to have someone seemingly know me but also a buzz. And I think that came from the espionage element of his reveal. The subterfuge. He didn't come out and mention the group, it was a verbal wink. Sure, he pranced around it for a minute with slimy flirtation but he got there in the end.

And it's got me thinking ... Can it be done? Is there a way to be the leader of Psychopaths Anonymous without anyone outside of the group knowing that I started it? Can you be the leader of a group and maintain your anonymity? I've always thought that cult leaders let their status go to their heads and that is one of the reasons these things often end so badly.

Newton, Koresh and Malcolm X were all assassinated. Was there a way they could have got their messages across without being known, without being in the spotlight?

Is there a way to set up a cult where nobody knows you are the leader?

No Name #1 pauses for a microsecond when he sees me. It's so subtle but I clock it. I don't know whether he is shocked that we've ended up at the same place in our personal lives or whether he somehow knew I would be here.

The snake at the fridge knew me.

Maybe there are more.

Maybe everyone here is on to me.

'Hey, DJ. Do you have Kokomo?' He's been playing contemporary dance and pop hits since I got here. He could download the Beach Boys' back catalogue in minutes, but this isn't the place.

'I'm sorry, miss. I don't have that one, I'm too young and attractive.' He smiles, twists a few knobs, presses a button or six and one song melts into another.

Everybody at this party seems to have an inflated sense of self. Every last beautiful one of them. I take a look around and it's like the Stepford wives all found Stepford husbands. Where the hell did all these people come from? I do a lot of work with various tech companies and almost zero percent of the employees scrub up this well. I've seen uglier contestants on *America's Next Top Model.*

'What are you doing here?' I ask.

No Name #1 doesn't answer me straight away. He holds one hand on his right headphone and bobs his head along to the beat of the track, then carefully slides something to the right to bring up the sound on the next track.

Then, 'What do you mean? I'm the DJ.'

He's playing it so much cooler than the fridge guy.

'Nobody is listening. It's okay.'

He looks around, seemingly as paranoid as I am.

'I'm doing what you said I should do.'

'What I said?'

'Yes. Step six. Make amends with people.' He holds out an empty glass and flicks his eyes towards the bottle in my hand. I hold it up to the light to make sure there will be enough left for me if I pour No Name #1 a drink. I'm not sure, so I finish my glass, top it up and pour whatever is left into his.

'Well, fuck. The kindness of strangers, eh?'

'I'll drink to that.' I raise my glass and laugh.

I ask him how deejaying for a cult of thriving narcissists was making amends with anybody. He tells me he's doing the gig for free. He'd been hired for their weird, little *Eyes Wide Shut* thing a year ago and he'd managed to get a lot of business out of that one gig. He was being hired all over town. Private functions. Corporate gigs. So, when James called him in a panic saying that the live band he'd booked for this year had fallen through and asked whether he would be interested in doing it again, No Name #1 jumped at the chance.

He said he'd do it for free.

'I'm not sure you caught the point I was trying to make. You're not supposed to do something nice for someone who has helped you out. That's not making amends. That's not what I meant.' I look over my shoulder. Seth is walking through the kitchen with James, towards me. I don't have much time left with No Name #1 on my own.

'Oh, I think I did get it. I'm not here for James, I'm here because I fucked his wife in every way imaginable and she fucking called it off with a text and ghosted me.'

I almost spit my drink out but I don't like to waste alcohol.

'You fucked Anna.'

'All the ways you can think of plus a few you couldn't dream up. Kinky as shit. Into all that cosplay stuff. Insisted on wearing a mask all the time. At first, I thought they had one of those open relationships but it was clear after a few times that she was just a cheat.'

'This is so beautiful.' My grin will not be contained.

'Honestly, though, Maeve, if you are not into all of that mask-wearing, sex-show, wife-swapping nonsense, you might want to book a cab in advance because things are going to get a bit gropey after midnight. Who knew being rich and beautiful was so fucking boring, eh?'

He holds a finger up to me and goes back to his station, flicking switches tapping along to a song that sounds about twenty years too young for me.

No Name #1 is still fiddling about with things when Seth and James come over.

'Hey, you. What are you doing out here? Dancing already?'

James looks down at the empty Champagne bottle in my hand. Seth only looks at my eyes. He can see only me.

'Can you believe this guy doesn't have Kokomo?'

Seth laughs.

James fake laughs.

It wasn't even a full bottle. And I gave some to the DJ. Who fucked your wife behind your back, James. You poor, cuckolded sap.

'This is such a great party, James. Thank you so much for inviting us.'

'You're welcome. There's plenty more to come. Are you both okay for drinks?'

I'm about to tell him that it's not a problem, I know where to get them from, when Seth steps in.

'We're okay, actually, James. Thank you. The legs feel a little looser, I think we're going to dance. Right, Maeve.'

'I guess so.' I place the empty bottle next to the DJ booth but keep the rest of my drink. I take Seth by the hand and start to strut backward towards the other dancing idiots.

'I should probably go and find Anna, anyway.'

He probably should. The house is deceptively larger than it looks and she could be in any of a number of rooms, balls deep with one of the guests.

'What the fuck was that? Who are you right now? "Thanks so much for inviting us." That was a bit of a turnaround.' He imitates my voice badly.

'It's called *making an effort*, my dear.'

I'd love to try to enjoy the night but I know Seth came here last year because he knew James from before DoTrue. And I wonder whether he was so adamant about going because he wants to put a mask on and share things about when this day ticks into the next.

I should just ask him but I always find a way to make things more complicated.

'I know things were getting pretty hot before we got here and we've already spoken about getting back home but I think it'll be okay to stay later if that's what you really want.'

'Well, I was going to talk to you about that. I booked a cab to come and get us just after midnight.'

'Very presumptuous.'

'Ha. Well, of course I want to get you back. But ... I didn't want to say anything at the time because it already seemed like you didn't want to come and I kind of have to because of work and...'

'Spit it out already.'

He leans in closer to me.

'I know it all looks pretty glamorous but let's just pilfer the good drinks and get out while we can. Things will turn a bit debauched later.'

I look at him as though I have no idea what he means.

'Trust me. It's best we just go. And we can have ourselves to ourselves.'

We dance like fools beneath the stars, surrounded by some of the most attractive people in North London and it feels like we are the only ones here.

Me. And my man, Seth. The liar.

The switch started happening at around fifteen minutes after midnight. And things descended pretty quickly.

I'd been trying my hardest but eight bottles of Champagne is too much, even for me; no way I was getting through them. Seth wasn't that much help because he was working his way through whiskies that he had never tried before. I think I could have made it if I'd come here with Jill but bringing her would only have only ended with me shutting the door on her, down on her knees, with eight naked men rubbing themselves hard for her.

It feels like everyone is dancing, then suddenly they are not.

I look over in one corner and two men are kissing like it's leading somewhere. Nothing out of the ordinary. It's a party. People are going to hook up.

Seth nudges me, nods his head over his shoulder for me to look. There's a couple, a man and a woman, sitting either side of another woman and they are kissing either side of her neck. They each have a hand on the inside of one of her legs.

'It's happening,' he mouths.

I screw my face up.

'What?'

Seth looks at his watch and nods to himself as if telling himself that he's right. He beckons me closer.

'We don't have that long until the cab comes,' he assures me.

'Or one of those guys in the corner by the looks of it.'

No Name #1 is standing in the DJ booth with his hands behind his head. It looks strange. He's not spinning discs or swiping at buttons. His eyes aren't even open. I see him shudder and, a few seconds later, a woman's head rises.

He's very open about his promiscuity so this isn't as much of a shock as the blossoming threesome over Seth's shoulder.

'Let's get off the dance floor before it becomes the orgy epicentre, shall we?'

'Good idea.' Seth takes me by the hand and leads me back towards the kitchen. 'Let's grab a bottle of something nice each. I reckon we can probably just walk out the front door. Everyone is gearing to get sucked or fucked in some way.'

It's worse in the kitchen.

Some drunk bikini model (probably) lying on the dining table, her clothes bunched around her neck, her breasts on show, is being fucked by some guy while everyone watches. He has her legs spread apart and is holding her by her ankles as he thrusts in and out.

It's not like a Kubrick film, nobody is wearing a mask and, strangely, nobody is filming anything on their phone.

It's an anonymous group.

Maybe James and Anna are the leaders, it's their party, but maybe they are just supplying a venue. This could be a monthly thing they all get together for.

I'm no prude but I don't want to be in here.

I don't want to hear a mob cheer some stud's climax.

I signal with my hand that I'm going to the fridge and point Seth in the direction of the whisky. He looks like a naughty schoolboy. It's cute. Funny, even.

There are three bottles of Champagne left that are the same brand as the one I brought but the spaces have been filled with some other option. I don't know who has been refilling and restocking but I haven't seen Anna since we arrived.

I take one. For the road.

'Where's your bag?' Seth is back next to me and has a bottle in each hand. A Macallan and something else; I can't see the label.

'What?'

'Your bag.'

'I don't have a bag. I never had a bag.'

'What the fuck? How are we supposed to get this out?'

'Calm down, Seth. You don't have a balloon filled with cocaine stuffed up you. We're not crossing the border. It's a bottle of booze. We're going to walk out the front door.'

'That's your plan?'

'That's my plan. I'd just like to say goodbye to our hosts.'

I want to laugh but there's a moan of apparent pleasure from the dining table before the man announces that he's going to come.

It's our cue.

No Name #1 is back to mixing tracks. I'm guessing he is going to enjoy making amends this evening. A different couple has taken over the dining table. A woman has been bent over it while the man is on his knees behind her, burying his face in her scent.

We just need to get down the hallway and out the front door but the corridor appears to have grown limbs, there's no way we are getting down there without touching someone or being touched. I take the lead.

People are being pressed against the wall. They're kissing or stroking or licking or biting. One man has his dick in his hand as he watches a couple who are minutes away from penetration. I reach my hand back and grab Seth by one of the wrists; he won't let go of his whisky.

We get to the door relatively unscathed.

Then, 'Seth. Maeve. Going so soon? Things are just getting going.' James's smile is unsettling. I can see how turned on he is now that the party has evolved into what he has been wanting from the start.

I hold the bottle of Champagne behind my legs but Seth has frozen with the stolen whisky in plain sight. I speak to take James's focus in my direction.

'Great party, James. Thanks so much but we have a stupidly early start in the morning.'

'Maybe next time,' he says, as though we've missed out on a game of tennis. He doesn't really care about us. There's more than enough flesh on display for his amusement.

He asks if either of us have seen Anna recently. I'm guessing she's in some darkened area getting filled out like an application form but I tell him that I saw her getting friendly with the DJ. He tries to hide his jealousy, bids us farewell and paces off through the corridor of wandering hands and out into the garden.

Seth shrugs his shoulders and lifts up both bottles of whisky. It makes him laugh. Which makes me laugh.

Our cab is waiting outside.

It's not a long drive home but takes a little longer because part of Hampstead appears to have been closed off with police tape and we have to take a slight detour.

I pop the cork in the driveway and send it shooting out into the street. Seth's hands are full and I pour Champagne straight into his mouth before taking a swig myself.

I want him.

Inside. Shoes off. Whisky down. Kiss. Drink. Kiss. Zip. Wall.

Those shameless swingers don't know what they're missing. Seth picks me up in the doorway of the lounge. I wrap my legs around him and he pushes my back into the frame. I still have the Champagne. I drink. I pour. We kiss.

He takes me into the lounge and sits me on the back of the sofa. It's the perfect height. I hand him the bottle and take off my top and bra. He hands it back, pulls my underwear to the side and moves forward between my legs, pressing himself against me.

I don't let go of the bottle the entire time we are fucking. With my free hand, I pull on Seth's hair and dig my nails into his back. We drink and fuck and sweat and, when we are done, we lie on the sofa, sharing the last of the Champagne and breathing heavily. Our clothes are screwed up or torn or wet with sweat and booze.

'That's how it's done,' Seth says.

Two people. No audience. No strangers.

'Yes. Good work, soldier.'

I don't want to move. I want to just bask in this moment for a little longer. I'm not thinking about anything other than where I am now and who I am with. It's silent apart from our breathing.

And then the television turns on.

'What are you doing?' I ask.

'Putting the TV on. I figured we could watch something while we have a nightcap of posh whisky.' His usually disarming smile isn't working because he's ruined the mood and the moment somewhat.

The screen shows a house surrounded by police and tape. The bottom right corner says that the scene is taking place in Hampstead.

'Must be the bit that was shut off on our way home.' Seth suggests.

We both sit up.

'Turn it up,' I tell him.

The reporter is saying that the authorities have been hunting this man for over a year and believe him to be responsible for several murders across the capital.

And then we see it, a dishevelled detective is escorting a man from the building. He's handcuffed. His head hangs low but you can see his face on the camera.

It's Eames.

LIST OF PEOPLE I HAVE (RECENTLY) HARMED

THE PRIEST

~~CLYDE~~

~~JAMIE KEACH~~

THE MAYNARDS

EAMES

STEP **SEVEN**

'Continue to take your personal inventory. Continue to make amends. Continue to spread the word.'

It's all anyone is speaking about when I get to work.

There has been a serial killer in our midst.

~~You stupid, ignorant idiots.~~

The majority of murders are committed by somebody that the victim knows. This is not something that differs from country to country, culture to culture. Crimes of passion. Momentary lapses in judgement or sanity. There's a fascination with somebody who kills for sport. For the hunt. Because they enjoy the way it feels.

There's the distance of miles and time to the golden age of serial killers, who dominated the headlines in America in the sixties and seventies but when one shows up in your neighbourhood, that fascination you once had turns into fear.

Whispers of 'you never really know a person' and 'one could be living next door' permeate the morning with a hiss.

Jill is at her desk, hitting the keyboard loudly with her heavy fingertips. She swivels in her chair as though she feels my presence.

'I'm guessing you've heard...'

'It's all over the news.' I stop and take a gulp of the coffee I brought from home. My head feels like I drank nearly eight bottles of Champagne last night and I can still sense Seth between my legs.

'I think people are freaking out because it's so close to home.'

'The guy got caught, what is there to freak out about? He can't kill anyone now.'

Jill gives me a look that says, 'Oh, yeah. I never really thought of that.'

'Can you hold all my calls for the next hour, Jill?'

'Of course. You need more coffee?'

'Strong and black.'

I walk into my office and shut the door.

Within seconds my computer whirs into life and I'm clicking and scrolling my way through the tabloid and broadsheet websites and all the news channels to glean as much information as possible.

Names. Dorothy Penn. Amy Mullica. Carla Moretti. Richard Pendragon. Stacey Blaine. All killed in some strange and horrific ways by a man that I know. Someone I thought was charming and interesting and mysterious. Someone who wanted to protect me from Clyde, it seemed. Someone who was a member of a group that I started. A group called Psychopaths Anonymous. Someone who always had the potential to be violent.

It's a small group but I already know for certain that two of us have killed people. Maybe there's more. Sam Ramirez may not have done anything yet but he certainly seems as though he would gain some satisfaction from doing so.

No Name #1 seems like he is more of a sex addict but fucking around the way he does is a surefire way to get yourself into scrapes with people in the height of passion.

Maybe Bob is into more than revenge.

Maybe Eddie works as a surgeon because it gives him the power to decide who lives and who dies.

Maybe Jake. Maybe all of them.

At some point, every one of these men could be showing up on a news feed for something they did that they hoped would never be found out.

You think there are fewer female serial killers out there than male?

Or is it that the men are stupid and narcissistic enough to get caught?

Seth calls me on my mobile phone. He feels rough. Last night was too much for him. I'd left him in the house this morning, he was in the shower as I picked up my coffee to leave. I don't like him being there alone for too long.

He sounds tired. Groggy.

'Everything okay?' I ask.

It turns out that the scalding shower had not been enough to wash away the pain in his head from all that whisky, or the images of all that depravity. Seth tells me he got dried but didn't get dressed and got straight back into bed. In fact, he has only just woken up.

'Did you call work?'

It turns out that a few people from the office had called in with something that morning so it looks like they all have the same bug. I wasn't introduced to any of Seth's DoTrue colleagues at the party but I'm guessing some were there and have woken up in a much sorrier state than Seth.

My brain starts clicking.

Have I left dirty underwear anywhere that he could find it? Will he go looking for my vibrator? Who is in the freezer? Will he count the bottles in the recycling box? What have I overlooked that could alert him that Eames is not the only local psychopath?

'I know you find it a bit weird if I'm here and you're not but I hope it's okay as a one-off. I honestly feel like utter shit. I'm going to stay in this bed in this position until you get home and then, if you want, I'll stay and make you some dinner but it's probably best to have a night off the drinking.'

I love that he understands how I feel – I don't need questions about why I keep a drill underneath the bed or why there is half a car that I still need to dispose of in the garage. But I also don't need somebody telling me when I should or should not drink.

'If you're feeling that bad then you probably shouldn't drink anything this evening.' My subtle way of saying that I managed to get up, get ready and drive myself to a full day of work, so, if I want a glass of wine when I get in, I will damn well have one.

I'm nervous but I tell Seth to stay in bed, sleep it off. I'll head straight home after work with a sports drink to help replace his electrolytes. We can order some food if he's up to it.

'You're the best, Maeve. I love you.'

'Okay, see you later.'

I know I shouldn't keep avoiding it and I'm sure that I feel it, I just don't know about saying it.

There's a knock at my office door.

'Come in,' I call out, so that Seth can hear. Then, to him, 'Got to go. Rest.'

Jill brings my coffee in. She's looking healthier.

'I'm not sure any work is going to get done out there today. I think people are really shaken up about this thing.'

It's not that they're shaken up, it's that they are fascinated. It's the same morbid curiosity that has passengers craning their necks to search for death or mutilation at car crash sites. Even though it's now very real, it still doesn't feel it.

It's like the fascination with reality television. The twelve people stranded on the island are real people but the situation they have been thrust into is not a reflection of anybody's life. There are real people that have been killed but the idea of a serial killer living in the next street is absurd because they only exist in books and films and urban legends.

'Well, I hope it's not distracting you too much.'

'No. I'm fine. I've seen some things, Maeve.'

There's a knowing silence between us.

She's seen her fair share of beatings and sexual assaults but a news site said that one of Eames' victims was found with her ankles and wrists bound together behind her and 156 cigarettes stuffed into her mouth and lit. Having the Maynards wipe their dicks on your curtains before they leave does not prepare you for that image.

Part of me doesn't really want to bring it up but there's going to be a lot of talk at our next meeting.

'I knew him, Jill.'

She wants to say 'What?' but it won't leave her mouth.

'He was part of the group.'

I want to go to Pilates. That's what I tell him.

Another lie.

The foundation upon which our relationship is built.

Seth is in the kitchen when I get home from work. He's sitting at the table with a cup of coffee and there is half an onion on the side that has been diced and left on the chopping board.

'Hello, lightweight. You're up, then?' I kiss him on the cheek. I imagine that this is how a married couple might act.

He tells me that it hasn't been that long. That he tried to make a dinner but cutting up the vegetables had turned his stomach so he sat down.

'I said I'd order in. Don't worry about that. Get this in you.' I hand him the bottle of sports drink I picked up at the petrol station on the way home. Then I'm at the fridge and I'm pouring myself a glass of wine. I don't even realise I've done it until Seth comments, it's my habit now.

'Jesus, Maeve, you're an animal. I feel like I've been hit by a truck.'

'You're not getting any younger, those hangovers will stay around all day if you let them.'

The trick is to never let yourself be fully sober.

I say that it's just one glass because work has been crazy today and there was a real knock to morale because of 'the guy that got picked up by police from around the corner'. I have to check myself from referring to him by name.

'Just one before I head out to Pilates. It's good for my mind and my relaxation.'

'The wine or the Pilates?'

Both. Although the Pilates isn't real.

'Ha. The Pilates, of course. Stretch things out. Relieve some tension.'

I should really look into what Pilates even is.

Seth offers to come with me. 'Yeah. Maybe it would be good for me, too. Blow off the cobwebs. Get me centred or whatever.'

'You'd be better off centring yourself on the couch with a glass of water.'

'No. Really. I could come with you. We could do it together.'

'That doesn't work for me.' I see his reaction, his rejection, and I know I need to tone down the psychopathic response a little. 'It's just that, I really love having you here, it's great. I'm glad you felt comfortable enough to stick around all day. I just ... well, it's something I have that's just for me, you know? Those things are important in any relationship.'

He takes a moment to think it over. It's a little more rational than my immediate response.

'Of course. You're right. Of course you're right. How long will you be?'

'A couple of hours. Not long. We can eat when I get back'

'Yeah. I should probably open the laptop and see what I've missed today. I found a file on a shared drive that has the details of all our end users. Email addresses. Contact telephone numbers. Products purchased. I'm trying to collate it into some kind of directory. Might be useful. Maybe you could use it for marketing.'

'There you go. Work on that. Clear your emails and I'll be back before you know it.'

I take my glass of wine upstairs and get changed. I have to find something that looks like I could wear it to work out, so that Seth thinks I am at an exercise class, but also not too casual that the psychopaths I am going to see think I have come straight from the gym. I don't really own any activewear but I have some black leggings and a grey vest. I stuff a jumper into a bag, finish my wine and head back downstairs.

I say goodbye to Seth, who is already in the lounge with his laptop open. He tells me to enjoy my class and I thank him.

Then I'm back in the car and heading over to the community centre so that I can talk about the local serial killer with a bunch of people that knew him for a short time before I let them know that I am shutting down the group.

†

I'm deliberately late. If I get there too early, I'll have to speak to Bob about Eames and what a shock it was to see that on the television. Then Jake will arrive and say how Eames always seemed like a stand-up guy. I already know how cocky No Name #1 will be after getting his balls drained by three different women at the party, I don't want to also have to have the same conversation five times about our former member.

I don't apologise for my tardiness. It was deliberate. I don't feel sorry.

I can't.

'Okay. The plan for today was to discuss how we are getting on with our making-amends lists. Hopefully we will get to that but I know that you are all dying to talk about what you've seen in the news. That one of our former members has gone off and killed a bunch of people.'

In no other setting would I be able to speak so matter-of-factly about such a subject.

'Remember that guy who was delivered in a box to Canary Wharf with his dick cut off? That was Eames that did it.' Of course, Sam Ramirez has a new idol. But nobody in the group is shocked to their cores. We may as well be discussing the football scores down the pub.

'Killed a woman with a bow and arrow, too.' Eddie chimes in.

Eddie isn't always fully in the room. I sense some kind of compulsiveness. He's always counting. He pinches his fingertips on one hand then does the same on the other. If he scratches his left shoulder, he has to scratch his right. There is something unbalanced about the way he seems to crave balance.

Now I know that Eames is like me, I'm looking for signs in everyone.

Sometimes, when you want something badly enough, you make it fit your theory.

The things you are seeing, you are not really seeing.

The things you think you are doing, are not really being done.

I think Jill is staring at No Name #1. Statistically, based on the number of people they have fucked between them, their paths may have crossed. There's no way he pays for it but Jill is always happy to give it up for free.

Perhaps I'm forcing that.

'If you ask me, it's a waste of time talking about the guy. I mean, talk about an unrecoverable relapse.' And he laughs.

Jake Killey joins in. 'What do they say at AA? "Even a sip is a slip." I don't know what the equivalent is for this situation.'

And then they try to come up with something for four minutes. None of them are any good. 'A kill is a spill' was probably the best and that wasn't great.

No Name #1 says that he crossed Anna off his list. He had planned to go to the party to torment her and leave her wanting him because she hadn't really given him any closure, he was going to do the same to her. He tells the story about the stranger in his DJ tent, going down on him for no other reason than the fact they were both in the same place at the same time.

But he couldn't stay away from Anna. A few drinks and a blow job and he wanted to see her. He found her in the utility room, sitting on the counter above the washing machine, kissing some guy that wasn't her husband, James. She was shocked to see him. He told the guy to get away from her. 'She's mine.' He left. And No Name #1 stuck it to Anna one last time. He didn't talk to her, just fucked, finished on her stomach, and left.

He found the room where James was watching two people having sex. And somehow, No Name #1 ended up fucking Anna's husband.

'Honestly, by that point, there was nothing left. I blew a puff of smoke into the guy from behind and I got the fuck out of there. Screwed them both with a dirty, little secret. Cross them off.'

He looks proud of himself.

'Sounds like a pretty dirty lifestyle those guys are leading, man. I bet they've got a fuck-load of secrets.' Jake isn't convinced.

Eddie tells us how some idiot got drunk, drove his car into a couple, killed one of them and ripped his arm off in the process. Eddie had to operate on the selfish prick and reattach the severed limb.

'If I'm operating on my own, you know that I'm either putting it on the wrong way round or I'm leaving it off ice for just long enough that it can't go back on. But I can't do that because there's a team of us in there.'

'So, what did you do?' Bob asks. 'Cut some nerves so he can't grip? Something like that. Can you do that?'

Eddie smiles.

'I like your style, Bob. I mean it. Nobody does revenge like you. But, no. I successfully reattached his arm. And I added him to my list.'

There's not a lot of time left. I have been so focussed on everybody this evening that I haven't looked out of the door once. The priest could have been there the entire time. I don't care.

'I'm glad we seem to be progressing with this latest step. It's really a case of continuing to take that personal inventory now, and continuing to make amends. Now, ideally, we would like to start spreading the word, putting out our message, recruiting, but I think, in light of recent circumstances, we have to shut down the group for a while.'

They all say something at once:

We've only just started/what has it got to do with us/we can't just quit.

Sam Ramirez and Eddie don't say anything and I understand that they are in the same boat as me. Having a convicted killer among us will draw attention to the group in a negative way. I can't have that. I still have a dead rapist taxi driver's car in my garage and, from their silence, I am guessing that Sam and Eddie are the ones that may also have their own violent stories they would like to remain hidden.

I want to let them know that I know. Just a look. A glance.

One killer to another.

Jill pipes up. She wants to know whether we should all stay in touch, whether they could still meet up without me.

I glare at her. I know I'm doing it.

'You try to take over what I started and I will cut out your diseased womb while you watch. You fucking parasite. After everything I have done for you. I will add every last motherfucking one of you to my list.'

I don't say this but my eyes do. And to anyone who has had a thought like this, it's obvious.

Sam Ram sees it.

'Jill, I know that comes from a good place but this is Maeve's train. She is the driver. We have instructions, advice, suggestions. We keep going with our own lists. We continue.' He nods in my direction, echoing what I said. 'And when it's the right time to come back, there will be even more friends of Maeve.'

'He's right.'

Thanks, Eddie.

'We don't want to get caught up in this investigation or the coming trial. It doesn't matter that we only met the guy a couple of times, he killed a bunch of people and our group is called Psychopaths Anonymous, for Christ's sake.'

And it is settled. We stop.

We press pause.

When the time is right, I will place a notice on the board again.

We have to stop meeting, and I have to stop killing.

Everybody disperses in different directions. Only Jill seems sad. The others took it well. It makes me wonder whether she really belongs with us.

'I'll see you in the morning, Jill.'

'See you then, Maeve.'

And like that ... it's over.

It's always so much easier to quit the things that are good for you.

PART FIVE

'It all led to here. To this point. Outside, on the driveway, with Seth down on one knee. Jill is inside the house.

He's asking me to trust him.

Forgive him.

Marry him.

Is marriage the way that I keep hold of Seth? Things have been off recently. Distant. And he looks so different, tonight. I can see he is nervous but he also looks so pale and tired. He hasn't been coming to bed at the same time as me and he stays up so late doing whatever it is he does.

You see those couples, two kids in, exhausted, evaporated libidos. They are not the same as they were when they met. Their life paths have not been travelling in parallel. They want different things, different people. They want to feel the way they used to. They want to recapture what has been lost.

So they try for another baby.

Like that will solve their problems. Sure, it gets them fucking again but it's not for joy. It's not for fun or recreation. There's an end goal in sight and that is another life that they can bring into this shitty world, and they hope it will pull them close again. It will remind them of their love.

It reminds them of sleepless nights and painful breasts and pressure and finding more money and how they now have to love somebody else with everything they have left so there is no room for one another.

And sometimes, that is what marriage is like. Two people get bored of each other and need a project. Something to do. Something to look forward to. Something to plan. So they get married. Hell, all their friends are doing it, anyway.

Seth and I are not there yet. Things have slowed recently since I stopped attending meetings but we haven't got anywhere near the point where we hate each other enough to get married.

It's not the most romantic of proposals but I can see he is trying. 'I want you to say yes. Because I love you. I've loved you from the beginning and I'll love you until the end.' But it's the ultimatum that doesn't sit well. 'And, because if you don't say yes, if I don't know that you are completely with me, I can't show you what I have in the car.'

'Oh, Seth, I don't think you're in the position to be saying things like that to me. You are down on your knees. You want me to trust you, you want me as I am, you say you love me, you can show me what you're hiding before I give you my answer.'

The door is still ajar and Jill is inside. I just know it, she's going to ruin everything.

Seth gets himself off the floor and stands still for a moment. Weighing up his options, it seems.

I wait. I won't speak.

Seth opens the boot of his car.

He's shaking.

I take a look inside and then return my gaze to his.

'Yes. My answer is yes.'

STEP **EIGHT**

'Stop killing people.'

Let me tell you how it got to this.

I needed to stop killing people. I had to stop. Cold turkey. No easing down. One day you're stabbing a guy through the throat with a key you have had sharpened for such an occasion, and the other, you're letting three abusive, sexually demeaning, wannabe gangsters off the hook so you don't get found out for the whole throat-stabbing incident.

I threw myself into work. Into Seth. And even harder into the drinking.

You quit a pastime, you have to fill that time with something else.

Jill slipped into the role of being purely my colleague and assistant. I had to leave it all behind. Our conversations became entirely professional or superficial. Even though I was drinking more and more, and she was always entertaining to go out with, I kept her at arm's length.

Jill was a part of my old life where I had hobbies and interests that existed outside the walls of my home and office.

I wanted to go and visit Eames. A ridiculous notion, of course, I may as well rent the fourth plinth at Trafalgar Square and regale the crowds with my tales of passion and destruction.

Without violence, revenge and making amends, I would feel lopsided. Unbalanced. Perhaps prone to mistakes.

I wanted to visit the priest. Again, an idiotic idea to take a pillar of the community at such a turbulent time. The reason that so many killers take prostitutes and homeless people is the same way I feel about murdering a priest. Who would really miss them? Don't we have enough? We need more holy men inviting kids into their quarters after communion? No, we don't.

He will have to wait.

I want to watch the Maynards. I want to stalk their every move, get to know their routines. And wipe them out, one by one. Saving the father for last. For every month I delay it, Jill has to take their fists and their fingers and their dicks until their will grows tired.

But I don't see this option as risky because they must have a ton of people who would want them dead. And police would probably look towards other criminal families.

I keep the Maynards in my back pocket.

In case I need a taste.

They are my nicotine patch. My methadone.

A sip is a slip.

I went three weeks before I started to itch for a kill.

I went thirty minutes before I started itching for a drink.

When I returned home from breaking up the group, Seth was in the same position I had left him in. Clicking away on his laptop.

'How was Pilates?' He calls out when he hears I am in the doorway behind him.

'What?' I'm distracted.

'Have you stretched out all your stress?'

'Oh. Yeah. I feel so centred.' I'm being sarcastic. Seth laughs along.

I'm leaning on the back of the sofa. He looks at me upside down and we kiss. I tell him to find a website where we can order food. I want Chinese because it's the worst for my health and it always makes me feel disgusting the day after. That's how I want to feel.

I give Seth my card and tell him to order it.

'I'm going upstairs to shower.' ~~Sweaty from Pilates~~.

The scalding water beats my face and I let it massage my shoulder for a couple of minutes.

Then I hear the door open.

Seth has decided to join me. I wanted to condition my hair but it isn't long before I'm bent over with my hands against the tiles and

Seth is thrusting himself deep into me while I rub between my legs, hoping we can get where we need to go and arrive at the same time.

Then we are dry and downstairs and in comfortable clothes on the sofa. He still can't face the drink but I have a large glass of Sauvignon Blanc and we are both starving after having sex.

The crispy beef arrives. And the noodles. And the rice. And the sweet-and-sour pork balls. And whatever Seth ordered for himself. It's all so brown and beige and disgusting. I feel full almost immediately but continue to stuff my face.

We watch some American show where a bunch of estate agents vie for the craziest of commissions, selling properties in New York that cost millions. And I wonder why we don't hear of more realtors being murdered because they appear to be no better than priests and bums. Maybe even a notch below recruitment agents.

It becomes real.

I can't kill anybody.

I'm a quitter.

This will be my every day from now on. Oh, God. What have I done?

Then Seth starts to drift.

At first, I put everything I had into my work and my man. He couldn't be a rock in my difficult time because I couldn't tell him what was going on. So he had to be my distraction. My unknowing distraction.

I showed him love and affection. I was attentive and engaged. But addiction eats at you. It doesn't go away. Once you are in, it is a constant battle to avoid the thing you want.

An alcoholic who no longer drinks is still an alcoholic.

I haven't killed anybody for three weeks, but that doesn't mean I am no longer a killer.

I start to think about my list and whether there might be a way to get rid of the priest without anybody noticing. There's not. I know that. But just thinking about hurting him gives me some release. I meditate on that God-fearing charlatan more than I should. And it means that the level of contact with Seth suffers.

The more I crave what I'm missing, the less attention I pay to the things that I have.

When I feel him slipping, I reel him back in with sex. Something new and exciting. Something spontaneous. Passionate. I let him put his hand around my throat even though I don't like it as much as he does.

Then there are the Maynards. I've left them in a safe place like the bottle of vodka one might keep hidden at the back of the airing cupboard, or a head in the freezer.

Break in case of emergency.

I'm still pretending to go to Pilates but I end up driving around for an hour or going to a bar for a couple of glasses of something. It's not living.

Seth is being neglected. I don't even know if I am drinking more than I used to but I know I don't feel the same enjoyment. I'm preoccupied.

Sometimes I park up next to the community centre and watch the drunks head in to New Beginnings. I keep an eye out for the priest. The longing makes me angry. Itchy.

Two more weeks and I find that I'm falling asleep on the sofa because I *am* drinking so much more and Seth either wakes me to go up to bed and be more comfortable or he leaves me there and goes up himself. In the mornings, he will say how he tried to wake me but I hardly moved.

Seth is staying over more frequently, it's almost as if we live together. But it's starting to feel separate. We don't sleep together. I don't mean sex, we have sex, but we don't *sleep* in a bed next to one another.

I appreciate there is a distance between us but he hasn't mentioned anything. He never says I drink too much. He's a man. His needs are far more simple.

When you go from all that adoration to not sharing a bed, you start to look for that warmth elsewhere. You crave it. It's a drug just like anything else.

I start to suspect Seth. Perhaps he will leave me for somebody new. Maybe he already has.

This is the drink talking.

And the lack of killing.

~~It accentuates the madness.~~

I'm thinking about Seth's adultery and the priest prancing around with impunity and the Maynards emptying their balls all over Jill just because she won't fight back. And how the alcoholics still get to hang out together and worry about whether or not a made-up man in the sky will show them the way but the psychopaths no longer have the opportunity to discuss the manner in which they exacted their revenge on someone who wronged them.

I've become a thinker and not a doer.

So, even though I know that I shouldn't, I make myself get up, go out, and do something.

My name is Maeve, and I'm a psychopath. It has been four weeks since my last kill.

I take a drive to the community centre. It's not the usual night. I don't want to bump into anyone I might know. I'm feeling sluggish. I'm drunk all the time. I'm not even sure I want it this much, I'm just doing it so that I can feel like I'm doing something. I shouldn't be driving.

There's music playing inside.

I thought I saw the priest when I got out of the car but then there was nothing.

The music is awful. Salsa or rumba. I don't know. The beat is so jovial and the woman's voice I can hear, barking out instructions of when to twist and where to step is grating my eardrums.

I peek through the window. Seven overweight women in their thirties and forties are wriggling around a room that drunks piss and moan in on a Tuesday and kids sing and praise in on a Sunday. They're not here to get fit or lose weight, they just want to say that they were here at a class if anyone asks them what they were doing last night.

They want to be able to say that they did something.

I understand that.

On the notice board I can see the poster for Gina's Zumba. Three classes a week. Tonight is beginners. Makes sense. Those women were all over the place.

The weaving club are still going strong. As are the cub scouts and the alcoholics. There's a new life-drawing session every couple of weeks.

'Feet together. Step to the right. Bend your knees.' She likes the sound of her own voice. 'Now ... return to the middle. And step to the left.'

I need to sleep.

I need to not drink.

I won't sleep.

I will drink.

~~I'm growing more intolerant.~~

My focus moves back to the board. I want to see which club has their flier where mine used to be.

And there it is. White background. Black text. Simple. Easy to miss.

Every Tuesday
18:00
Friends of Maeve

***

The polluted London air hits me as I exit and I feel more drunk. The damn priest is walking in my direction. The way I feel in this moment, I don't believe I could avoid a slip. He's getting closer.

I run. Straight to the car. No stopping.

I take out my keys and grab the sharpened one by accident. In the bushes just beyond I see something.

Clyde? Still there? Nobody can be bothered to discover him?

I don't realise that I'm squeezing my hand around the sharpened key until it cuts my finger.

'Ow. Fuck.'

When I look up, Clyde isn't there. Just a dog, rustling about beneath the bush, searching for a ball.

I need to get home. To safety. To Seth. To wine.

On autopilot now, I don't know if I recognise anything around me but I somehow know that it is the right way. On the other side of the road there is a man who looks so similar to Not Jack that it makes me double-take and I don't realise that somebody has stepped out onto the crossing.

I blink and turn back just in time to slam on my brakes. The man on the crossing jumps back in shock then taps his hand on my bonnet a couple of times before continuing on his way. But before he does, he looks straight at me. I see Gary, my old sponsor.

They're everywhere.

I need to get home.

Now I feel sober but panicked. I focus my sights dead ahead until I pull into my drive.

Ignition. Bag. Keys. Door. Open. Shoes. Off.

Silence.

There's a handwritten note on the kitchen counter from Seth telling me that he's probably not going to make it over tonight because he has some things to take care of. Bullshit. He could have sent a text but I would have gone straight back to him.

I have felt him drifting away for the last couple of weeks.

He's doing something he doesn't want me to know about.

I'm going to slip.

I am definitely going to slip.

A fortnight of mildly diminished attention was all it took for Seth to disconnect. How did I think that I would find a way to keep him?

Two weeks and now I am alone.

Maybe this is how Jill felt when I stopped talking to her about personal things. Who else does she have? A kid she can't bring herself to truly love? Men who abuse her? A sister who never lets up?

I call Jill.

'Maeve. This is a surprise. Is everything okay?'

I explain to her that I have been a little too focussed on my job recently and have neglected the things that should matter the most.

'Let's get together and have a drink.'

'Now?' She's pretending like she wouldn't come for a drink right this second.

'No. Not now. Tomorrow night. Seven o' clock. My house.'

'Your house? I've never been there.'

'I'll send a cab. You in?'

'Of course, I'm in.'

I know she wants to talk now but I can't. I have things to do.

'Great. I'll see you then. I have something for you, too.'

~~Your freedom.~~

I hang up and jump straight on to every social-media platform I know. If I'm going to give Jill her gift, I'm going to need to know where the Maynards will be.

And it's so easy with those sub-mental, show-off, beer-soused, walking hard-on, daddy's boys. Eighteen minutes ago, one of them took a picture of himself, flexing a bicep while posing in front of his new car. An obvious penis extension, it tells me that I won't need my best knife to chop off his favourite appendage.

The other brother – the eldest, I think – has the most recent status, 'Sunday drinking starts at midday. Good Mixer. Who's in?'

The same pub as before.

I know exactly where to be and what time.

I'm in, boys.

And I'm jumping off the wagon.

That brings us up to speed.

This is the day. Sunday. God's day. It's perfect.

Today, I cross the Maynards from my list, I give Jill back her freedom and Seth comes home with a proposal. If I can fit it in, the priest is going, too.

~~I just feel like killing a lot of fucking people.~~

I just feel like killing a lot of fucking people.

The morning drags. I didn't sleep well. Excitement coupled with worry over what Seth was doing did not make for a comfortable bedfellow. I know the Maynard boys are starting their drinking from noon and I have decided to give them a couple of hours of celebration before I descend on them.

This is not impulsive. It's not the same as clocking a homeless guy around the head with a heavy-bottomed whisky bottle. It's not like stabbing someone in the throat for lying on your car. This is deliberate. It is planned.

It is happening.

I haven't heard from Seth. Jill has sent me a text saying that she is looking forward to catching up later.

I eat breakfast, drink coffee, shower and get dressed. Something classy but sexy. Not slutty. I know what the Maynard boys like but I'm going to show them something that they *want*. I'll make it as easy as I can for them, and their tiny infantile minds.

From twelve until one, I am nursing half a bottle of wine. That's enough to stave off a hangover, keep the demons at bay and allow my body and mind to function normally.

I'm in control.

I decide to walk there. It's forty minutes away by foot. It will give me an opportunity to reflect and to work myself up. It's only six minutes away by tube. Two stops on the Northern Line. That's my route home.

The weather is pretty good by English standards and the Maynards have a bench outside the pub and are drinking with four or five other men, who laugh along at their shitty jokes and make them feel important.

My plan is to sit around for a while, drinking and listening in. Then I want to make myself seem vulnerable. Like I've had a little too much and maybe one of those kind Maynard men will help me home. Maybe order a taxi. Maybe take me home. Perhaps I could go back to theirs for a drink.

Idiots. It's too fucking easy.

I think I could get them both at the same time. I already know they've been screwing the same whore. They are brothers. Related by blood. And they have both seen the other one ejaculate. The world will be better off.

My job is made even easier when I arrive because parked next to the pub is a shiny black BMW I saw in an Instagram post yesterday, neatly framed by a Maynard bicep.

The way they behave is deplorable. And that's coming from a serial killer who has no plan or desire to quit. I understand how fun it is to drink and I know that inhibitions get left at the kerbside when you've had too many but it's the lack of respect they have for anything and everyone. They smash glasses. They shout at strangers. They wolf whistle like there is even a 0.1 percent success rate of that behaviour getting you laid.

They think they rule the world and that they are indestructible.

So when they see a tipsy, decent-looking woman in a tight skirt hanging around their new car, they think they've won the fucking lottery.

'Hey. Are you okay?' The Neanderthal actually sounds concerned for my welfare.

'No. I've had some drinks and my friends have gone to a different bar. I figured I could call a cab or get on the tube but I saw this beauty and wondered whether a dashing knight might be able to give me a lift.' I'm slurring a little, but not so much that he thinks I could be sick in his car, just enough that he thinks I can't put up a fight.

'Well m'lady. It's your lucky day. That is my brother's car. We've only had a couple of drinks so I'm sure we could get you to where you need to be.' I have my head dropped but I can hear his smile as he thinks his double entendre has gone unnoticed.

He's also lying about how much he's had. I've been watching him like a good little stalker.

He asks me to hang on a moment while he goes to get his brother.

Two birds with one stone.

I lean against the car as though I need the support. Twenty seconds later something clicks and beeps and one of the Maynards returns.

One bird. One stone.

It's still early.

I have one dead Maynard on the floor of his flat, which looks like it has been decorated by the half-blind president of the Scarface fan club. Such a boring cliché. He even has a pet snake.

It was so predictable. I told him that I didn't live that far away and that I was a bit annoyed with my friends because I hadn't finished drinking. He said he knew a place. I agreed. Pretty soon, we were back at his apartment and he was whipping up cocktails and telling me facts about the things he had collected and put in his immaturely furnished home. He sounded young and enthusiastic and even a little sweet.

But that didn't make up for that fact that he had pushed his dick into Jill's anus so his father could teach her a lesson about respect. So I slit his throat with the knife from my bag and cut off that disgusting piece of gristle between his legs.

It was in my hand when I heard the knock at the door.

I froze.

Another knock. And his voice. The old man.

'Come on, son. Open the door. I want my go, too.'

That piece of shit must have messaged his dad and told him to come over so they could both come for me. I want to spit on him.

Instead, I open the door for the old bastard. Nice and wide, so that he can see his dead son bleeding out on the floor beneath his samurai-sword collection.

You would expect the father to attack. But he runs. Perhaps it is the sight of the knife in my right hand or the penis in my left. Maybe the blood on my face.

Maybe the smile.

He doesn't get far.

A knife to the back of the neck and he drops like a bag of rocks. I slash behind both his knees because I don't want him getting up. He's light. I can drag him easily back into his son's shithole apartment.

'Who the fuck are you?'

'Ballsy for a guy who just got dropped by a one-hundred-pound woman.' I know this will aggravate him because he thinks we are a lesser species.

Now, I know how some might gain some satisfaction by explaining themselves, saying why they are doing this, who they are doing this for and blah blah.

That's not me.

~~Eat a dick.~~

I shove his son's amputated penis inside his mouth and hold it shut for a few seconds. He spits it out and starts gagging. I'm bored of his shit. I take his mobile phone from his trouser pocket, hold it up to his face and it unlocks. I cut his throat, too, and take his dick off his body.

But not in that order.

He deserves worse.

Then I text the last Maynard boy and tell him he needs to come to his brother's place, now. Alone. 'Won't take long.'

I know he'll come. Because he does whatever daddy tells him to do.

This is fun.

It's really scratching my itch.

Again, those long, thought-out diatribes delivered by the villain before he is thwarted at the last minute or the hero gains justice and bleats on for three minutes to explain their position and ultimately give a satisfying resolution, they are not a requirement for a psychopath.

We just don't care.

So, when the final Maynard comes knocking, I use the peephole to make sure it is him, I open the door and wait behind it. When he sees his dickless family lying on the floor he rushes straight in like the dolt he is and I swing the knife around from behind the door.

I wanted his throat but went high and hit him in the open mouth. I felt the handle butt against his front teeth. He went down to the floor as quick as the others. I pounced and thrust the knife into his back as many times as I could before I started to lose my breath.

And now I am looking over them all before I leave. I took a hooded sweatshirt and some jogging bottoms from Maynard #1's wardrobe and I put Maynard #3's penis into a small Tupperware box so that I can present it to Jill later.

There's a bottle of Champagne in the fridge, which I also take.

The tube is relatively empty. Six minutes later, I'm back in Hampstead. I want to shower, burn these clothes, and start on that Champagne.

Still no word from Seth.

LIST OF PEOPLE I HAVE (RECENTLY) HARMED

THE PRIEST

~~CLYDE~~

~~JAMIE KEACH~~

~~THE MAYNARDS~~

EAMES

THE GROUP

One down.

Balance.

Next, I give Jill her peace.

There was no time for the priest, which I'm annoyed about. I guess three kills in a day is still a success. I got myself clean and put the clothes I wore into the burn barrel with the outfit I took from Maynard. I wanted to keep the hooded sweatshirt – it was so comfortable – but it would be a mistake, of course. Evidence. By the time I'd finished and had a couple of glasses of wine and some food and watched an episode of *Real Housewives*, there wasn't enough left to traipse back across town and cut the heart out of that holy moron while he screamed out for a God that has stopped listening.

I booked a cab for Jill. I'm tracking it on my phone. She's eight minutes away.

The Champagne I took from the Maynards is chilling. The penis I took is in the freezer, I'll show it to Jill once I've got some red wine down her neck. I'm sure she'll be thrilled.

There's a cheese board in the fridge and some grapes. I have music playing downstairs – a playlist I found called 'Piano Bar' that fades perfectly in the background. We will be able to talk.

She's four minutes away.

I can't sit down. I'm edgy. Or energised. It probably looks like nerves but it's not. Things might be strained at first because I still see Jill most days but I haven't been telling her anything about my personal life. She does divulge information, still. An anecdote when she brings my morning coffee. She'll say something about her daughter. Like I care. I've made my position clear. Things between us need to be professional.

Jill won't give up, though. She keeps trying to tell me things. But I know there are some things she is keeping back.

Two minutes away.

I pop the cork on the Champagne and pour two glasses to kill some time. Then I open the Sangiovese I bought for Jill to let it breathe.

As I check my phone screen, the doorbell rings.
She's here.

'Your. Place. Is. Amazing.' She's stunned that I live in such an affluent part of the city. It's a world away from her home.

'Well, come in.'

'I feel like I should take my shoes off.' She feigns awkwardness.

'Go with it. I'm not wearing any. Take this.' I hand her a drink. 'I know you prefer red but I got some Champagne and it's nice to kick things off with a bit of a toast, don't you think?'

'Sure. What are we toasting?'

I raise my glass. 'To peace.'

She clinks her glass against mine and downs half the Champagne in hers.

We fall straight into a rhythm. There's no awkwardness, no need for surface conversation. I take out the cheeseboard and place it on the kitchen worktop so that we can pick at it. Jill quaffs the wine like it's a house red. She may have more of a handle on her drinking now but I can't expect her to also have taste or any kind of refinement.

She's still fucking guys for extra money on the weekends even though I told her she shouldn't.

I guess she only has to do what I say at work. In her own time, she does what she wants.

She confides in me. She's worried about the Maynards.

'They usually come around once a month to rough me up a bit. I think it's been five weeks. So it could be any night now.'

'Let's not let those arseholes ruin our night, eh? Besides, I don't think they'll be bothering you any more.' I smile brightly and savour the last mouthful of the expensive Sangiovese I bought to go with our cheese selection.

'You can't know that, though, Maeve.'

'Wait here.' I place my glass back on the side. 'Top me up.' And I turn around to the freezer where a frozen Maynard dick is waiting.

Jill pours while I fish out the container.

She is drinking. I give her the cold box.

'What's this?'

'It's little Maynard's little Maynard.'

'What?'

'I cut their dicks off, Jill. They won't bother you ever again.'

Jill doesn't know what is happening. The wine is in her right hand, the frozen penis in her left. She lifts the box up and tries to look through it from underneath because the top is frozen. That's the moment I take the large knife from the block and thrust it into her stomach.

She drops the glass and the dick.

'What the fuck, Maeve? What are you doing?'

She's confused. She doesn't think it's real.

'You kept my group going when I told you not to, Jill. I saw the noticeboard and I see your handwriting every damned day. It's you.'

'You fucking psycho.' She pulls away but realises it hurts more when the knife starts coming out of the body. She's crying.

'Yes, Jill. That's the fucking point.'

I let go of the knife handle and she holds it with both of her hands. She wants to pull it out and try her luck at thrusting it in to me. She wants to take that risk. Or she wants to make sure she takes me down because she knows she won't make it.

It all happens quickly.

As soon as I let go of the knife, I am already reaching for the corkscrew. I pick it up and jam it straight through Jill's left temple.

She drops to the floor on her side, the knife still protruding from her stomach. I drop down to her level and turn the handle so that it screws deeper into her brain.

Jill is dead. I can't make her any more dead by screwing.

I do it because I like it.

I want to know what it feels like.

'There you go, Jill. How does it feel?'

Finally at peace.

I've dragged Jill out into the garage. That fucking rapist's car is still in here.

All the people I killed because of Jill and then she turned on me. She asked for this.

There's blood in the kitchen. I don't want to spend my Sunday night cleaning that up but it would be worse if I'd pulled the knife out of her stomach, so it's pretty contained.

Then the doorbell.

I have Jill in my arms. We wait. Maybe they'll go away.

It rings again.

Fuck. I manage to open the chest freezer with one hand and push her inside. There's not much in there. A few bags of ice for my gin. Frozen chips. Frozen peas. Two tubs of vanilla ice-cream.

It had better not be that detective. I thought I saw Gary in the road, yesterday. It wasn't him. I couldn't be. But why would that detective be sniffing around again.

I edge out into the hallway.

Not the detective.

It's Seth.

What is he doing here?

He has a key. Fuck. He has a key. Why is he not using his key?

'One second,' I call out, but I run into the kitchen and throw a tea towel on the floor to cover the blood. There's some kitchen roll. I pull off more than I will ever need. 'I'm coming. Hang on.' I soak up as much as I can and then dump it in the bin.

I have to answer the door.

I don't know whether to be panicked or relieved or angry.

Seth tells me that I'm everything he's ever wanted. He is standing on my doorstep and he looks as though he has been crying and maybe his collar is ripped and he's talking about how much he loves me and that he needs my help and I have to trust him and he takes me by the hand and is leading me out on to the drive towards his car and it's maybe the most exciting thing that has happened for weeks.

I want to ask him where he has been for the last couple of days. Instead, I tell him that I have Jill inside, so that he doesn't think about going in the house.

He's sweating and shaking. He looks unwell.

'What's going on, Seth? You look wrecked.'

His knee crunches into the gravel of my driveway and he's telling me that he will love me until the very end. He wants me to be his wife.

I can't say yes right away. There's something off about this proposal. He hasn't messaged me for two days. It feels like he is asking me because he wants to make sure that I am his. I want the same thing, but marriage is not the way to future-proof our relationship.

There's something in the boot of his car that he wants to show me but is also anxious about showing me. I wonder whether it is part of the proposal, some grand gesture I didn't see coming. He has always been so kind and thoughtful and attentive. It will be something I have never even thought of or knew I would like. I imagine the boot is empty apart from an engagement ring.

But Seth doesn't want to show me until I say yes.

And I don't want to say yes until he shows me.

I get my way.

Seth clicks a button on the key fob and the boot pops open. I look over at the front door. Still ajar. Jill inside. Seth reaches down and lifts the boot open all the way.

And there it is. Thin. Young. Blonde. The opposite of me.

'Is she dead?' I ask.

'Very,' he answers. And he's crying again.

I take him tightly by the arms and make him look in my eyes.

'Yes. My answer is yes.'

~~Now I've got you.~~

~~Now, you are mine.~~

But…

The fact that I was distant for a short while is not a reason for anxiety or low self-esteem. Not getting every ounce of my attention because I was fighting to protect myself, shutting down my group, not killing all the people I wanted, when I wanted, does not need to trigger your insecurity.

Only having sex twice in a week is not a free pass to make surreptitious, late-night calls, searching for some kind of connection. We never lost what we had. It may have seemed like it was on hold, perhaps. It happens. It doesn't mean that you meet up with some blonde tramp. I don't care if you had no intention of taking it anywhere, it's already too far.

Coffee is too far.

Arranging a rendezvous is too far.

Talking in the first place is too far.

This is the kind of behaviour that will likely get you killed.

Seth explains himself. He says I became distant but that none of this is my fault and that he is not blaming me. He was just talking to her and she was listening. They met up a couple of times but nothing happened. He didn't fuck her. He didn't kiss her. He backtracks and says that anything they seemed to have was nothing compared to what we had together, when it was working. When we were both present.

It doesn't matter to me that she had no brains, I can see her beauty through the bloodied hair that sticks to her face and I know that intellect was not a consideration.

I don't know what she did to end up here like this. I don't ask. I don't care.

~~You can't leave me now.~~

All that matters is you are mine.

What would tear other couples apart will only bring us closer together. But I still want to bleach her out of our lives. She is a blip on our history. A footnote. A smudge.

And I know that alcohol will dull my mental faculties and affect my memory in an irreversible way, at some point.

I know that every unprotected sexual encounter is a game of Russian roulette.

And I know that every killer eventually screws up and makes an idiotic mistake that will get them caught.

But I can't quit.

I won't.

Doing the right thing is so much harder than getting things wrong.

And it's not as much fun.

I love the things that are bad for me. And you can't make yourself stop loving.

They're all mine.

LIST OF PEOPLE I HAVE (RECENTLY) HARMED

THE PRIEST

~~CLYDE~~

~~JAMIE KEACH~~

~~THE MAYNARDS~~

EAMES

~~JILL~~

SETH

Whatever works.

Love is strange. Some people skip merrily through life with one partner, others get married several times. Some couples don't want kids. Some don't want to be in a couple. Sometimes one of you is a psychopathic serial killer while the other accidentally murdered a woman and needs help covering it up.

Whichever camp you fall into, people seem obsessed with this idea of happiness. They think they want it. They think that the meaning of all life can be boiled down into this concept. Perhaps we just need to make the journey to the end as best we can and not think that feeling unhappy means you are not living.

Seth is pencilled on my list because he has obviously done something wrong to get into this situation. I don't know who this woman is and I know that I have him now, but there could come a point in the future where my addiction to him is cured.

For now, he needs my help.

'Get her out of the car and into the house.' I have to take control here. He's not like me.

'But what about Jill?'

Jill. Fuck. I forgot about her.

'Don't worry about Jill. She's not here any more. I said it because I didn't want you to come in. But now I do.'

I go in ahead of Seth and the mystery blonde. It gives me a minute to finish cleaning up the blood a little more. When I get back into the kitchen, there isn't any blood. I must have done a better job than I realised when I panicked at the sound of the doorbell.

I can hear Seth struggling through the door. I open the cupboard beneath the sink. There are three bottles of bleach and one half bottle. I take them out and meet him in the hallway.

'Put her down and shut the door.'

He does as I tell him.

He looks lost.

'Listen. Seth. It's going to be okay. Just do what I say. Nobody will ever find out. Okay?'

'How do you know that?'

'Just do as I say.'

I tell him that I don't want to know what happened, how he knew her or what he did with her, I just want to get any trace of him off the body. I shake the bleach at that point.

'She's going to take a bath and you are going to make a drink.'

'I can open a bottle of wine.'

Fuck. The corkscrew is still in the side of Jill's head.

'I think this calls for something stronger, don't you? A couple of gins would work. I'm going to get things started upstairs. I'll be back in a moment.'

I have a bathroom that I rarely use because my bedroom has an en suite. I put the plug in, run some warm water, and empty the contents of all three and half bottles of bleach into the tub. I leave it running and go back downstairs to get the body.

Seth is not in the kitchen. There are two large goblets and a bottle of gin on the kitchen counter but Seth is not in there.

He emerges from the side door, which goes straight into the garage. And he's holding a bag of ice.

My mind is racing. Am I going to have to kill him now? We just got things sorted.

It's all going to come crashing down. The priest, the Maynards, my sponsor, Not Jack, Psychopaths Anonymous. Oh, shit, I'm going to have to kill Seth. There's no way he didn't see Jill in there.

'What are you doing? I thought you were making gin.' It's accusatory. Like going into my garage is the worst thing he has done today.

'There was no ice in the kitchen freezer, so I went outside to the garage.'

Maybe he won't say anything. I just told him that I would help him cover up a murder. Maybe this makes us even.

I thought I had him but maybe now he is the one who has me.

Why did I have to kill Jill?

~~Because I've wanted to since that first meeting.~~

'I saw some ice-cream in there, too, so I picked that up.'

I know there was ice-cream in there. Two tubs. Along with some oven chips and the dead body of my assistant from work. Why is he being so calm?

Where is Jill? Was she not dead? Has she escaped? Was she ever really here? I've been drinking so much recently, I'm starting to question things. How did I kill three men? That's the kind of thing that will be all over the news. Sure, the dead hobo will be squirrelled away at the bottom of a column on page thirty-six but what about Clyde? I left him in a bush. I didn't even bury him. How are people not talking about that.

It's all about Eames on the news channels.

Eames is real. I met him. He was part of my group. I'm not just making things up because I'm a drunk. I killed my sponsor. I drilled through his skull. There was a detective. I saw him. He gave me his card. I have it somewhere. I'm sure of it.

Why is Seth not saying something? He was freaking out about what he did to that woman, if he just saw Jill, which he must have, then he shouldn't be acting this calm.

I nearly ran over a man who looked exactly like Gary yesterday. And that priest is out to get me. And Not Jack. He was on the other side of the road, even though I saw him hanging from a bridge by his neck.

Why is he not asking me anything?

'Er, ice-cream sounds great.'

He starts to walk towards me. The dead woman is to my left, crumpled in a heap on my hallway floor.

'That's everything you got from the freezer?' I ask. Trying to sound breezy.

'Yeah. Ice for the gin and ice-cream for our sin.'

She can't be in there. Jill is not there. He didn't see her because I never killed her. I never killed any of them. I need to look. I need to know.

'You didn't find anything else out there?'

'There was something I couldn't quite understand, yes.'

Here it comes.

'Why the fuck do you have half a Toyota Prius in your garage?'

Oh, thank you, rapist taxi driver.

I know who I am.

Seth and I drink the gin and toast our impending nuptials.

~~In sickness and in health.~~

We eat the ice-cream like we've just been dumped.

~~For better or for worse.~~

And we fuck like he's just returned home from war.

~~If anyone has any reason why these two psychopaths should not be joined in unholy matrimony…~~

When we are done, Seth helps me upstairs with the dead woman. We take off her clothes – they will have to be burned – and place her in the bath.

It doesn't get you clean. Not that much bleach. Sure, there are face creams that you can buy that will help with dry skin or dark patches left from overexposure to sunlight and they're clinically proven to help. But it's a trace amount.

And, for those suffering with eczema, a bleach bath may be recommended. Your dermatologist will tell you that the bleach can significantly decrease the infection of staphylococcus aureus, a bacterium prevalent in those who are plagued by this skin condition. Still, it is recommended to use no more than half a cup of bleach in one half-filled bath of water.

Because it won't make your skin sparkle like it does your toilet basin. It will burn. It will blister. You will bleed. It will hurt like hell.

Unless you're already dead.

ACKNOWLEDGEMENTS

I'll keep these short. Partly because I can't really remember writing this book but also because West says I only have a page this time.

I have to thank Karen for allowing me to write two this year. Neither one had a detective and one had no hook. I know I make things difficult but thanks for making things so easy for me by giving me the freedom to explore.

West, of course. No locked horns on this one and we turned it around in record time.

My agent, Kate, who always has my back, and Louisa for getting the film/TV world interested in my stuff.

Fourbears Books for getting behind a local writer and pushing all my words.

Fellow writers, reviewers and bloggers for liking my stuff and telling other people about it.

Anne, for smashing the blog tour(s).

My kids for making things light as the world got darker.

Kel. My love. I know that being with me is a non-stop thrill ride, unless I am writing, editing or waiting for feedback. Or a book has just been published. Or I get a three-star review. When I feel like a fraud, you make me feel like a superstar. I love you, woman.

Oh, and January David. See what I did? Nearly got you back…